A DATE TO DIE FOR

A HOPGOOD HALL MYSTERY

E.V. HUNTER

Boldwood

First published in Great Britain in 2023 by Boldwood Books Ltd. This paperback edition published in 2024.

I

Copyright © E.V. Hunter, 2023

Cover Photography: Deposit Photos

A CIP catalogue record for this book is available from the British Library.

Paperback ISBN 978-1-83561-887-5

Large Print ISBN 978-1-80483-567-8

Hardback ISBN 978-1-80483-566-1

Ebook ISBN 978-1-80483-564-7

Kindle ISBN 978-1-80483-565-4

Audio CD ISBN 978-1-80483-572-2

MP3 CD ISBN 978-1-80483-569-2

Digital audio download ISBN 978-1-80483-563-0

Boldwood Books Ltd

23 Bowerdean Street
London SW6 3TN
www.boldwoodbooks.com

PROLOGUE

'Don't even think about pulling the rug now. You're in too deep.'

'I don't respond well to threats,' he snarled.

'This is no threat, and we both know it.' She jerked at the sound of a fox barking. Typical townie, he thought. 'You owe me.'

'And I've paid.'

'Not nearly enough.'

She smirked, fully aware that she held the upper hand, and something inside of him snapped. A red mist of anger caused spots to dance before his eyes, blurring his vision. Without conscious thought for the consequences, he reached for her and grabbed her by the throat. She fought him with everything she had, pummelling his chest with her fists and desperately trying to kick out as he ruthlessly crushed her windpipe. He watched dispassionately as her face contorted and his anger slowly abated.

A rational corner of his brain warned him to stop. He was no murderer. It wasn't as if she could report the attack without drawing attention to her own nefarious activities. Oh yes, he knew what she used to be, and sometimes still was. What would that scandalous snippet of gossip do for her fledging business in a village this size? Why hadn't he thought of that before? There was no need to kill her. He could simply fight fire with fire.

He released his hold on her neck and she fell forward, chest heaving, wheezing and coughing, hands resting on her bent knees.

'You bastard!'

She recovered faster than he'd expected and launched herself at him. He instinctively put out a hand to ward her off, shoving her backwards with considerable force. She fell with a sickening thud and cried out as her head struck the ground. There was blood. Too much blood. She groaned, then stopped moving. He felt for a pulse and didn't find one.

That's what happened when you went soft, he reflected. He'd been willing to let her live but she'd brought her fate on herself. His thoughts now turned to survival. He couldn't leave her here but had plenty of time to cover his tracks. There was no need to panic.

Calm and methodical, he threw her over his shoulder. Strapped to the back of his quad bike, she lolled like a rag doll. He rode to a more isolated spot and dug a shallow grave. Then, once the body was wrapped in an old blanket, he tossed it unceremoniously into its final resting place, glad to be rid of the threat she posed once and for all. He filled the earth back in, sweating from his efforts, and scattered leaves and branches over the disturbed soil.

'Rest in peace,' he said sardonically, before remounting his bike and returning home to a stiff drink and a warm bed.

1

Alexi's heels echoed on the boarded floor of her loft as she made a final check for rogue possessions. The space felt devoid of character as it awaited someone else's imprint. Outside, a spring drizzle turned London monochrome, reflecting her own grey mood. She looked at her reflection, ghosted in the picture window against a backdrop of rain. She shuddered at the defiant image that glared back at her and turned away. At the flat's front door, she paused to say mental goodbyes to her old life.

'Okay, Cosmo, let's hit the road.'

Her black cat rubbed his head against her calf and stalked through the door ahead of her.

In the underground car park, Alexi stowed her case in the boot of her Mini and placed her computer bag behind the passenger seat, into which Cosmo had already installed himself. Alexi pulled the seatbelt across and fastened his leash to it. The police could be funny about unrestrained pets in vehicles, unenlightened as they were when it came to Cosmo's idiosyncrasies. There were cats, and then there was Cosmo, whose oddities she was still getting to grips with herself, and the last thing she needed was an altercation with the law.

Alexi climbed into the driver's seat, stowed her handbag, and turned the key in the ignition. Apprehension, anger, and relief fought for supremacy as she pulled out into the flow of traffic on the Battersea Road and watched her old home grow smaller in her rear view mirror.

Twenty minutes later, they were on the Westway heading towards the M4, music blasting on the radio, the windscreen wipers on intermittent to counteract the light drizzle that continued to mirror Alexi's mood. She automatically lifted her foot off the accelerator when she saw a warning sign for a speed camera. Always in a hurry, Alexi put her foot down once she was clear of the danger zone, only to lift it again almost immediately.

'You know what, Cosmo,' she said, 'we don't actually have to be anywhere. For the first time in living memory, I don't have a deadline.'

Cosmo's ears twitched.

Alexi felt a flash of optimism filter through her anger and insecurity. When had she last not had at least one assignment to keep her dashing from pillar to post? When had she last taken time for herself, rather than channelling every second into her career?

She'd made it, too, or at least thought she had. She had won the respect of some of her fiercest critics through hard work and persistence. But now it had all come crashing down in a spectacular ball of flames, and she was left with... well, with Cosmo and two bags of possessions. Not much to show for all that ambition.

Perhaps it was time to reassess.

She sighed, the sound of her mobile pulling her from her reverie. She moved to pick up the call without screening it. As a journalist, she never allowed her phone to go unanswered. Then she remembered that she no longer *was* a journalist – at least not a gainfully employed one – and checked to see who wanted her.

'Patrick,' she muttered, pressing the reject button.

She was well and truly over the two-faced schemer. *He* still had his cushy number on the *Sunday Sentinel*, with plum additional duties – *her* duties. He claimed to love her, but he'd known what changes were in the offing weeks before the announcement and hadn't warned her. That didn't add up to love in Alexi's book. She blew air through her lips and bashed the heel of her hand hard against the steering wheel. Cosmo opened an eye.

'I should have known there was something wrong when you kept trying to bite his ankles,' she told her cat.

Cosmo shot her an *I-told-you-so* look and went back to sleep.

Alexi hummed along with the radio as other cars sped past her, feeling calmer with every mile she put between herself and London. Driving slowly was cathartic. Who knew? The motorway rolled out through open countryside she'd never had time to look at before, and she decided to leave the busy road a couple of junctions short of her destination. The drizzle had stopped and a weak sun threatened to break through. The Berkshire fields undulated gently as she drove through small villages. She slowed to the speed limit on the road into Lambourn, a pretty town lying within a fold of the chalk downs. A large sign welcomed her and asked her to drive carefully. The area was dotted with large houses and stables, the fields fenced with post-and-rail; barely a leaf out of place. She could almost smell the money. A few leggy horses grazed in one of the fields but most of them appeared unoccupied, as did the roads. It was peaceful, pristine, and eerily quiet.

'I hope you like fresh air and horses, Cosmo,' she said as the cat finally stirred, sat up, and took notice. 'And remember what we talked about. No terrorising Cheryl's dog.'

Cosmo arched his back and sent her an appraising look through piercing hazel eyes.

* * *

Alexi followed the directions issued by the disembodied voice from the satnav, feeling guilty that she needed guidance to her best friend's door; a door she hadn't passed through since Cheryl's wedding ten years before. She'd been too busy building a career but in her hour of need, her neglected friend had welcomed her with open arms.

It was humbling.

She drove to Upper Lambourn, past a pub called the Malt Shovel, curious about the origins of its name. Turning left, she took a right through brick gateposts that she still remembered, a discreet plaque advising her that she had reached:

Hopgood Hall
Boutique Hotel.

The gardens on either side of the gravel drive looked pristine. What Alexi knew about gardening could be written on the back of a postage stamp but even she recognised a display of late daffodils and tulips. After the drizzle of London, a chilly breeze had sprung up, blowing away the blanket of cloud and showing the rural setting in its best light.

The old manor house had a façade of honey-coloured stone, wisteria climbing against it, its pendulous purple flowers giving off a heady perfume. Alexi breathed the scent deeply into her lungs. Hers was the only car in the visitors' parking area, she noticed, but before she could decide if that was a bad omen, the front door burst open and Cheryl flew down the steps, messy blonde curls dancing around her face.

'You're here!' she cried, launching herself into Alexi's arms and almost knocking her from her feet. 'And you look fantastic, damn you.'

'You don't look so bad yourself,' Alexi replied, wondering how she had let something as inconsequential as work get in the way of their friendship. The warmth of her reception caused the years to fall away and she knew she had done the right thing in coming here to lick her wounds. 'Thanks for the invite.'

'Where else would you go in your hour of need?'

Alexi's reunion with her old friend was interrupted by a series of indignant meows from inside Alexi's Mini.

'I'd best let him out before he frightens the horses,' Alexi said.

Cheryl peered into the car, only to be hissed at. It didn't seem to faze her. 'Wow, I've never seen such a huge cat.'

'I did warn you.' Since being adopted by Cosmo, Alexi had heard him described as anything from a panther to a racoon, or various combinations thereof. 'Are you absolutely sure he's welcome? I wish I could say the bad mood was a big act, but it isn't.'

'I'm sure we'll get along just fine.'

Alexi shrugged, crossed the fingers of one hand behind her back, and released Cosmo's leash with the other. Her cat indulged in another slow stretch, his eyes fixed speculatively upon Cheryl. Alexi tensed when Cheryl reached out a hand and waited for the explosion that didn't come. Instead, Cosmo submitted to Cheryl's ministrations and then regally stalked off into a nearby clump of bushes.

'My god, he remembered his manners. That's a first.'

They watched his rigid tail disappear deeper into the bushes.

Alexi grabbed her handbag and linked her arm through Cheryl's. 'I want to hear all your news. How long is it since we last had a chance to catch up face-to-face?'

Cheryl screwed up her nose. 'When I came to London and stayed with you, more than two years ago. Come on, Drew just put the kettle on. Although the sun's no doubt over the yardarm somewhere, and if your arrival doesn't count as an excuse to break out the bubbly, then I don't know what does. Oh!' Cheryl clapped her free hand over her mouth. 'There I go again, letting my tongue run away with me. I guess you're not in a celebratory mood.'

'I'm *always* in the mood for bubbly.'

'Attagirl!'

They made their way into a large, homely kitchen at the back of the house in which a bear of a man was setting out tea things with remarkable delicacy. He saw Alexi, gave a whoop of delight, and swept her clean off her feet.

'Thank god you're here,' he said. 'Cheryl's been listening to the traffic news all day, convinced that every time there was mention of an accident, you had to be involved in it.'

'Well, you have always been a bit of a reckless driver,' Cheryl protested.

'I got more responsible.'

Cheryl stifled a disbelieving laugh. 'So come on, tell us about it. What happened to you?' she asked, her smile fading. 'You've been working so hard. I don't really understand why it all fell apart.'

'Let the poor woman get some tea down her before you interrogate her, love,' Drew said mildly.

Cheryl shrugged. 'I didn't think a lot of that Patrick guy. You're worth way more than someone that self-centred.'

'Yeah, well... oh no!'

A strangled howl from the back garden had Alexi leaping from her seat, already guessing the source of the noise. Cosmo was on the lawn, squaring up to a little terrier.

'Cosmo, what did I tell you?' Alexi demanded, joining him outside and placing her hands on her hips.

Cosmo backed down and fixed Alexi with an innocent look. With his tail rigid, he approached a trembling Toby and rubbed his head against the dog's body.

'I'll be damned,' Drew said, shaking his head.

Cheryl grinned. 'It seems they've worked the pecking order out,' she said. 'Come on in for that tea, Lexi, then we can legitimately crack open a bottle or six.'

Alexi didn't move. Instead she stared at the ugly row of prefabricated chalets occupying a big chunk of the manor's large garden. They were on the far side, away from the windows in the main house, which is why she hadn't seen them before.

'What happened?' she asked.

'Come on in and we'll tell you,' Cheryl said, grimacing.

Cosmo preceded them through the door and meowed for food. Toby followed behind and barked in support.

Drew guffawed. 'They're a bloody double act already.'

Grinning, Alexi reached into her bag and found a pouch of dried cat food she'd had the presence of mind to keep close at hand. Cheryl took it from her and decanted the contents into a plastic bowl.

'Right,' Alexi said, as they sat around the scarred pine kitchen table drinking Earl Grey. 'Spill.'

'We just couldn't get the bookings to keep the hotel afloat.' It was Drew who answered her. 'It's all seasonal here. We rely on well-off people who want to rub shoulders with the elite of the racing world. Problem is, if the weather's crap, they abandon that idea and sod off to sunnier climes.'

'Plus there're a lot of cheaper hotels springing up in the area,' Cheryl added.

'Don't you get owners and other high-end horsy types?'

Drew shrugged. 'Owners either stay with their trainers or just come in for the day.'

'We get a lot of their business in the bar and restaurant,' Cheryl said in a cheerful tone that sounded strained.

'We have a prima donna chef who knows his own worth and causes almost as many problems as he solves,' Drew said. 'But at least he draws the punters in. Trainers who want to impress potential owners, stuff like that.'

'But the... er... annexe?' Alexi asked, bewildered. 'How does that fit with your posh image?'

'Something had to be done. No way was I going to let Drew lose his family home,' Cheryl said defensively.

Cheryl and Drew had met in a pub during Alexi and Cheryl's final year at university. The two of them had hit it off immediately and were married the day after Cheryl graduated with a degree in hotel management. Drew had taken out a bank loan to buy out his siblings' shares of the family home, with plans to turn it into an upmarket hotel.

'You've been holding out on me,' she said, frowning at her friend.

'Pride goeth before a fall,' Cheryl replied, her chin supported in her hands. 'I wasn't about to admit to my hotshot journalist friend that we'd messed up.'

'Oh, Cheryl.' Alexi leaned forward to give her a hug. 'I might have been able to help. I could have got our travel section to give you a good write-up, stuff like that. I did mention the place several times but readers don't look for travel tips in the stuff I write... wrote.'

'Sorry, hon.' Cheryl squeezed Alexi's hand. 'Take no notice of me. I'm on edge all the time nowadays.'

'You haven't told her?' Drew asked.

'Told me what?' One look at their soppy grins and Alexi realised what ought to have been immediately apparent when she saw Cheryl's expanding waistline. She slopped tea over the table as she jumped up and hugged them both. 'About time too. Congratulations!'

'Thanks,' Cheryl said.

'When's the baby due?'

'Another four months yet,' Cheryl replied, grimacing.

'A late-summer baby then. Do we know what you're having?'

'No,' Drew replied. 'We're being old-fashioned and prefer a surprise.'

'I plan to make up for being a crap friend by spoiling the baby rotten.'

'You'll have to join the queue,' Cheryl warned, nodding at her husband who was still sporting a goofy grin. 'Anyway, we hope you'll agree to be a godmother.'

'With pleasure, although what spiritual guidance I can offer is debatable.'

'You have good morals, which is all that counts nowadays,' Cheryl said.

'Those... er, whatever they are in the garden.' Alexi reminded them. 'You still haven't told me what that's all about.'

'We let them to grooms and trainee jockeys from a local yard,' Drew admitted. 'I know we were full of lofty ideals when we started out.' He shrugged. 'But this is the real world and needs must.'

'We would have gone under without them,' Cheryl added starkly.

'Most trainers either have staff accommodation on site or

make arrangements locally.' Drew rubbed his chin. 'But last winter, one major trainer had a fire on his premises—'

'Graham Fuller,' Alexi said. 'I remember there was a lot of speculation about that.'

'Right. There were suspicious circumstances,' Drew said. 'Fuller was on bad terms with another trainer. The other guy accused him of poaching one of his top owners, and the row escalated.'

'Didn't Fuller cry arson?' Alexi asked, her interest piqued.

'I think my friend senses a story,' Cheryl said, grinning.

'Professional curiosity. Can't turn it off just because I'm unemployed.'

'Yeah well, I don't think anyone will ever really be able to prove what happened. Graham uses our bar and restaurant a lot, told me about his problem with housing for his lads, and Cheryl and I decided to bite the bullet.'

'I get why you did it, but I'm surprised you got planning permission.'

'We had to jump through hoops,' Drew admitted. 'But Graham has a lot of sway with the local council. I don't know what strings he pulled, and I don't want to. We put the units to the side, so guests in the main house don't have to look at them.'

'What we didn't realise when we agreed to do Graham a favour—'

'—And save our own bacon...' Drew added.

Cheryl waved the reminder aside. 'We didn't know it would affect our five-star status.'

'You lost a star because of them?'

'We don't have tennis courts any more,' Cheryl explained. 'None of the guests ever used them, but it seems they matter when it comes to a hotel's place on the totem pole. Anyway, the annexe is fully occupied year round, the residents fend for themselves, and we send in cleaners once a week to make sure they haven't completely trashed the place.'

Alexi could see Cheryl and Drew were putting a brave face on things. 'I'm glad they saved the day, and I promise never to say another word about the way the huts look.'

'If things pick up, or when Graham rebuilds his own staff accommodation, we can have them taken down again,' Cheryl said.

'We're just about making ends meet right now.' Drew sighed and stood up. 'Come on love, I'll get your stuff from your car and show you up. You've got the big room, centre front.'

'But that's your best room,' Alexi protested. 'Cosmo and I don't expect star treatment.'

'We don't have anyone else in the main house right now, although we're booked up for the weekend,' Cheryl replied. 'You deserve to be pampered, at least until then.'

'All right, but I insist upon paying the going rate.'

'Are you trying to insult me?' Drew asked indignantly.

Alexi refused to back down. 'You're in business,' she reminded them.

'We'll work something out,' Drew said gruffly. 'Come on now, let's get you settled, then we'll have drinks before dinner and you can catch us up with your news.'

'I can't have drinks,' Cheryl said, patting her belly and pouting. 'But I can inhale yours vicariously *and* feel all virtuous in the morning when you two have headaches from hell.'

Alexi laughed. 'The sacrifice will be worth it.'

'You hear that,' Cheryl said to her stomach. 'You are going to be *so* worth it.'

'Don't forget,' Drew said as he lugged Alexi's bag up the stairs. 'You can stay with us for as long as you like. Take some time to think about what you want to do. Cheryl will be glad of the company.'

Alexi the hardnosed, self-sufficient journalist who didn't need anyone and never accepted favours, glanced out the window and noticed spring shower-clouds building on the crests of the downs. For no apparent reason, the sight caused her eyes to swamp with tears.

2

Cosmo stalked up the stairs with them, Toby following two paces behind.

'A right pair,' Drew said, laughing at Toby's expression of total adoration.

'If Cosmo takes a liking to someone, he tends to inspire devotion. Mostly he doesn't like people and is suspicious of them—'

'He's a feral cat, right?'

'Yeah.'

'Well then, it stands to reason that he'll have learned to be selective. It's a survival skill. But I have to say, he's the largest moggy I've ever seen, especially since he doesn't have an ounce of fat on him.'

'I'm not sure why he's so svelte. He eats me out of house and home.'

Drew opened the door to her room and placed her case on the stand. He chuckled as Cosmo, erect tail twitching, prowled imperiously around his temporary accommodation. 'What made you take on a wild cat?'

'I was doing a feature a few years back about the homeless

living under Waterloo Bridge. He was there, keeping both humans and rodents in line. He was a feral tom in every sense of the word, but for some reason, he took a liking to me. The third time I went down there, he followed me back to my car, jumped into the passenger seat and hissed at anyone who went anywhere near him.' Alexi shrugged. 'What could I do?'

Cosmo leapt onto the four-poster bed, took a position in the middle of it, and set about washing his face, sending Alexi and Drew occasional glances.

Drew laughed. 'He must have been a domestic cat at one time if he likes cars.'

'That's what I figured. And I think he's forgiven me for taking him to the vet—'

Drew winced. 'Tough luck, Cosmo.'

'Hey, safe sex shouldn't be restricted to humankind. Cosmo is probably responsible for a good number of stray moggies already. He doesn't need to add more notches to his bedpost.'

Drew reached forward to scratch Cosmo's head. Alexi tensed, then relaxed again when the feline pushed his head against his hand. Toby jumped up, too, and curled up against Cosmo's body.

'I'm really glad you're here, Alexi. Cheryl's been worried about you.'

'The nicer you guys are to me, the worse I feel about not having seen more of you.'

Drew shrugged. 'Life has a nasty habit of getting in the way of friendships.'

'That's no excuse.'

'You're here now and that's all that matters. Have you got everything you need?'

'This is luxury.' Alexi glanced around the high-ceilinged room with its full-length windows looking out over the downs. Those windows were covered with floral curtains that matched the bedspread. There was a comfortable sofa beneath the window and a desk and chair where she could set up her computer. Eventually. She peered into the spacious en suite with its rack of fluffy towels and basket of toiletries. 'How could I possibly want for anything?'

'Okay, I'll leave you to get settled. Come down as soon as you're ready and we'll have that bevvy.'

'You've got yourself a date.'

* * *

Left alone, Alexi swiftly unpacked her case and hung her clothes in the closet. Then she stripped off and took a long shower. Half an hour later, feeling refreshed, she dressed in cotton trousers and a light top, brushed her hair, dabbed on a slash of lip gloss, and waved the mascara wand at her lashes. Dog and cat accompanied her downstairs again and she followed an enticing aroma into the kitchen.

'Hey.' Cheryl looked up from stirring something in a pot. Kitchens terrified Alexi. She'd lived on take-away in London and would have trouble scrambling an egg. Cheryl, on the other hand, had always loved cooking.

'Can I do something? I can chop, peel, or dice without wrecking anything.' Alexi winced. 'Probably.'

'You're good. Grab a pew. I'll be right there.' Cheryl grinned. 'Although, on second thoughts, I'm betting you can still wield a corkscrew as well as you used to back in the day.'

'Show me where, sister!'

With a glass of wine in front of her, and orange juice for Cheryl, the friends sat at the kitchen table and clinked glasses. Cosmo, failing in his transparent efforts to extract food from Cheryl, sent her the feline equivalent of an injured look and curled up in Toby's basket. Toby hopped right in with him, wagging his tail as he occupied the small amount of space Cosmo allowed him.

'Congratulations again,' Alexi said. 'I'm really happy for you. I know you're going through a rough patch with the business, but you and Drew still appear to be joined at the hip.'

Cheryl grinned. 'Yeah, we're lucky that way. And on the subject of relationships, can we clear the air about Patrick?'

'Who?'

'Lexi!'

'What do you want me to say?' Alexi spread her hands. 'You were right about him. He's a skunk. He claimed he was sworn to secrecy and couldn't tell me about the impending changes at the paper. If he had, I'd have known I was for the chop and it would have given me more time to prepare a countermove.' Alexi sighed. 'If you love someone, you put their feelings first, don't you?'

'Yes,' Cheryl replied succinctly. 'Always. I'm sorry you've been hurt but I gotta say, you're worth way more than Patrick. You *will* find that elusive someone, probably when you least expect to.'

'Right now, I'm off men and definitely not looking.' Alexi leaned over and gave Cheryl a hug. 'The organisation was top heavy and haemorrhaging money. It was obvious something had to give. I just didn't figure that I'd be one of the casualties – I was in a relationship with the political editor, who wouldn't feed me to the wolves, at least not without giving me a heads-up.' She managed a wry smile. 'Quite a blow to the ego, that one.'

'You wrote brilliant, insightful pieces,' Cheryl said defensively.

'Which was my downfall, apparently. If it doesn't have *celebrity* status, people don't want to know any more.'

'You were too good at what you did. The *Sentinel* has made a mistake if it's trying to sensationalise. They seem to forget there are still people who actually have functioning brain cells and want reasoned opinion along with the cornflakes.'

'Not so many people buy papers at all now; that's part of the problem, to be fair.' Alexi leaned an elbow on the table and rested her chin in her cupped hand. 'It's all instant, online stuff.' Alexi expelled a resigned sigh. 'Anyway, Patrick is now covering the dumbed-down version of what I did, and seemed to think I'd be happy to run the equivalent of a political gossip column.'

Cheryl's bosom swelled with indignation. 'The fink!'

'Yeah well, that's not quite what I called him.'

'All this only happened last week, and yet you've arranged to let your flat and hot-footed it down here already.' Cheryl grinned. 'I like your style.'

'I haven't seen or spoken to Patrick either, although he keeps calling.'

'Any idea what you intend to do now?'

'Nope, not a clue.' Alexi took a healthy sip of her wine. 'It's liberating in a scary sort of way.'

'You have no job, no home, and your mum recently died. I wouldn't call that liberating. More like consecutive kicks in the teeth.'

'It's forced me out of my comfort zone, which is good in some ways. I was in a bit of a rut. And, on the bright side, I have no financial worries. Sorry,' Alexi added when Cheryl flinched. 'I sold Mum's property, inherited her investment portfolio, plus I got a golden handshake from the *Sentinel*. Not that they wanted to cough up. They reckoned they'd offered me an alternative role and that by refusing it, I'd sacked myself.'

Cheryl blew air through her lips. 'Cheapskates.'

'Fortunately I'd studied my contract and found a clause that said they couldn't *demote* me without just cause, so I threatened them with legal action if they tried it. I also intimated I'd write about the way I'd been treated, offer it to their rivals... it worked. They paid up, so I can take my time deciding what next *and* pay you for my keep.' She raised a hand to stop Cheryl from protesting. 'I've had a few offers from other London papers, but nothing that tempts me. I think it might be time for a complete change of direction.'

'What, move from London altogether?' Cheryl widened her eyes. 'I thought you were a city girl through and through. Do you even own a pair of wellies?'

Alexi laughed, feeling herself begin to relax as the wine worked its magic. 'Do they come with four-inch heels?'

The back door opened to admit Drew. Cosmo, seemingly resigned to the fact that he wasn't going to be fed any time soon, stalked through it, his faithful disciple tagging along behind him.

'Any luck?' Cheryl asked.

'Sorry love, no sign.'

'No sign of what?' Alexi asked, sensing their joint anxiety.

'It's Cheryl's friend, Natalie.' Drew poured himself a generous glass of wine and topped Alexi's up. 'She's missing. We're worried about her. I just stopped by her place but no one's been there since I checked yesterday.'

'Who is she?' Alexi asked.

'She moved to Lambourn a couple of years ago. She's into floral art. Does bouquets, table decorations for weddings, stuff like that. We've used her here, which is how we became friends.'

'How long has she been gone?'

'Three days.'

'Too short a time to worry, surely?'

'She *does* go away quite a bit, but never without telling us,'

Drew explained. 'We have her keys and keep an eye on the place for her.'

'It's just so out of character,' Cheryl said, frowning in a manner that drew attention to the dark shadows beneath her eyes. Either she was really worried about her friend or those visible signs of stress were caused by their financial problems.

'She isn't answering her mobile or emails either, and that's just not like her. She runs a business and has to keep in touch with her clients, or risk losing them.'

'What about her other friends? Husband. Men friends.'

'She's divorced,' Cheryl replied. 'With no significant other. No kids. Truth is, she's lonely, but never seems to have much luck with men. They take advantage of her... well, I suppose she's so desperate to be loved that she attracts the wrong sort.'

'She's got a lovely house, drives a nice car, and she's good-looking; takes care of herself. The moment those losers she dates see that, I'm betting they think they're on to a good thing,' Drew said, scowling. 'Her car is in the garage, but her laptop, iPad, and mobile are gone, along with her handbag.'

'That does seem odd,' Alexi replied, her journalistic antennae twitching. 'Have you told the police?'

Cheryl rolled her eyes. 'They didn't want to know. Natalie is over forty, she often goes away, so they say there's not much they can do. When Drew went to our part-time police station yesterday they all but laughed him out the door.'

'I know it's not what you want to hear,' Alexi said, 'but there probably isn't any action they can take. People make out of character decisions all the time and unless there's clear evidence that a crime's been committed, the police have got more urgent things to do. They'll list her as missing, make a few enquiries, and that's about it.'

'That's more or less what they told me when I reported it,'

Drew said, giving his wife's hand a comforting squeeze. 'They implied she'd taken herself off for a naughty weekend.'

'I know a few people,' Alexi said. 'I could get one of them to run a trace on her mobile.'

Cheryl's expression brightened. 'Could you? I was hoping perhaps—'

'That would give us some idea where she is. If she's in an urban area, they might be able to get within fifty metres of her location. But fifty metres in a densely populated area is still a lot of space to get lost in. If she's out in the sticks, there could be miles between antennae stations, impossible to pinpoint her exact location.'

'I told her it was a mistake to...'

'To what?' Alexi asked when Cheryl's words trailed off and she sucked in a shuddering breath.

'Natalie has signed up to an online dating service,' Drew explained.

'Ah.'

Cheryl sighed. 'What if she was being cyber-stalked by some creep, that's what I keep wondering?'

'If she's with one of the reputable... what the hell was that?' Alexi asked when shrieks and then raucous laughter interrupted their conversation.

'The grooms returning home,' Drew said, standing up and looking through the window, a broad smile on his face. 'I think your cat is providing a welcoming committee.'

'Oh god, I'm sorry! Cosmo hisses at everyone.'

'It makes up for all the times they've disturbed us with parties they're not supposed to hold,' Cheryl said.

'Whenever one of their horses has a win, the groom usually gets a cash gift from the owners,' Drew explained.

'Ah, I get the picture. Any more problems with your grooms, say the word, and I'll get Cosmo to up his game.'

'Hey, Mrs. H,' an attractive young man waved in the window. 'Can you call your guard cat off?'

Laughing, Alexi got up, opened the back door and shouted at Cosmo. Cheryl followed Alexi out of the door.

'Fine feline,' the young man said, looking at Alexi rather than Cosmo. 'Here you go, Mrs. H. The guv'nor asked me to give you this.'

'Thanks, Tod.' Cheryl took the envelope he held out to her. 'Are you going to introduce us?'

'Alexi, this is Tod Naismith, Graham Fuller's head lad and self-appointed leader of this motley crew.' She waved a hand negligently towards the annexe. 'Tod, this is my good friend, Alexi Ellis.'

Alexi shook Tod's outstretched hand. 'Nice to meet you,' she said.

'You too.' Tod waggled his brows. 'Do you plan to stay with us for long?'

'She's out of your league, Tod,' Cheryl said, laughing as she and Alexi returned to the house. 'Sorry,' she added as she closed the door behind them. 'I should have warned you about Tod. He's incorrigible.'

'He seems like fun.' Alexi winced at the sound of banging doors. 'Or not.'

'Graham's sent over the cheque he owes us,' Cheryl said, handing the envelope to Drew.

'At last!'

The noise gradually subsided, but Alexi could see the damage the grooms would do to the hotel business. People who paid through the nose for quality accommodation expected peace and quiet and the grooms' presence was unlikely to encourage repeat bookings.

'Anyway,' Alexi said, returning to their conversation. 'If your friend is with one of the more reputable dating agencies, I'd say she'd be pretty safe. Those sites conceal members' true email addresses and block their personal details.'

'Yes, but what if she's met someone and revealed those things?' Cheryl asked. 'I warned her about it, and she promised me she wouldn't, but if she really liked and trusted a man...'

'Do you know if she went on any dates?' Alexi asked.

'To begin with we had a good laugh about some of the men she'd met, and how different they were to the images they projected on the site.' Cheryl became pensive. 'But recently she'd become quite tight-lipped about her activities. She seemed distracted, and I hoped it was because she'd met someone nice.'

'She promised us she would only meet dates in public places,' Drew added. 'Bars, restaurants, stuff like that, and if she *did* invite anyone back to hers, she also promised to let us have his details in advance, just in case.'

'But she didn't do that?'

'No.' Cheryl shook her head. 'Natalie is a good business-woman, but when it comes to personal relationships, I wouldn't put it past her to have been sweet-talked into keeping stuff to herself. Some charismatic guy would only have to spin her a line and she'd fall for it.'

'It might not be so bad,' Alexi replied, even though she had a nasty feeling about the circumstances. 'Between a quarter and a half of all new relationships start online nowadays. Did you know that?' Cheryl and Drew both shook their heads. 'Welcome to the cyber age. Online dating has got an iffy reputation—'

'With good reason,' Drew said.

'It's like anything; opportunists will find a way to exploit it, but the majority of people don't have any problems, if they're careful.'

The wine bottle was empty. Drew opened a second while Cheryl dished up the food.

'Oh god, I'm in love!' Alexi cried, groaning as she took a mouthful of Cheryl's homemade lasagne. 'I'd forgotten what a good cook you are.'

'Now you know why I married her.'

Cosmo, presumably attracted by the smell of food, appeared in the open kitchen window. Toby's pathetic barks from outside had them all laughing as Drew got up to let him in.

'Do you think we're wrong to be worried about Natalie?' Cheryl asked.

'What dating agency did she use?'

'Heart Racing,' Cheryl replied, giggling at the name. 'Apparently online dating has gone interest-related.'

Alexi grinned. 'Whatever happened to opposites attracting?'

'People don't have time for *proper* relationships nowadays,' Cheryl replied. 'Like you just said, everything's virtual. Except that now, dating agencies are targeted at specific interests.'

'I got in touch with Heart Racing,' Drew said. 'I wanted to put Cheryl's mind at rest, but they wouldn't tell me who Natalie dated. They gave me all the spiel about confidentiality and wouldn't even confirm she was registered with them.' Drew scowled at the wall. 'They wouldn't open up even when I told the snotty woman I spoke to how worried we were about Natalie and threatened them with a visit from the police.'

'They could get sued, I suppose, if they revealed anyone's details.'

'Even if they have a pervert on their books?' Cheryl demanded hotly.

'They probably have a get-out clause when it comes to perverts,' Alexi said in a futile attempt to lighten the mood.

All sorts of questions filtered through Alexi's journalistic brain, but pregnant women with money worries didn't need stress so she let the subject drop. While Drew stacked the dish-washer and put the coffee on, Alexi mentally ran through the steps she would take if this was an assignment.

Locate Natalie's mobile phone, hack into her email and see who she'd been talking to, check her bank account to make sure it hadn't been cleaned out, check her social media sites to see how open she was about herself online. If she'd registered with Heart Racing under her true name and given an honest picture of herself, it would be child's play for a cyber-stalker to get all her personal information elsewhere without asking Natalie any intrusive questions. More troubling was the fact that if the guy's intention had been to steal her cash, he wouldn't want her around afterwards to identify him. But one woman wouldn't have enough cash to see him set for life, so he'd want to do this again. And again. Which meant he would go for wealthy, needy women.

Women like Natalie.

3

By the time she returned to her room, Alexi's curiosity had got the better of her. She fired up her computer, just to see what a little creative surfing might throw up about Natalie. Alexi had what the old hacks referred to as a 'nose' for a story, and right now that nose was twitching like it was hay fever season.

It couldn't hurt to poke about a bit.

The absolute peace and stillness of Lambourn – no traffic noise, no sirens, no hustle of a city on steroids – made it hard for Alexi to concentrate. She switched on the television news with the volume turned down low. The background noise helped her to focus upon what might have happened to Natalie. The more she thought about it, the more convinced she became that this other woman was still alive.

Working on the assumption that she'd been targeted by a fortune hunter, the guy had probably whisked Natalie off to some exotic location, spinning her a line about wanting her all to himself and persuading her to cut herself off from the outside world. He'd wine and dine her; give her his undivided attention, and ply her with the best of everything.

Those types of men were always charismatic, Alexi knew. They chose their victims carefully, then traded on their looks and charm, relying on the woman's desperate need for a man to nurture to seal the deal. Having gained Natalie's trust, it would be comparatively easy for a computer-savvy guy to access her online banking. Alexi hadn't lost sight of the fact that Natalie's electronic devices were all missing. If he didn't clear Natalie out, the chances were she'd take the hit and be too embarrassed to report it.

'Okay, Cosmo, where do we start?'

Cosmo completed his ablutions and then curled up in the middle of the bed, sending her a condescending look before closing his eyes.

'Fat lot of help you are,' she chided.

Alexi quickly checked her email. There was a long missive from Patrick, which she told herself she wouldn't read.

She read it.

He was sorry, and he could explain. Where was she? He loved her. He'd only been trying to protect her. He had a proposition for her. One that was right down her street and would be more financially rewarding than slaving away on the *Sentinel*.

'Yeah right,' she muttered, deleting the email with only a slight pang of regret for what they'd once had.

Cheryl didn't know what picture of herself Natalie had used on the Heart Racing site; nor could Alexi access that information unless she either hacked into the site or registered with them. She had no intention of doing the latter. The former was a possibility.

Natalie's business website was easy to navigate and professional. It showed a pleasant image of an attractive woman in her early forties with blonde hair cut in a neat bob and an open, friendly smile. There was a contact form for those wanting information about Natalie's services. It would be child's play for anyone who knew their way around a computer to trace the IP address. The chances of it not being registered to Natalie's business, which was located at the same place as her home, were slim.

'Oh, Natalie,' Alexi muttered, shaking her head.

She was on Facebook, Twitter, LinkedIn, and half a dozen other social media sites. Her chatty posts on Facebook said enough about her daily activities to offer a stalker a good idea of her interests. She liked horses which, given where she lived, wasn't exactly a surprise. She was thinking of investing in a part-share of a racehorse, which *was* news to Alexi, who audibly groaned. Easy enough for a potential date to pretend a similar interest, along with a passion for hiking, flowers, and photography.

By the time Alexi finished her initial foray into Natalie Parker's life, she'd become as worried about her as Cheryl was. Her eyes began to droop, which surprised Alexi since she normally did her best work after the witching hour. She figured the overdose of clean, country air had messed with her lungs, which were accustomed to unhealthy doses of carbon monoxide and second-hand smoke. Then there'd been the physical and emotional upheaval, too, as well as the big meal and too much wine.

'Face it, Cosmo,' she said with a wry twist to her lips. 'I can't take it like I used to.'

She had a quick wash, slipped into a tank top and boxers, and crawled between crisp, cotton sheets. Cosmo crept up to the pillows and wrapped himself around her head, a bit like a furry nightcap, purring like a traction engine.

'Shut up, baby,' she murmured, falling almost instantly asleep.

* * *

She was woken at some ungodly hour by a noisy army on the march: presumably the grooms heading for work. She felt remarkably rested, so pushed back the covers and had a good stretch. After a quick shower, she pulled on a pair of favourite old jeans and a sweatshirt. Cosmo deigned to stir only when she slid her feet into her shoes. Pathetic whining noises from outside her door indicated that Toby was pining for his new buddy.

'Come on then,' she said to Cosmo. 'I think I can smell bacon frying.'

Toby bounded in when Alexi opened the door, wagging and jumping all over Cosmo in a frenzy of delight. Cosmo gave Toby a gentle head butt and the two of them led the way down the stairs.

'Morning,' Drew said, turning back from the stove where he was frying the bacon that had lured her into the kitchen. 'Did you sleep well?'

'Like a log. I never sleep like that in London.'

Drew screwed up his nose. 'Too much going on in the big, bad city.'

'Actually, it's so quiet here, I thought it would stop me from sleeping.'

'Grab a seat. Breakfast won't be long.'

Alexi opened the cupboard where she'd stowed Cosmo's food and extracted a packet. He wound himself around her legs as she placed his bowl on the floor.

'Where's Cheryl?'

'Just getting up. I had to almost tie her down at first to make her rest—'

Alexi warded him off with the flats of her hands. 'Too much information.'

Drew laughed. 'She's finally being more sensible. Anyway, have you had any more thoughts about Natalie? I'd rather you told me first, especially if it's not good news.'

Alexi explained about her online search. 'That was just a short foray and I already know a ton of stuff about her life.' She frowned. 'That's why this so-called social media age is dangerous. Why did she feel the need to tell the world she's thinking of investing in a share of a racehorse? That implies money and will attract all sorts of unsavoury people.'

Drew put aside his spatula and gave Alexi his full attention. 'You think she's been groomed?'

'It's a possibility, but let's not jump to conclusions. I wouldn't mind taking a look at her home later, just to get more of a feel for her, then we'll decide where to go from there.'

'Where *can* we go? I mean, the police aren't too bothered, I don't suppose the dating agency will tell us anything, and—'

'I could take a peek at her email. See who she's been talking to.'

'You can do that?'

'Comes with the territory.' Alexi laughed at Drew's horrified expression. 'I did a story once on computer security and a master hacker taught me the rudiments of his *modus operandi* just to demonstrate how easy it actually is. Anyway, let's not get ahead of ourselves. Despite what you think, I don't make a habit out of invading people's privacy online, just because I can. It's a last resort.' *Well, usually.*

'Sorry, we can't come with you.' Drew placed Alexi's breakfast in front of her and she tucked in. 'We have a lunch party for twenty people this Sunday and we have to be here to talk to the customer. There's really no need, but I think they're a bit starstruck and insist upon meeting Marcel.'

'Marcel?'

'Our chef. I hope to Christ he behaves himself. It's impossible to know. He's a bit like your cat. If he takes a dislike to someone, he can be incredibly rude.'

'Ah, one of *those*.' Alexi rolled her eyes. 'Thanks. Breakfast was great, as you can see.' She nodded towards her cleared plate. 'I'll get out the way then. Give me the address and Natalie's keys and I'll find my own way.'

* * *

The gardens to the front and side of Sundial Cottage told their own story. Bursting with orderly colour, it was obvious that whoever lived there had green fingers and a talent for making flowers thrive. Jack recognised all the usual suspects for that time of year – daffodils, tulips, primroses – but that was as far as his knowledge went. There was a mass of colourful stuff crawling over a wall, and a whole patch of white things in the bed below it. An ancient sundial sat in the centre of a well-tended lawn. The curtains were half-closed and he knew before he knocked that no one would be at home.

Time for a good snoop.

He peered through the living room window and saw nothing to excite his interest. No signs of a scuffle or a hasty departure; everything neat and tidy, which told him absolutely nothing. He would have to get inside and take a closer look. Sighing, he rounded the left flank of the cottage, looking for a more discreet point of entry. This was a quiet lane with little passing traffic and no immediate neighbours, but even so, it paid to be cautious.

There was a newish, navy-blue Mini Cooper with a garish pink roof parked at the side of the cottage. It hadn't been visible from the lane. Preoccupied by thoughts of its ownership, he almost failed to notice a massive black ball of fury launch itself from the branches of a tree like a guided missile.

'Whoa there!'

He instinctively held up his arms to protect his face. The missile landed at his feet, hissing like it bore him a grudge. It was a cat. The largest, sleekest, most pissed off cat he'd ever seen. It had obviously been camped out in the branches and now seemed to be debating whether or not to attack Jack.

'Hey, puss.' He held out a hand and the feline sniffed his fingers. He wondered where such an odd-looking creature had sprung from.

Instead of attacking Jack, the moggy eventually rubbed its large head against his jeans.

'Glad we got that one sorted out,' Jack said, reaching down to scratch its flat ears. 'Who do you belong to, big guy?'

'Who the hell are you?'

A woman rounded the corner of the house, wielding a garden rake. From the hostile look in her eyes, he figured she was about to take over where her cat had left off.

'Ms Parker?' he asked, immensely relieved that Natalie Parker was at home, alive and well, even if she did seem a tad aggressive at having her privacy invaded.

'I asked first.'

'Jack Maddox.' He delved into his pocket and produced a business card from his wallet. She reached forward and took it from him with one hand, but kept a firm grip on the rake with the other. 'Private investigator.'

'Investigator? What are you investigating?'

'We received a report that you might be having trouble with a guy you were dating.'

'Who reported that?'

'Hey, no need to be so defensive.' He held up his hands, palms forward in a placating gesture. 'I'm on your side.'

She looked at him with open suspicion, which is when Jack realised he'd probably jumped to the wrong conclusion. The picture he'd been given of Natalie Parker showed a woman a good decade older, with a blonde bob and soft-grey eyes. This one was taller; at least five eight, without an ounce of spare flesh on her. She had slim legs that looked good in tight denim. She sported a waterfall of brunette hair that tumbled over her shoulders, high cheekbones, a pert little nose, a wide, lush mouth and huge, arresting, silver-green eyes. Eyes that remained fixed upon him with misgiving while he took her measure. She looked familiar, too. He'd seen her somewhere before but couldn't place her.

'You're not Natalie Parker, are you?'

Without replying, she pulled an iPhone from her pocket, placed the rake against the wall where she could reach it again in a hurry, and started pressing buttons. Jack figured she was checking him out. Smart lady.

'Fenton-Maddox Investigations in Newbury,' she said, as though speaking to herself.

'That's me.'

'I know. I'm looking at your website.' She glanced up at him, then back at her phone. 'This picture looks like you, except you've grown your hair longer.'

He shrugged, not knowing what to say to that. The silence worked for him and, appearing to make up her mind that he wasn't an axe murderer, she extended her hand.

'Alexi Ellis,' she said. 'Natalie's friends are worried about her. They sent me to check her place out.'

'You're the journalist,' Jack said slowly. 'That's where I know you from. I've seen your picture often enough above your by-line.'

'Right.' She looked as though she was about to say something more, then closed her mouth again.

'I take it you have a key to the cottage.'

She nodded. 'Who are you working for?'

Alexi Ellis could be the break in this case that Jack had been hoping for. She was a journalist, probably on the trail of a story, and he wasn't sure if he could trust her. But still, if he didn't tell her something, he doubted whether he'd get anything in return.

'Heart Racing Dating Agency.'

She brightened. 'Ah, so they're taking this seriously. Have there been other problems?'

Jack shook his head. 'You know better than that.'

She flashed a non-apologetic smile. 'Can't blame a girl for trying.'

'What did you find in there?'

'Sod all,' she replied, shrugging. 'But I don't suppose you'll accept my word for it so you might as well come in and see for yourself.'

Jack followed her into a neat cottage with a musty smell that implied it had been shut up for a while. There was a small lounge, an eat-in kitchen and two bedrooms upstairs. Books lined the walls, mostly about flowers, photography, and horses. Nothing looked out of place.

'All that's missing is her laptop and phone. I gather she had an iPad and I can't find that either.'

'When did your friends last see her?'

'Four days ago. Who was she dating? Come on, Jack,' she coerced when he hesitated.

'Let's look at the rest of the place first,' Jack replied, playing for time. 'What's that big building out the back?'

'I was about to investigate when Cosmo found you.'

'Cosmo?' Jack quirked a brow. 'Cute name.'

This time her smile was uncontrived. 'I've heard many adjectives used to describe Cosmo, but cute is definitely a first.'

'He likes me,' Jack replied, bending to give his ears another scratch, just to make a point. 'Do you always take him on investigations?'

She grinned. 'Face it, he's pretty damned efficient. He scared the living daylights out of you.'

'Flying felines with attitude are a new one on me and I thought I'd seen it all.'

'You're not the first person to mention that,' she said as Cosmo trotted along between them towards the outbuilding.

He chuckled. 'I believe you.'

Alexi sorted through her keys and found one that fitted the lock.

'This must be her work space,' she said as they stepped inside. There was a long surface with vases, ribbons, wires, and other stuff that Jack failed to recognise, all neatly arranged beneath a large window. There was a desk in one corner and, tellingly, a phone with the message light flashing. Alexi saw it before Jack did and pressed the play back button.

The first was from someone named Cheryl.

'Your friend?' Jack asked.

Alexi nodded. The second was from Cheryl, followed by several business enquiries before Cheryl's voice came through again, sounding more concerned. Then a frantic voice.

'Ms Parker, I was expecting you this morning with my husband's wreath. How could you let me down at such a time? I am very disappointed.'

Jack and Alexi exchanged a look.

'From what Cheryl has told me, she simply wouldn't renege

on an order,' said Alexi. 'I wasn't absolutely convinced that anything had happened to her, but now I'm not so sure.' She fixed Jack with an accusatory glower. 'Your clients must think so too. Otherwise they wouldn't have called you in.'

'Let's call the lady back and see what she has to say,' Jack replied. 'Then we'll talk about it.'

4

Alexi left a message for Mrs Dixon, Natalie's aggrieved client, and then turned to look at Jack, wondering if he had any ideas about what to do next. He was standing closer than she'd realised, watching her deliberate. What the heck? Did he imagine Mrs Dixon might know something about Natalie's whereabouts and that Alexi wouldn't share the information? She hated the alpha male posturing she saw all the time in her line of work and wanted to tell Jack she wouldn't have survived five minutes in the still predominantly male domain of journalism if she couldn't play the big boys at their own game.

She was unsure how she felt about having run into Jack and less sure still whether she trusted him. Working alone and guarding her sources was second nature to Alexi, but she reminded herself that this time she didn't have to worry about being scooped. It was more serious than that. Natalie's life could hang in the balance.

Part of her was glad that the dating agency was taking things seriously. Two heads were better than one, especially if Jack had access to the agency's database. She could sense he didn't entirely trust her. He would almost certainly hide behind client confidentiality and try to keep her in the dark if things look bad for his employer. *Good luck with that one, buddy.*

At least six-two, Jack Maddox was far too easy on the eye and Alexi figured he had to know it. She might be off men, but she wasn't blind. She could appreciate his rugged profile as well as the next woman without allowing his good looks to affect her judgement.

Probably.

He had thick, dark curls falling across intelligent, chocolate-brown eyes, a strong, chiselled jaw sporting a day's worth of stubble, a high forehead, and features that had no business being quite so symmetrical. To add insult to injury, Cosmo appeared to like him. Damned if her cat wasn't in danger of gaining a sociable disposition. She put it down to all that fresh country air messing with Cosmo's metabolism, and hers. They'd both return to normal once they got back to London.

If they went back.

Whoa, since when had that been in doubt? Alexi hadn't thought much about her future but had assumed she would end up back in journalism in London, which is where the action was. *So why did you lease out your apartment?*

'Let's get out of here,' she said curtly. 'You have some explaining to do.'

'Café Lambourn in the High Street. Do you know it?'

'I'll find it.'

'Okay, see you there in a bit.'

Alexi watched him climb into a BMW that was several years old and drive away. She and Cosmo locked up carefully and took their time getting into the Mini as Alexi pondered upon developments. Part of her wanted to go straight to the police and demand that they take action. But she needed to find out what

Jack knew first, and establish why Heart Racing had put him on the case. Besides, she had the edge on Jack. Before he'd interrupted her, she'd gone through Natalie's things and found statements for two bank accounts concealed beneath a pile of sweaters in her walk-in wardrobe. Hidden there by accident or design? One of the accounts was personal and one business-related. Both had healthy balances, or had the last time she'd received paper statements. Those statements were quite old so she'd probably moved onto banking online. Still, at least she now knew where she banked.

There had been files containing household bills, the usual stuff, in the drawers of a small desk in Natalie's sitting room, but nothing else pertaining to her finances. Odd, Alexi thought. Odder still that she hadn't found anything personal in the short time she'd had to search before Jack interrupted her. No birth certificate, divorce record, old letters, photographs... nothing, nada, zilch. The lady carried no emotional baggage.

She drove slowly back to Lambourn, thinking Jack wasn't much of a PI if he hadn't thought to look for Natalie's financial records while he was inside the cottage. Unless he was holding out on her and planned to go back alone later on.

'We'll see about that, Cosmo.' She took one hand off the wheel and stroked her cat's head. 'Don't get too attached to your new buddy. He might be pretty but may not be around for long. First we need to play nice and figure out whose side he's on.' Cosmo cocked his head to one side and fixed her with a sceptical look. 'Yeah, that's what I thought too.'

The café was easy to find. Alexi pulled her car into a spot next to Jack's. She cranked a window and told Cosmo to stay put. He blinked up at her and went back to his slumbers.

Jack was standing just inside the door to the café, waiting for her.

'What will you have?' he asked.

'A skinny latte, please and... er, are those blueberry muffins fresh?'

'Homemade this morning,' said a motherly lady from behind the counter.

'Then yes, please.'

Jack laughed, sounding superior as he ordered just a black coffee for himself. Men! Alexi refused to feel guilty about the muffin following so closely on the heels of a large cooked breakfast. She *was* on holiday. Kinda.

'Okay, Maddox, give,' she said, once they'd settled themselves at a quiet corner table. 'How long have you been on this case and what have you found out?'

'So you can put it in your paper?' He gave his head an irritated shake. 'I don't think so.'

'This is nothing about work. I'm doing this as a favour to my friends.'

'People in your line of work can't disassociate.'

She sent him an appraising look. 'You don't have a very high opinion of me.'

'Not you specifically, but what you do to earn a crust. Don't take it personally.'

Alexi took her irritation out on her latte, stirring it aggressively even though she hadn't added sugar. She'd lost her appetite and picked distractedly at the muffin with her fingers.

'No offence taken,' she said in a sweetly sarcastic tone. 'What have journalists done to make you so dead set against us?'

He was quiet for so long that she didn't think he intended to answer her. She stole glances at him, trying to get the measure of the real man beneath the film star looks. She prided herself on being a good judge of character and reckoned there was more to this guy than the admittedly attractive package he showed to the world.

'I'm guessing you'll check me out properly first chance you get,' he said, breaking the uneasy silence between them.

Alexi nodded. 'Count on it.'

'Then you'll know soon enough, so might as well hear it from me.' He paused, a faraway expression gracing his features. Whatever he was about to tell her, she sensed it wasn't something he found easy to talk about. 'I was a detective with the Met until a couple of years ago. The press conducted a witch hunt when a drug dealer we arrested cried police brutality.' He sighed. 'You'd think the same lament would have gotten old by now, but I guess it was a slow news day. Anyway, I was the sacrificial lamb.'

'I think I remember something about it. The tabloids made it a *cause célèbre* because the kid had some crusading lawyer grandstanding on his behalf.' She canted her head as she continued to observe him and softened her voice. 'If it's any consolation, those of us who report news objectively rather than going for the populist and sensational thought you got a bad deal.'

'Yeah well, I was encouraged to jump before I could be pushed. Not that it took much encouragement. I'd had enough. All those regulations, the impossible-to-achieve targets, endless paperwork, and all the other crap that got in the way of what most of us signed up to do, which was to keep the streets safe for Joe Average.' He lifted his shoulders, the casual gesture at odds with the tension in his expression. 'Beats me why anyone would want to be a copper nowadays when the odds are stacked so heavily in favour of the bad guys.'

'How did you get to be a PI?'

Alexi took a bite of sinfully delicious muffin and closed her eyes, groaning with pleasure as she absorbed the sugar hit. When she opened them again, he was watching her intently.

Alexi shook her head, determined not to be drawn in by him. She still wasn't sure about his interest in Natalie.

'Seemed like a logical direction to take. I had a buddy—'

'Mr Fenton?'

'Nothing gets past you.' He flashed a megawatt smile that she found it hard not to react to. 'Actually it's Ms Fenton. Cassie Fenton.'

'Your significant other?'

He chuckled. 'Not exactly.' He leaned his elbows on the table, bringing his face closer to hers. 'Now, your turn. What's a hot-shot journalist doing down here?'

Alexi opened her mouth to tell him it was none of his damned business. Five minutes later, he knew it all. How she'd been shafted by the corporation that had employed her since she'd left university. How she'd crawled her way up the greasy pole, working twice as hard as her male counterparts to prove herself at the sacrifice of a personal life, only to be left high and dry. He was a good listener, and didn't interrupt.

'Can't think why I told you all that,' she said sheepishly, staring at her hands.

'People tell me stuff all the time.'

She shook her head. 'I'll just bet they do.'

'Sounds like you and I both grew too big for the organisations that spawned us. What will you do now?'

It was Alexi's turn to shrug. 'Stay here for a while and lick my wounds. Feel sorry for myself.'

'And try to find Natalie Parker?'

'I can't seem to help myself.' She took a swig of her rapidly cooling coffee. 'Why did Heart Racing call you in?'

'They got a visit from the local plod, were worried about their reputation—'

'The police *are* doing something about Cheryl's report. She will be relieved.'

'I doubt it. They'll be going through the motions, covering their backs.'

'Well, I guess you would know.' Alexi scowled at him because what he'd just said really annoyed her, even though it didn't exactly surprise her. 'Presumably the agency had nothing to tell them that aroused their suspicions.'

'Nope.'

'But they called you in so they must have concerns.' Alexi paused to reason it through. 'I suppose the police aren't the only ones covering their backs. If something *has* happened to Natalie, they'll come across as being uncooperative and uncaring about their clients' welfare.' Alexi rolled her eyes. 'Typical. People with that sort of attitude do deserve to be crucified by the press.'

'Not this particular organisation,' he replied, an edge to his voice.

'Well, of course you would say that. They're paying your outrageous fees.'

'Actually they're not. I'm doing this one *pro bono*.'

'Why?' she asked scathingly. 'Don't tell me you're having trouble getting a date.'

He leaned back in his chair and fixed her with a penetrating look. 'My sister, Katie, owns the agency,' he said.

'Oh.' Her mouth fell open and her cheeks turned pink. 'I guess that puts a different complexion on things. Sorry if I spoke out of turn.'

'No apology necessary and yeah, it changes things.'

* * *

Jack didn't understand why he'd told her about Katie. He didn't entirely trust Alexi. How could he? She was a journalist, and journalists had tried him in the court of public opinion and found him guilty without a shred of evidence to back up their hysteria. No, he didn't trust her, but the man in him liked what he saw.

They were drawn together by a common goal in that they both had their reasons for wanting to find Natalie. If Alexi went to the papers when this was over, he'd make sure his sister's organisation came out of it with its reputation intact. He owed her that much, and a damned sight more.

'Does your sister suspect one of the men Natalie dated?' She sat forward and watched him intently.

'Nope.'

'Presumably you have a list of the men she's spoken with electronically, or has been out with. You must have looked into them.'

'Cut me some slack.' He spread his hands. 'This is my first day on the job. Katie rang me last night, told me about your friend Drew's rather aggressive accusations, and the visit from local uniforms. I agreed to come down today and take a look around for myself.'

'Ah, right.'

'Katie started this agency from scratch five years ago. She's put everything she owns into it, including re-mortgaging her house. Now she's between a rock and a hard place. If it comes to light that she's given away confidential information needlessly, she will be finished. If she doesn't and something's happened to Natalie at the hands of one of her punters, she can also kiss her business goodbye. She has liability insurance, but still, she will lose credibility.' Jack shifted position and sighed. 'It's a hell of a worry for her. She wants to do the right thing, but...'

'The agency is local to Berkshire?'

'That's the whole point of it. According to her, people are too busy nowadays to hook up by traditional means, so they go online and are drawn together by common interests. Katie lives locally. This is horseracing country, so...' He spread his hands, refraining from stating the obvious.

'Do you ever worry that computers are taking over our lives?' Alexi asked pensively. 'When I was a kid we played outside, climbed trees, fell off bikes, and god forbid, even walked to school. We got fresh air, exercise, *and* we interacted personally with our peers.' She flashed a rueful smile. 'I sound like an old crone, but you get my drift?'

'I agree with you, Grandma, but times change.'

'Not always for the better.'

'Do you want to put the world to rights or concentrate on finding Natalie?'

Her hurt expression made him regret sounding so impatient. They'd been talking like normal people, almost enjoying one another's company, but now her hackles were up again.

'Sorry.'

She shot him a look. 'You're right. Natalie is all that matters.'

'Right, well, as I say, busy professionals want to meet like-minded people with similar interests and don't want to travel the length and breadth of the country to hook up. So Katie figured keeping it local would be a good way to go. She's well aware of the pitfalls, too. The Online Dating Association—'

'The what!'

He chuckled, resisting voicing the jibe that sprang to mind about her not having done her research. 'They have a code of conduct, which she adheres to, doing all she can to protect her clients' interests. She's earned herself a good reputation, which is why she really doesn't need a scandal.'

'I understand, but—'

'Look at it from her clients' point of view.' Jack's voice cut through her objection. 'You're an average Joe, perhaps embarrassed about having to turn to the internet for a date. But you meet some nice, regular people, get comfortable with the idea, and then get the likes of us crawling all over you, accusing you of stuff you probably haven't done. If they sued, Katie would lose everything she's worked for.'

'The punters wouldn't know we were looking at them, unless there was something to arouse our suspicions. That's one way in which the internet works in our favour.'

'Katie knows that, which is why she called me in. She is worried because she hasn't been able to get hold of Natalie, either. She had a date arranged and the guy contacted Katie, complaining Natalie didn't show up.'

'When was the date for?'

'Yesterday lunchtime.'

'You're close to your sister, aren't you?' she asked after a short pause.

'She saved me from self-destructing when I left the force. It cost me my marriage, and my self-respect. I gave up for a while and viewed the world through the bottom of a glass. Katie came along and gave me a well-deserved kick up the backside. Anyway, I heard from Cassie, who was expanding her business and needed a partner with an injection of cash. That was a year ago.'

'I can relate because I'm going through the *what-the-heck* stage right now, too.'

'Don't let the bastards grind you down.' He grinned at her. 'Well, I say that now, having come out on the winning side of a deep depression.'

'Do you have any kids?'

'Come again?'

'You said you were married. I wondered if you were a dad.'

'The marriage didn't survive the test of time so no, no kids.' He stared off into the distance, marvelling at her ability to get him talking about himself. 'Grace and I were never really suited. She hated being a copper's wife, and I knew she wasn't happy about my career choice before we married. That ought to have told me something. Anyway, we're good friends now. She's got herself another guy and I wish her well.'

'I'm not the right person to talk to about relationships. Ask Cosmo.'

He smiled at her, guessing she was thinking about the guy at the paper whose name she had mentioned several times. Feeling her need to change the subject, which suited him just fine because this was getting way too personal, Jack obliged.

'Fill me in on what you know about Natalie,' he said.

'Most of what I know I gleaned online last night. The rest I learned from Cheryl and Drew. Basically, Natalie is a successful businesswoman with no close relations, stating online for the world to see that she's thinking of buying a share in a racehorse.' Jack flinched. 'Yeah, that was my reaction, too. I get the impression she's emotionally needy and really wants to be in a relationship.'

'Ideal fodder for the stalkery type.'

Alexi looked serious. 'We both know something's happened to her, don't we?'

He nodded. 'It's looking that way, but more digging's necessary before we can be sure.'

'Into her dates?'

'I'll let you know what I find out.'

'Oh no! We're in this together, buster. You want to find Natalie and save your sister's business. I want to find Natalie and put my friends' minds at rest.' She fixed him with a malevolent glare. 'How does that make us enemies? Oh, I get it,' she added, before he could reply. 'You think I'm gonna write this up and sell it to the *Sentinel*'s competitors because I'm the resentful type looking to get one over on my previous employers.'

'Are you?'

'I could do that anyway.' She leaned forward, arms folded on the table, determination radiating from hostile eyes. 'I'm not any happier with the idea of having a partner than you are, but I am going to try and find out enough about Natalie to get the police actively involved, with or without your help. It seems daft both of us covering the same ground. Accept my word for it that I won't write a single paragraph until we find Natalie, and perhaps not even then.' She held out a hand. 'Do we have a deal?'

Jack relented. What she said made sense. Besides, she was sharp, and would definitely be more of a help to him than a hindrance. He took her hand in a firm grasp. 'Deal,' he agreed. 'And in the spirit of open partnership, I think the first thing we should do is look at her financials.'

Alexi removed the bank statements she had found at the cottage from her bag and waved them beneath his nose in a flourishing gesture. 'I helped myself to these.'

'Damn, you're good!'

'Normally I'd agree with you, but I got lucky.' She explained where she'd found them and how odd she thought it that Natalie didn't keep a file for her banking documentation.

He shrugged. 'Odd, I agree, but not unheard of.'

'As to being good, I have my limitations and I'm not sure I know how to hack into bank accounts.'

'Who said anything about hacking?'

'Well, I thought...' Alexi spread her hands. 'How else can we...'

Jack took the papers from her. 'Her bank's here in Lambourn. Why don't we go and see the manager, ask if there's been any unusual activity on her accounts?'

'He won't tell us diddly squat.'

'No, but if we tell him Natalie's missing and the police have been informed, if there is anything odd going on, we could encourage him to take his concerns to them.'

Alexi pouted. 'You think like a policeman. You're used to having the authority to demand answers. I think like a journalist, used to having doors slammed in my face and having to find a back way in. Therein lies the difference between us.'

'Oh, I don't know.' He allowed his gaze to lazily travel the length of her body; what he could see of it with the table separating them. 'I can think of one or two others.'

'Get your mind out of the gutter, Maddox.'

He sent her a sheepish grin. 'Sorry.'

'Okay, let's call the bank first. Then we'll look at the details of the guys she's dated. No hacking required since you can get us those legitimately.' She gathered up her bag. 'Where are you staying?'

'Nowhere. I just drove over from Newbury for the day. I was planning on going back.'

'Well, don't take this the wrong way, but if we're in this together, it might make more sense if you stay in Lambourn.'

He sent her a long, speculative glance. 'What do you have in mind?'

'Not what you're thinking, obviously.'

He shrugged. 'Shame.'

'Cheryl and Drew have a hotel with empty rooms. I'll put in a good word with the owners,' she said, grinning. 'I might be able to persuade them to give you a discount.'

5

'Why don't you follow me back?' Alexi suggested.

He flashed another of his devastating smiles. 'Sounds like a plan.'

Damn it, Alexi thought as she climbed into her Mini, fired up the engine, and floored the accelerator, *why did he have to have such a killer smile?*

'He's wasting his time, Cosmo,' she told her cat. 'I'm immune to whatever game he's playing.'

She used the short drive back to Hopgood Hall to think over the agreement they'd reached, wondering if it was a good idea. She could simply go to the police with what she knew and use the power of her press credentials to force them to take Natalie's disappearance more seriously. What did she know about investigative work? If she played Nancy Drew down here in the valley of the racehorse, where she stood out like a townie on an away-day who didn't know a fetlock from a farthingale, she could put Natalie's life in danger.

Supposing she was still alive.

With such sobering considerations rattling around inside her head, Alexi felt a tad reassured when she thought about having Jack Maddox in her corner. He *did* know how to conduct an investigation. While they waited to see if the bank took any action, Alexi could pretend she was fully on board with Jack. Then she'd get to see who Natalie had been dating through legitimate means. It would also give her time to take a look at Natalie's email, which *would* require a basic hack. Hopefully they would be able to amass enough evidence to convince the police to up their game, minimising damage to Jack's sister's operation. It surprised Alexi how badly she wanted to help a woman whom she had never met.

'Go figure,' she muttered as she pulled in between the Hopgood Hall gateposts.

Jack parked, climbed from his vehicle, and shaded his eyes with his hand as he took a look at the house. As soon as she released Cosmo, he went straight across to Jack and rubbed his head against his legs. Toby came bounding down the steps and launched himself at Cosmo. Jack laughed as he watched cat and dog go through their meet-and-greet routine.

'Cosmo has an identity crisis,' he said.

Alexi rolled her eyes. 'Tell me something I don't know.'

'Nice place.' Jack's gaze lingered on the refined old Georgian building.

'It's been in Drew's family for several generations.'

'And we're hanging on in there. Somehow,' Drew's voice remarked.

Alexi turned to see him and Cheryl standing on the steps, eyeing Jack with curiosity. Alexi made the introductions and explained how their paths had crossed.

'It's nice to meet you, Jack. I'm so glad someone else is worried about Natalie,' Cheryl said. 'Do come in and tell us more.'

'Actually, Jack needs a room for a night or two,' Alexi said 'I said I thought you could probably oblige.'

'I expect we can find you a broom cupboard,' Drew said with a wry smile, indicating the visitors' car park, empty but for their two vehicles.

They followed Cosmo and Toby into the kitchen, where Cosmo set up an almighty racket, demanding food. Alexi relented and allowed him a snack. It had been a busy morning for him too.

Seated around the table, Cheryl gave Jack the third degree. Alexi didn't know whether she was more annoyed or amused with the way he fielded her questions without giving much away about himself.

'I managed to find Natalie's bank account details,' Alexi said, explaining what they planned to do with that information.

'Good thinking.' Drew nodded his approval.

'Given the police have already asked a few basic questions at Racing Hearts,' Alexi added, 'they can't ignore new information.'

'Let's make that call,' Cheryl said, fidgeting with impatience.

'In a mo,' Alexi replied. 'And while the bank's deciding what to do, Jack and I are going to take a look at the backgrounds of any men she might have dated and see what her email throws up.'

Cheryl elevated both brows. 'You can get into her email?'

'It's easier than you might think,' Jack told her. 'Simply a case of cracking her password and there are a ton of programmes you can buy online to do that job.'

'At least in this instance, it'll be in a good cause.'

'Can we use the guests' sitting room to set up our laptops?' Alexi asked.

'Consider the room as your personal working space, at least

until we fill up at the weekend,' Drew replied. 'I'll show Jack to his room, and he can join you once he's settled.'

As soon as Drew and Jack departed, Alexi braced herself for a barrage of questions.

'Only you could go out on a simple assignment and come back with *him*,' Cheryl said grinning.

'Don't get too cozied up. His first loyalty is to his sister.'

Cheryl shook her head. 'If you're saying he'd let something happen to Natalie rather than have his sister's reputation tarnished, or that he'd try to cover up her organisation's involvement if something has happened to her, then it won't wash. He has way too much integrity.'

'How can you possibly be so sure?'

'A mother instinctively knows these things,' Cheryl replied loftily.

Alexi guffawed. 'You're still a mother in training.'

'Even so.'

'You're letting his pretty face influence you.'

Cheryl fixed Alexi with a knowing look. 'And you're not?'

Alexi shrugged. 'I've never been in a life and death situation like this one before. I need help.'

The implication that Natalie was in danger caused the smile to fade from Cheryl's lips.

'Don't worry.' Alexi gave her friend a swift hug. 'We'll find her.'

* * *

Jack let out an appreciative whistle when Drew showed him into the room directly across the hall from Alexi's.

'I could get used to this,' he said. 'But really, you don't need me cluttering up your best rooms.'

'Since you're doing us a favour in a roundabout sort of way, you might as well be comfortable.'

'Well then, thanks.' He threw his overnight bag on the bed, thinking it was large enough to accommodate four with ease. Two could have an absolute ball. *Don't go there!*

'What are the chances of finding Natalie alive?' Drew asked bluntly.

Jack shrugged. 'Until we learn more about her activities it's hard to say, but something's definitely happened to her. There's no way to sugar coat that. Hopefully, by the end of the day, we'll have got the police fully involved, but we need more than we have right now to make them prioritise her disappearance.'

'Like a body,' Drew said, grimacing.

Jack slapped his shoulder. 'Don't think the worst just yet. If she's alive, we'll find her.'

'I'll let you get on with it then.' Drew paused in the open doorway. 'Let me know if you need anything.'

'Will do.'

Jack sat on the edge of the bed for a while after Drew left him, thinking about the speed with which this enquiry had escalated. His partner wouldn't be happy. The agency was busy right now, this assignment didn't pay, and paying work was the only kind Cassie took on. Jack needed to make her understand that he couldn't walk away and leave Katie in the lurch.

Hopefully he and Alexi could absolve Katie's clients of involvement before the police got their teeth into the investigation. It was looking increasingly unlikely that Heart Racing could keep itself out of the case. In spite of what he'd just told Drew, Jack wasn't optimistic about finding an innocent explanation for Natalie's disappearance. It was a question of degree. If they could find another thread to Natalie's life – personal or connected to her business – to account for her vanishing act, it would take the heat off Katie.

He pulled his phone from his pocket and called his sister up. She answered on the first ring.

'Hey, what have you found?'

'Good morning to you, too.'

'Sorry, Jack, but you know how worried I am.'

'Yeah, I do know.'

He told Katie where he was, who he was working with and why.

'A journalist?' Her groan echoed down the line. 'You hate journalists. Besides, I thought you were going to help me keep this thing under wraps, not have the spotlight shone on my problems.'

'She's on this anyway, sis. Better we work together, so I can keep control of what she makes public. Besides, I think she's more concerned about finding her friend's friend than she is about making headlines.'

'Well, that's something, I suppose,' Katie said dubiously. 'And you're right. Natalie's welfare is the primary concern. Let me know if you need anything and keep me posted.'

'Will do.'

Jack took a moment before making his next, more difficult, call. Jack knew that Cassie Fenton, a few years older than him, divorced and attractive, was angling to become Jack's partner in all senses of the word. Jack liked Cassie. He admired her quick mind and tough, no-nonsense attitude. He valued her friendship but didn't want more from her than that. She would be annoyed because he needed to stay in Lambourn for a bit longer. That was bad enough but if he mentioned Alexi, Cassie would put two and two together and come up with ninety-seven.

'Hey, Cas,' he said, when she picked up. 'How's it going?'

'Hectic. When will you be back?'

'Er, that's why I'm calling. There've been some developments. Looks like this woman has definitely gone missing and when the alarm's raised my sister's organisation will be in the direct firing line. I need to stay, dig around a bit more, and manage damage control.'

'Damn! I'm sorry about your sister, and about the missing woman, but we're up to our eyes here.'

'I'm sorry, too, Cas, but this is something I have to do. Get Larry in to help you,' he said, referring to an ex-copper they sometimes used when they were busy. 'I'll get back just as soon as I can.'

'Yeah, all right.'

'Oh and, Cas, can you run a few checks for me?'

She sighed. 'Okay, I guess. What do you need?'

'See if you can get a fix on Natalie's mobile.' He reeled off the number. 'It's a longshot. I'm guessing it's either switched off or in a poor coverage zone, but we need to give it a go.'

'Okay, I'm on it. Anything else?'

'Well, yeah. Natalie dated three guys.'

A longer sigh echoed down the line. 'I suppose you want background checks on all of them.'

'Just the basic stuff,' he replied in his most persuasive tone, giving her the details he had. 'Oh, and while you're at it, see what you can find for me on the missing woman herself, Natalie Parker.'

'Just the basics, huh?'

'Sarcasm doesn't suit you,' he said, chuckling.

'Leave it with me. I'll get back to you.'

'Thanks, Cas.'

Jack cut the connection, picked up the bag containing his laptop, and found his way to the residents' lounge.

'Nice,' he said, looking around the light, airy room that had been tastefully renovated and furnished with what appeared to be genuine antiques. Alexi was sitting at a walnut secretaire below a window that offered a pleasant view over the gardens.

'The furniture has been in Drew's family for generations,' she said, immersed in something on her computer and not looking up as he approached.

He peered over her shoulder. 'What are you doing?'

'Running a programme to crack Natalie's email password.'

Jack set his own computer up on a table next to her desk, and told her what arrangements he'd just made.

'Good.' Finally she looked up and gave him her full attention. 'I think it would be better if you rang the bank,' she said. 'If I give my name, the connection might be made to the paper, which doesn't always work to my advantage.'

'Whereas being a PI opens all sorts of doors,' he said flippantly.

'I've got the bank's number here,' she said, reeling it off. Jack punched the digits into his mobile. 'Put it on speaker.'

Jack elevated one brow and complied with her request. He jumped through a few hoops and was finally put through to the assistant manager, a guy called Cole. He quickly identified himself and told the man why he was calling.

'I can't tell you anything about a customer's account,' Cole replied crisply.

'She's gone missing,' Jack repeated. 'We don't expect you to tell us anything, but we do know she had healthy balances in both her business and private accounts.'

'I can't confirm that.'

Jack blew air through his lips and strove for a patient tone. 'We wondered if there had been any unusual activity on those accounts. Large sums of money being transferred, that sort of thing. If so, the police would be very interested.'

'They haven't been to see us about it. If they suspect Ms Parker has been targeted for her money, we ought to be the first place they look.'

'It's still early days and the police prefer to think she'll reappear.'

'Well then, I—'

'If you have concerns about activity on her accounts you can contact...' Jack extracted the card from his wallet that the PC had left with his sister. 'PC Taylor at this number.' He read it off. 'Concerned friends reported Ms Parker's disappearance to Lambourn Police but, as you probably know, the local station is only open part time. PC Taylor knows all about it and can be reached any time on the number I've just given you.'

Having secured a promise from Cole that he would make the call if he thought it appropriate, Jack cut the connection.

'You'd think I just asked him for the combination to his bank's safe,' Jack said, screwing up his features in disgust. 'If something happens to Natalie because he procrastinated, I shall make his life a living hell.'

'Do you think he will call?'

'If there's anything there, then he probably will. Eventually. His own arse would be on the line if he didn't and fraud is subsequently uncovered. I recorded that call so he can't deny it took place.'

'Very trusting of you.' Alexi grinned. 'I like your style.'

'All Cole cares about is his career.' Jack allowed his impatience to show. 'Anyway, if he does contact Taylor, he's just a local bobby. I'm betting he's given Natalie's disappearance a case number, made a few desultory enquiries, and left it at that. But if he gets more solid information that implies a crime's been committed, he'll have to pass the case on to the Thames Valley Police.' Jack stretched his arms above his head and smiled at her. 'Okay, so let's take a look at Natalie's dream dates.'

'How many of them are there?'

'Three.'

'And she dated all three of them?'

'Two of them just once. One of them three times.'

Alexi brightened. 'The three-time winner sounds hopeful.'

'Let's take a look-see.' He pulled up the Heart Racing site and accessed the restricted area. 'Ah, the power,' he said, grinning.

Alexi stood behind him, resting her hand on the back of his chair. She smelled of a light floral fragrance and herbal shampoo. He liked the way she smelled. He liked everything about her, which irked the hell out of him. Reporters were bad news. Reporters were responsible for him being hounded out of the police under a cloud of suspicion.

'Pull up a chair,' he said easily.

'You've accessed the female clients' list,' Alexi pointed out to him. 'Looking for a date?'

'I was looking to see what Natalie posted about herself.'

'Oh, right. Good thinking.'

There were several pictures of Natalie: arranging flowers, playing with a dog, out walking along a country path.

'They look like the real deal,' Alexi said. 'I don't think they've been photoshopped, but Cheryl will be able to tell us.'

'Tell you what?' Cheryl's voice asked from the hallway. She poked her head around the door. 'I just came up to tell you it's lunchtime and heard my name being taken in vain.'

'These are the pictures Natalie posted of herself on the dating site,' Alexi explained. 'Is this how she looks in real life?'

Cheryl peered over their shoulders. 'That's her,' she said.

'A pretty lady,' Jack said, printing off a couple of the better ones.

'Yes, she is.' Cheryl sighed. 'We're having lunch in the bar, if you'd like to join us.'

They both stood up.

'Sounds good to me,' Jack said. 'I could eat a... well, I probably won't be too popular around these parts if I finish that statement.'

'Stay, Cosmo,' Alexi said to the cat who, along with Toby, had come in from the garden and joined them. 'I'll be sure and bring you something.'

Cosmo sent her an assessing look, then curled up in a patch of sunshine on the window seat. Toby hopped up to join him.

Cheryl laughed as they made their way down the stairs. 'You'll just have to stay with us permanently, Alexi. Toby will be heartbroken if his new best friend leaves again.'

'Don't tempt me.'

* * *

A wide archway led from the vaulted entrance hall to a welcoming, tastefully appointed bar with racing memorabilia decorating the walls.

Jack knew a bit about expensively refurbished houses, and could tell a fortune had been sunk into this one. The original fireplace had been restored, with a huge mirror filling the space above the marble mantle and a leather fire seat surrounding the polished brass fender. There were shelves of old books, and his feet sank into expensive, thick pile carpet. The bar itself appeared to be well-stocked. It was tended by an attractive young woman who chatted with a half-dozen racing types occupying the stools surrounding it, all of whom nursed meagre half pints of beer. Less than half of the tables were occupied, all by men who appeared to be immersed in conversations, eating and drinking sparingly. Jack suspected they were using the place to impress, but were obviously slow to put their hands in their pockets. He wasn't optimistic about Drew seeing a return on his investment any time soon.

There were closed double doors at one end of the bar with a sign above them indicating that the restaurant was behind them.

'We don't open it at lunchtime,' Drew said, following the direction of Jack's gaze. 'It's not cost effective. The demand is for bar food on weekdays.'

'It looks good,' Jack replied, glancing at a bursting sandwich being served to someone at an adjoining table.

'So, what do you fancy?' Cheryl asked, handing him a menu.

Jack perused it, noticing a clever combination of traditional sandwiches and soups, alongside sushi, tapas, and exotic salads. The work of the temperamental chef he'd already heard about, presumably. He opted for a roast beef sandwich.

'I'll take a Caesar salad,' Alexi said. 'I've already eaten more than usual today. I can't believe I'm hungry again.'

'So,' Drew said, after he'd fetched drinks. 'How's the sleuthing going?'

Alexi told them about Jack's call to the bank.

'We're going to look at the people she dated after lunch,' she added.

'My partner's looking into their backgrounds,' Jack said, taking a swig of local beer and nodding his approval. 'It's often the things people don't make public that hide the clues.'

'Doesn't your sister's agency vet them?' Cheryl asked, toying with the stem of her orange juice glass.

'She tries, but only so much probing is possible without invading a client's privacy.'

'There must be a limit to how many things you can get away with lying about, I guess,' Alexi remarked.

'Exactly. If someone goes on a date and finds the person they hook up with has lied about something important, like... say, their occupation, or if they're clearly a lot older than they implied, or behave inappropriately, then Katie's people give the offender the equivalent of a yellow card. If it happens a second time, they will be removed from the agency's database. Like I was telling Alexi earlier, the Online Dating Association has a code of conduct which Katie's agency rigidly adheres to.'

Their food arrived, which kept them all quiet for a few minutes.

'Tell me more about Natalie herself,' Jack invited. 'My partner is looking into her background, but—'

'Why?' Cheryl asked defensively. 'She didn't abduct herself.'

'No, but I need to get more of a picture about her private life. It might help us to figure out what's become of her. Does she have a sick sister, aunt, cousin, niece... I don't know, someone she cares about enough to drop everything and dash to the rescue without telling anyone.'

'I didn't see any family pictures in her cottage,' Alexi said.

'I don't think she has any family,' Cheryl said in a considering tone. She glanced at Drew, who shook his head. 'It's funny, but we never really talked much about what she did before she came here. She said she'd been married for a while but it didn't work out, and that she didn't have any kids. It was like she didn't want to talk about her past. She always turned the conversation on to her business, or her hobbies—'

'Photography and walking?' Alexi asked.

'Yes.'

'Did she belong to a photography club, or a walking group?' Jack asked.

Once again Cheryl and Drew shared a glance and simultane-ously shook their heads.

'She never said if she did,' Cheryl replied.

'We need to go back to her cottage,' Alexi said. 'Take a closer look at her files. After we've looked at her email, of course. That's the most likely place to learn more.'

'I feel bad not knowing more about her life,' Cheryl admit-ted. 'I'm a rubbish friend.'

'You trying to steal my crown?' Alexi asked.

Cheryl shook her head. 'I'm fairly sure she had no family at all. I do remember her telling me she was an only child and that both her parents were dead.'

'So,' Jack said musingly, 'where did a middle-aged woman who lives alone and runs a modest business out of her back garden get so much money?'

'Divorce settlement?' Drew suggested.

'Possibly, but it'll show up in Cassie's background check if that's the case.'

'We don't know how much money she actually has,' Alexi pointed out.

'No, but we know that two years ago, when she first moved here and had a paper statement from her bank, she had over a quarter of a million quid spread between her deposit account and various investments. And she didn't take a business loan to get started.'

Drew and Cheryl looked flabbergasted.

'Well,' Drew said, recovering first. 'We did wonder how she could afford a share in a racehorse. Now we know, I guess.'

'But not where the money came from,' Cheryl said. 'That's a lot of change.'

'Did she talk about horses a lot?' Jack asked.

'All the time,' Cheryl said, nodding. 'She was obsessed with the sport.'

'A lot of people are. That's why they buy shares. So they can go to the glamorous races, be in the owners' enclosure, stuff like that,' Drew said.

'Did she have any favourite trainers? Any horse she was seriously interested in?'

Drew and Cheryl looked at one another and shook their heads. 'If she'd found a horse, she didn't say anything to us,' Cheryl said.

'Same goes for trainers,' Drew added.

'Did she have any other particular friends in the village?' Jack asked.

'Not really,' Cheryl replied. 'She was friendly with everyone, but also very private. I think I was her only female friend. She dated occasionally, but there was no one special. That's why she started online dating. She said good men were rarer than an honest politician.'

Jack smiled. 'Interesting comparison. Okay, we'll have to wait and see what Cassie comes up with.'

Drew got up to speak to a couple of suits at another table when they beckoned him over.

'That happens a lot,' Cheryl said. 'It can be annoying, but if we want to succeed, we're never off-duty.'

'We need to get back to work, too,' Jack said, putting aside his napkin and draining the last of his beer. 'Thanks for lunch, Cheryl. Put it on my bill.'

6

'A lady of mystery,' Alexi said as they climbed the stairs, side by side. 'The more I learn about her, the less I feel like I know her.'

'Everyone has a past.'

'Sure, but I get the impression Natalie was being deliberately evasive. She seemed to avoid making female friends.' Alexi paused with her hand on the banister. 'I wonder if that was because she didn't want anyone getting close enough to ask awkward questions. Cheryl, the only girlfriend she had, knew nothing about her relationships and was too polite to probe. Even so, it still strikes me as odd that Natalie offered up nothing about herself.'

Jack shot her a look. 'Do *you* kiss and tell?'

'This isn't about me.' She resumed walking. 'Do you think Natalie kept people at arm's length because she had something to hide? The source of that money perhaps?'

'I can't see the issue arising. On the surface, she doesn't live the life of a woman with money to burn. Her home is modest and she works hard.' Jack opened the door to the guest lounge and ushered Alexi through it ahead of him. 'Anyway, there could be a genuine explanation for her bank balance. We don't know how long ago her parents died and if she came into an inheritance when they did. Her husband might have been well-off and she got a good settlement when they split.'

Alexi stroked Cosmo's head and fed him the pieces of chicken she'd saved him from her salad. She pulled her chair closer to Jack's table and waited while he fired up his laptop, ignoring the wave of awareness that streaked through her when their thighs accidently touched.

'Sorry.' She hastily moved hers out of the line of fire.

Jack grinned as he pulled up information on the first of Natalie's dates.

'Paul Keiser, forty-seven, a stockbroker based in Reading,' he said, reading off the guy's profile. 'Never been married. Lives alone. Interests include cycling and, obviously, horseracing. She dated him once two weeks ago. Her email will tell us if they've been in touch since.'

Alexi screwed up her nose as the image of a very ordinary-looking man, whose only redeeming feature appeared to be a kind smile, filled the screen. 'Wonder what she saw in him,' she said, making a note of the details.

'He's a stockbroker. That implies personal wealth.'

'Only if he indulges in insider trading. Otherwise it's just a job. Besides, Natalie has money of her own.'

'Perhaps she amassed it by targeting men like Keiser.'

'How? Unless she marries them, she wouldn't have access to their bank accounts. But then again, he's never been married, and would be flattered by attention from someone who looks like Natalie. That might get him spending on her.'

Jack shrugged. 'Let's leave him for a moment and see who else took her fancy.' Jack pulled up details of her second date.

'Divorced father of two grown kids, fifty-two, a freelance photographer—'

'Photography is one of Natalie's interests,' Alexi pointed out, again screwing up her nose when she looked at the guy's picture. 'Nothing else about him stands out.'

Jack shot her an amused look. 'Do you always judge a book by its cover?'

'If Natalie *does* want a personal relationship, of course appearances would matter to her. But I think she was equally concerned about what made the guys she dated tick.'

'Or she was looking for a lonely sugar daddy who'd be flattered by her interest in him, so appearances would be inconsequential.'

'Make up your mind, Maddox. One moment we suspect her dates of trying to fleece her, then you think it could be the other way around.'

'Doesn't do to focus on just one possibility. People never fail to surprise me with the lengths they're prepared to go to.'

'Fair point. But this guy doesn't fit the bill. Not if she planned to take him for his dosh. He has grown kids who would naturally be suspicious of any woman who got their hooks into their daddy, depriving them of the inheritance they probably think they're entitled to.'

Jack shook his head, grinning as he tutted at her cynicism. 'Okay, are you ready for this?' He sounded like a cheesy game show host trying to whip an indifferent audience into a fervour of expectancy. 'Guy number three is the one she dated three times, with Paul and Roger slotted in between. His name is Darren Walker, retired early aged fifty-five from the Civil Service and moved to Lambourn about a year ago.'

'He lives here, in the village?'

'In Hungerford, which is local enough and probably explains why she dated him so regularly.'

'Nothing else would,' Alexi said, glancing at his picture and grimacing.

Jack chuckled. 'Yeah, okay. Even I can see he's not god's gift, but perhaps he has a winning personality.'

'He's a widower with no kids,' she said, reading over his shoulder. 'That's a game-changer. He would be an ideal target, if she *was* the predator. I hate to admit it, but it's starting to look as though you might be right about that. We should pay him a visit.'

'Not yet. Give Cassie a chance to work her magic. Once she's found out about all three men's finances, we'll have a better idea if their interest in Natalie is fiscal.'

'I hate all this waiting around,' Alexi complained. 'Can't we go and have friendly chats with these guys?'

'And ask them what?'

She smiled. 'Okay, I take your point. Whatever we ask, as things stand, we won't have much idea if they're lying.'

'Right, and don't lose sight of the fact that we're trying to protect my sister's interests. Or rather, I am.' A hint of determination fuelled his expression. 'If we go knocking on Walker's door, we have no way of explaining how we know about his dates with Natalie. He will assume the agency broke its confidentiality clause and could kick up one hell of a stink.'

'We could pass ourselves off as friends of Natalie's. Say she's missing and we're worried about her. She mentioned dating Walker and we wondered when he'd last seen her.'

Jack shook his head. 'Let's look at her email before we decide, see what clues that throws up.'

Alexi moved back to her own computer. 'I have her password cracked.'

'Good, it's Cassie,' Jack said at the same time as an email popped into his inbox. 'Let's see what she's got for us.'

Jack read Cassie's message and then clicked to open a lengthy attachment.

'Paul Keiser isn't a stockbroker. He holds a middle-management position with an investment firm, salary forty thousand, and lives with his elderly mother. He pays for her round-the-clock care.'

'A nice guy who can't devote all his attention to a woman while his mother lives.'

'Right. So if Natalie's intention was to fleece him, she would know from one date that she was backing a loser. His mother owns her home, which Keiser presumably will inherit, but Cassie reckons it's only worth two hundred thousand. Not big bucks in this day and age.'

'No, and anyway, if Natalie is a victim, not the predator, leaving aside the fact that this guy doesn't have an obvious motive to wish her harm, he hasn't had enough time to figure out a way to kidnap her, or worse, so I agree with you. He's probably not our guy.'

'Good god, the woman agrees with me. Hold that thought.'

Alexi flapped a hand. 'Stop being an idiot and let's see what Cassie's found on Roger Dalton.'

Jack flipped to the second page of the attachment. 'Hmm, he has a photography business in Ascot, specialising in horses, but he's got a hefty business overdraft and a second mortgage on his house.'

'A good reason for Natalie not to have any interest in him, if he revealed any of that.'

'But plenty of reason for him to take an interest in Natalie.'

'We might need to take a visit to Ascot,' Alexi said.

'Looks that way. Still, let's see what's what with our number one contender.' The third page of the attachment was more detailed. 'He has a house on the outskirts of Hungerford, value half a million, bought for cash two years ago.'

'Where does a civil servant get that sort of dosh?' Alexi asked, frowning.

'His wife of thirty years died of cancer three years ago.'

'Life insurance pay out?'

Jack shrugged. 'Possibly. No kids or close relations.' He looked up at Alexi. 'If Natalie is motivated by money, or simply wants to find a decent guy to share her life with, either way Walker would fit the bill. I can see why she's dated him three times.'

'Then we must go and see him.'

'I agree, but after we've gone back to Natalie's cottage and taken a closer look at her papers.'

'I was about to say that.'

He sent her a sexy smile that caused her tummy to perform Olympic-standard backflips. 'Sorry.'

'You've redeemed yourself by finding all this stuff so quickly. How does Cassie do it?'

'We have our ways,' he said, smirking.

'Okay, don't tell me.'

'Hey, there's no big secret.' He waved her aside. 'You ought to know, in your line of work, how easy it is to find out just about anything on anyone these days, if you know where to look. The company Cassie worked for used to do some of the work the Met farmed out.'

'Is that how you met her?'

'Actually, no, that was coincidence. She was my ex-wife's close friend.'

'Oh, I see.'

Jack chuckled. 'I doubt it. Cassie got fed up doing grunt work for an organisation that thought a virus was something you saw your doctor about, and didn't pay her close to what she was worth. She set up on her own as a computer doctor, and kind of fell into investigation work as a sideline that finished up being more profitable than the day job.'

'Straying spouses, benefit cheats, stuff like that?'

'To start with. Now we get all kinds of obscure assignments.' He flipped a pen backwards and forwards between his forefinger and thumb. His body language was casual, but the business with the pen told Alexi he wasn't comfortable with this conversation. 'Anyway, my marriage broke up. Cassie stayed neutral and we kept in touch, had the occasional drink. Then, when she heard about my problems with the Met, she invited me to invest in her agency. She can make computers give up their secrets but needed someone with my background for doing the face-to-face stuff.' He shrugged. 'So far, we make a good team.'

I'll just bet you do! 'Glad to hear it. Now, what did your super-star partner find out about Natalie's background?'

'She's still working on that. Miracles, as she puts it, take a little longer.'

'Okay then, let's take a look at Natalie's email.'

Alexi moved back to her own desk and logged into Natalie's account. 'I haven't tried to crack her business email address yet,' she explained. 'I figured anything about her private life would be in her personal mail.'

'Good thinking.'

He scooted his chair over and leaned over her shoulder, distracting her. He had no damned business smelling so... well, so masculine. She wanted to put distance between them but that would imply she was affected by him.

'Do you notice anything?' Alexi asked, frowning as she scrolled through Natalie's inbox.

'Yeah, she's remarkably tidy. Very few files.'

'Make that no files, which is odd. I have tons on my personal email, and I keep my business files separate, just like Natalie must.' Alexi leaned back in her chair and glanced up at Jack. 'So, she either doesn't file her emails, or keeps them offline somewhere.'

'Actually, according to Cassie, a lot of people keep really important stuff off the web all together, simply because it's more secure. Nothing online is completely confidential. Hacking is the modern-day equivalent of tax evasion. Technically illegal, but anyone who's computer savvy can't resist having a go, and it's not really looked upon as being illegal.'

'Since I just cracked Natalie's password, I can't claim the moral high ground.'

Jack sent her a look. 'You're a journalist, so you can't anyway.'

The caustic comment took Alexi by surprise. She thought they had got past his resentment of her profession.

'Sorry,' he said, breaking the awkward silence that ensued.

'Apology accepted.' Alexi fell into momentary contemplation. 'I wonder if Cassie can find some sort of online storage for her. Dropbox, or something like that.'

Jack jotted a note on a piece of paper. 'It's worth a look.'

'Considering this is day four since she was last seen, there are surprisingly few emails waiting for her,' Alexi pointed out. 'The usual spam that we all get, but not a whole lot else. Certainly nothing from any of our suspects.'

'Anything marked dates? Or, more to the point, finances?'

Jack peered closer, all but resting his chin on her shoulder as his breath peppered her left ear. She shifted position, removing herself from the direct firing line, and caught a glimpse of his profile in the periphery of her vision. A smile flirted with his lips, leaving her with the impression that accidently touching her was a deliberate ploy. Nice try but Alexi didn't do casual sex. Then again, perhaps a no-strings-attached hook-up was what she needed to get Patrick out of her system. Only the fact that he so obviously thought he'd get what he wanted without too much effort made her determined to hold out.

'Nope.' She answered his spoken question, and the unspoken one, with the one word.

'I guess that would be too much to hope for.'

'What about the guy she stood up?' Alexi asked, turning her head so abruptly when the thought occurred to her that her hair whipped across Jack's face.

'Come again?'

'Your sister called you in because Natalie had missed a date. Had she seen that guy before? Could she have kept the date, but he said she hadn't to throw suspicion off?'

'I'll double check with Katie, but she assured me it was a first date. The two of them hadn't met at all.'

'As far as she knew.'

'Right. I'll ask for the guy's name, so we can check him out, just in case.' He fired off an email to his sister, typing with two fingers.

'What next?' Alexi asked.

'Let's take a moment and assess what we know so far. That's why the police keep whiteboards during investigations: so any new leads can be added, keeping everyone updated. Well, not always whiteboards nowadays, but fancy big touchscreen thingies. Still, I'm an old-fashioned guy and think *whiteboards*. Anyway, we know for a fact that Natalie Parker was last seen going about her normal business over four days ago. She has no close relatives that we are aware of, but Cassie will turn them up if they exist. It's out of character for her to go anywhere without telling her friend Cheryl, who looks after her place if she has to leave.'

'And she always answers her phone wherever she is because it could be business-related. But her phone is off and she's missed supplying a business commitment, which is totally out of character.'

Jack nodded. 'She has – or at least two years ago – had a lot of money in her personal account but lived modestly and didn't shout about it. Where did that money come from? I can't help thinking that if we can find the answer to that one, we'll find Natalie.'

'She's divorced, but we don't know how long she was married for, or anything about her husband and why they separated. We do know she now wants to have another relationship, hence joining Heart Racing, hoping to meet a guy with similar interests.'

Jack wrote Natalie's name at the top of a sheet of paper, and listed below it all the things they knew about her. On the right-hand side, he listed areas of dispute that needed further investigation if they weren't explained when Cassie reported her findings. Her husband's background and, significantly, the source of her wealth headed that list.

'Is she the genuinely nice, private person Cheryl thinks she is, looking for her happy ever after?' Alexi mused.

'Is she a female predator, using her sensuality to prey on vulnerable, wealthy men?'

'Or are the men preying on her need for companionship?'

'She's cautious about using the internet, but has a presence online because she's in business and doesn't stand much chance of surviving if customers can't find her on the net.'

'But,' Alexi added. 'There are anomalies. She's cautious about the internet but tells the world via Facebook that she's thinking of buying a share in a racehorse, which implies she has money. Why would she do that? It doesn't fit with her cautious approach to online activities.'

'Beats the hell out of me.'

'We need to hear from Cassie about Natalie's background.'

'And the fact that we haven't probably means there's hidden stuff to be rooted out.'

'There is one other thing to add to your list of unanswered questions,' Alexi said. 'Something rather important. Does she have a will, and—'

'And who inherits if she does turn up dead.' Jack nodded. 'Good thinking. I must be getting slow in my advancing years. That's always one of the first things we used to think about in my previous line of work.'

'Don't feel bad,' she replied sweetly. 'I have a naturally suspicious mind, and a generally low opinion of human nature. There's less chance of disappointment if you don't have much by way of expectations to start with.'

Jack grinned at her as he stood up. 'Let's go back to her cottage and take a closer look at her paperwork, then swing back past Darren Walker's place in Hungerford.'

'Come on, Cosmo,' Alexi said, standing up and grabbing her bag. 'This is no time to veg out. We have work to do.'

Cosmo got to his feet, dislodging Toby's head from his belly, and stretched.

'He looks so comfortable. Why not leave him where he is?'

'We're a team. Besides, he sulks if I leave him home too often.'

Jack chuckled. 'Oh well, we can't have that now, can we. Sorry, Toby,' he added, tugging the dog's ears. 'You're gonna have to make your own fun for a while.'

7

'Perhaps we should have looked at her business email before doing this,' Alexi said, as they followed Cosmo down the stairs.

'We can do that later if need be.'

'I'll just let Cheryl know where we're going.'

Jack nodded, still doubting the wisdom of joining forces with Alexi. He got more attention from women than he could handle, or looked for. Now he'd found one he'd actually like to get to know, but couldn't afford the distraction. His first and only concern was for his sister's business.

'Okay, let's go.'

Jack followed her out to her car and lifted the passenger seat forward so Cosmo could jump in the back. But Cosmo was having none of it. He simply sat down and gave Jack the evil eye.

'What?'

Alexi, already behind the wheel, chuckled. 'You don't really expect him to sit in the back, do you?'

Jack rolled his eyes. 'You have got to be joking.'

'Nope. Cosmo only travels up front.'

'Is that right?'

'Careful!' Alexi cried when Jack bent to pick the cat up. 'If anyone tries to make Cosmo do something he doesn't want to, it inevitably involves blood.'

'His or mine?' Jack placed the cat in the middle of the back seat. 'Hell, he weighs almost as much as I do.'

Cosmo let out an indignant meow.

'Don't listen to him, darling,' Alexi cooed as she fired up the engine. 'Apologise, Jack. You've hurt his feelings.'

Jack chuckled as he slid into the passenger seat, found the lever to push it back as far as it would go, and fastened his seat-belt. His smile abruptly faded when a feline ton weight landed on the back of the passenger seat and wrapped itself around his neck, a rattling purr coming from the cat's throat.

'You sure about that?' Alexi asked.

'I guess I can live with this arrangement,' Jack replied, stroking the cat's sleek body and creating an even louder purr.

'He likes you.'

'I like him right back but he senses I'm not about to put up with his theatrics.' He shot Alexi a cocky grin. 'Kids and animals need boundaries.'

A short time later, they parked at Natalie's cottage. Alexi and Jack headed for the front door. Cosmo stalked off into the garden. Jack took Natalie's keys from Alexi and unlocked the Mortis, then the Yale.

'There's no alarm system here on the cottage, but I noticed there was one on the workshop when you opened it up earlier.'

'Yes, Cheryl told me the code for it. I figured she'd have to have her business premises protected for insurance purposes.'

'Or because that's where she keeps anything that's important to her. It is where her laptop lives, I noticed.'

'Yes, but Cheryl says she kept her iPad in the cottage, along with a small printer and scanner.'

'The laptop for business, the iPad for pleasure.' Jack shrugged. 'That would work.'

'But there are no personal files in her office, or anywhere else. I found stuff in her living room relating to domestic bills and those old bank statements beneath some sweaters in her walk-in wardrobe, but they don't help much when it comes to figuring out who she was.'

Jack frowned. 'It seems awfully careless for such a careful person.'

'An oversight, perhaps?'

'The bank statements date back to the time just after she moved in. She was probably disorganised and they accidentally got buried.' They were now in the cottage's entrance hall. 'Show me where you found them.'

'Sure.' Alexi led the way up the stairs and into Natalie's bedroom. 'I suspect she had the walk-in closet specifically made to house her clothing. I reckon there was a third bedroom, a small one that she had converted into this closet and an en suite.'

Jack nodded. 'Makes sense.'

Alexi rummaged through the clothing that filled the racks and shelves. 'A lot of this is decent stuff,' she said. 'Designer labels that would make her feel good but don't scream money.'

'You'd know more about that than me.'

She turned her attention to the racks of shoes. 'Shoes tell you a lot about a woman,' she said. 'And all of these are top notch.'

Jack had moved back into the main part of the bedroom and methodically searched the drawers.

'Leave it to a man to find a girl's lingerie,' Alexi said, walking up behind him.

His responding grin caused her to shake her head and delve into another set of drawers. 'Oh my!'

'What you got?'

'Come and see for yourself.'

A large drawer was full of sexy – very sexy – underwear. And a number of toys. Jack let out a low whistle. 'This lady takes her pleasures seriously.'

'So it seems, but alone or did she invite men back?'

'Not much point in doing herself up in this stuff unless she had an audience to appreciate it.' Alexi nodded. 'We ought to talk to the neighbours, see if they've noticed any comings and goings.'

'She doesn't have any immediate neighbours. This place is pretty isolated.'

'Which makes it easier to have assignations that she wanted to keep under wraps,' Jack said speculatively. 'Perhaps that's why she chose it.'

'She doesn't need to keep her activities quiet. She has no ties.'

'But perhaps her caller does. And there had to be one.' He picked up a riding crop from her play drawer and slapped it against his palm. 'I doubt whether she used this on herself.'

Alexi giggled. 'She really does like all things equestrian, doesn't she?'

Jack didn't reply. This find showed Natalie in an entirely different light and had him wondering.

'Women are way more liberated these days,' Alexi said, 'and don't feel any need to apologise for their needs. But to hear Cheryl talk, Natalie Parker is Lambourn's answer to Mother Teresa.'

'Come on,' he said, 'there's nothing else to help us in here. Let's go and check out her work room.'

'Nothing other than meticulous accounts of her business transactions for the taxman, client invoices, and invoices from her suppliers,' Alexi said a short time later, pushing a strand of hair away from her forehead. 'Nothing about her personal life at all. Nothing to imply she even existed before she came here. No address book, no old birthday cards kept for nostalgic reasons, no letters... absolutely nothing.' She shook her head. 'I thought I travelled light, but this is just not natural.'

'It's lucky you found those old bank statements.'

'I would have smelt money when I looked more closely at her clothes but, yeah, that's our only break so far.'

'I wonder if she was checking her statements and was interrupted,' Jack said. 'That would account for their location. Perhaps she got a call from her guy to say he was almost there. She would have been looking through her post but then found herself in a hurry to get ready, deciding what to wear – or not. Standing in her walk-in closet, she found she still had the statements in her hand and simply dropped them on that shelf. They got buried beneath her sweaters and she forgot about them.'

'Possibly. Anyway, what now?' she asked. 'We don't seem to be—'

Alexi broke off when Jack's mobile rang. He checked the caller ID and took the call. 'Hey, Cas, what you got?'

'Are you on your own?'

Jack frowned, wondering why she'd asked, feeling the compulsion to lie. Cassie would get possessive if she knew he was with Alexi and he didn't need the hassle. 'Yeah, I'm alone.'

'Check your email. I've found a few interesting things about your saintly Ms Parker.'

'I know that tone of voice.' He winked at Alexi. 'Give me the highlights.'

'She's known to the police. Is that highlight enough for you?'

'She's been arrested?' He gaped at Alexi, whose jaw dropped open. 'What for?'

'Soliciting.'

Jack inhaled sharply.

* * *

Jack didn't look that surprised by what his partner had unearthed, but Alexi was stunned. Why, she couldn't have said. It wasn't as if she knew Natalie personally. Besides, she'd seen and heard it all during her years as a reporter and knew that women turned to the oldest profession for all sorts of reasons – usually financial necessity. The sexy underwear and extensive collection of sex toys ought to have told her something. Jack had obviously already made the connection, but she'd been slow on the uptake because she'd bought Cheryl's take on her friend. A basic error. Not that Cheryl had any reason to lie, but she did have a tendency to think the best of everyone.

'Tell me,' she said when Jack ended his call.

'Cassie says it's all in her email.' He logged into his account. 'Here we go.'

Alexi again found herself reading over Jack's shoulder.

'Natalie Parker isn't her real name,' she said.

'Nope. She's Natalie Seaton but changed her name by deed poll some years ago. She was given up for adoption at birth. No information available on her birth parents.'

'Since she never knew them, she can be excused for saying her parents died.'

'Perhaps she meant her adoptive parents are dead,' Jack suggested. 'She would have thought of them as her parents, presumably.'

'Most likely.'

'Her adoptive mother was a gardener, into floral art, whatever the hell that is.'

'Flower arranging,' Alexi told him. 'Natalie's adoptive mother's example must have persuaded Natalie to go down that path. How old was she when she got arrested?'

'Fourteen.'

'Fourteen?' Alexi was rendered temporarily speechless.

'Her juvenile records will be sealed so Cassie hasn't been able to look at them.'

'Will it be impossible for her to get them?'

Jack shot her an ironic look. 'You trying to insult my partner's abilities?'

Alexi answered his question with one of her own. 'Why did you tell Cassie you were alone?' She frowned when Jack hesitated to answer. 'You haven't told her about me, have you, Maddox?' A slow grin spread across her face. 'You're scared of her.'

'Yeah, right!'

Alexi wasn't buying his denial and the opportunity to have a little dig was too good to let it go. 'I thought you said your relationship wasn't personal,' she remarked sweetly.

'I *have* told her, but perhaps I underplayed the amount of co-investigating we're doing. She's already annoyed with me for spending more time down here when the paying jobs are stacking up. No point in making matters worse. She can be a tad overprotective.'

She tilted her head, pretending to be affronted. 'And thinks you're being traumatised by exposure to my conniving company?'

'Something like that,' he agreed with a self-deprecating smile.

Alexi shook her head, thinking she'd just learned something useful. Cassie Fenton had her sights set on Jack. Jack obviously knew it since he was prepared to go that extra mile not to antagonise her. Not personally involved, indeed!

'I wonder if Natalie's adoptive father got over-friendly,' she said in a speculative tone. 'It happens. A lot. I did a feature about abuse in the social welfare system once. The stories I got out of foster kids were heartbreaking. Those that tried to tell weren't believed and were labelled as troublemakers.'

'Don't jump to conclusions.'

'I don't work on conclusions. Just so you know, I always triple check my facts, otherwise the paper's lawyers would be all over me. I was thinking aloud, that's all.'

'Hmm.' Jack was reading Cassie's email and clearly only giving Alexi part of his attention.

'If she was a high-class escort then it would explain all that dosh.'

Jack let out a long, appreciative whistle. 'Wow!' he said.

Alexi looked at the screen and had to agree with him. The pictures that came up were from a website on which Natalie had advertised her former trade. She went by the name of Natalie Dwight and looked classy, sexy, and sophisticated all at the same time.

'This website is long gone, but Cassie found it. That's what took her a while.'

'Presumably she retired when she moved here two years ago,' Alexi said, watching as Jack flipped through the pages; each of them devoted to a different female, every hair, skin and eye colour featured, every customer's taste catered for. 'She was part of a classy escort agency. Does it say where it was based, Jack?'

'Mayfair Escorts. I'd put money on that being in London.'

Alexi rolled her eyes. 'Nothing gets past you.'

He grinned and winked at her. 'Cassie will be able to find out exactly where, and if it's still in business.'

'How will that help us? And why would the website be gone if they're still operating?'

'I'm not sure yet, but I'm guessing this agency, or whoever ran it at the time, was a big influence in Natalie's life. Top end joints like that one are very selective.'

Alexi regarded him quizzically. 'And you'd know this because...'

'I just do. The madams take a motherly interest in their girls. This one might actually have been the saving of Natalie, if she was going off the rails. And perhaps the agency has the type of exclusive reputation that no longer requires a website, or any advertising at all.'

Alexi nodded thoughtfully. 'She must have changed her name to Parker just before she moved here but perhaps she still sees a few of her old clients, which would be why she retained the tools of her trade.'

'That's possible, but if she was serious about settling down, why would she continue turning tricks in her own backyard?'

'I haven't figured that part out yet.' She frowned. 'Maybe she doesn't. Cheryl says she often goes away for a night or two on business.... she obviously neglected to say what kind of business.'

Jack chuckled. 'Good old Cas. She got into her bank accounts.' They peered together at the figures scrolling down the small screen. 'She retired with over half a million in the bank.'

'We already knew that.' Alexi sighed. 'I'm in the wrong business. None of the careers advisors at my school pointed out the financial advantages in Natalie's particular line of work.'

'Girls in the high end of the business get taken to swanky business parties and need to be able to look and talk the part,' Jack told her. 'If they're canny, like Natalie obviously is, they can make a small fortune.'

'Yeah, I get that part.'

'It looks like she bought this place for cash, then she applied for planning consent for the annexe. She got it approved, got business use, and paid for all of that in cash, too.'

'That must have made a dent in her nest egg,' Alexi said.

'It did.' Jack continued to read the figures. 'Those statements we saw dated back before she shelled out all the cash. She was down to less than a hundred thousand by the time her business premises were finished.'

'And now?'

'Double that amount.'

They looked at one another. 'Her business can't have made that much money so quickly, can it?' Alexi asked.

'She's been getting regular payments of a thousand quid a time ever since she moved here. But they've gone into her personal account, and we know that she only keeps fastidious records for her business activities.'

'Payment for services rendered? Would she be able to ask that much?'

Jack shrugged. 'Depends on how good she is at her job.'

Alexi took a closer look at the figures as Jack scrolled through the pages. 'What about these amounts? Seven thousand, nine thousand. There are quite a few deposits in four figures.'

'Made quite recently.' Jack looked pensive. 'What the hell did you get yourself mixed up in, Natalie?'

'Those amounts would fly beneath the banking radar, so she wouldn't need to explain where they'd come from,' Alexi said slowly. 'Where *did* they come from, Jack?'

'Beats the hell out of me.' He leaned back and stretched his arms above his head. His T-shirt rode up, giving Alexi a close-up view of washboard abs and the trail of curling chest hair that disappeared beneath his waistband. 'Putting the squeeze on ex-clients, perhaps?'

'Blackmail? The sort of thing that would get her killed?'

'Yeah, if she was daft enough to go down that route. And Natalie doesn't strike me as being stupid. She knows how the game's played and which lines are never crossed.'

'But if she crossed them?'

'Then we will definitely have to delve deeper into her murky past and see what's what.'

'You don't have to do that. Once we're sure this has nothing to do with your sister's agency, you can leave the sleuthing to me.'

He subjected her to a slow, lazy appraisal. 'Fed up with me already?'

'Your partner wants you back.'

'She's my partner, not my mother. And this business with Natalie has got me intrigued, so I'll hang around for another day or two, then see where we are.'

'Okay, but for what it's worth, I still think Natalie was serious about finding Mr Right and putting her previous life behind her. If she wasn't, she wouldn't have joined your sister's organisation.'

'I'm inclined to agree with you. Although she could have joined because she was lonely. From what she told Cheryl, she wanted normal.'

'Cassie didn't find any evidence of a husband?'

'No, she must have lied about that, too.'

'We haven't found a will, or even any mention of a solicitor.'

'We can find out easily enough who represented her in the purchase of this place and for building the annexe.'

'Except they won't tell us diddly-squat.'

Jack conceded the point with a nod.

'Well, I don't think we'll find anything else here,' Alexi said. 'Time to go and call on Walker, although I'm thinking it less and less likely that anyone connected to the dating agency has anything to do with her disappearance.'

'Katie will be glad to hear it.'

They froze when Natalie's landline rang. Alexi glanced at Jack, suspecting he felt as much like an intruder at that point as she did. The answerphone cut in and they heard Natalie's voice: a soft, well-modulated voice, asking the caller to leave a message. It was the first time they had actually heard her speaking voice. To Alexi, it made her seem more human somehow and reinforced her concerns for her welfare. She hated herself for the conclusions she'd jumped to. The fact that she'd started to think less of her since discovering how she'd amassed her nest egg. That was wrong, and Alexi gave herself a mental dressing down. Natalie had had a tough start in life and, without knowing more about her, Alexi was in no position to stand in judgement on the choices Natalie had made.

'Natalie,' said a male voice into the phone. 'This is Charles. I'll be down your way on Saturday and wondered if you could make some time for me. Please let me know.'

'Damn,' Alexi said when the message ended. 'He didn't leave a number.'

'And he withheld his,' Jack added, having dialled 1471. 'Never mind: he can't hide from Cassie.'

* * *

Alexi resisted the urge to make a noise and give her presence away while Jack chatted with his possessive partner. He asked her to check Natalie's phone records and discover Charles's identity.

'Right,' he said, pocketing his phone. 'Let's get ourselves over to Hungerford.'

They left Natalie's workshop, having set the alarm and locked the door behind them. Cosmo materialised from the undergrowth and preceded them to the car.

'How does he do that?' Jack asked.

'He's very perceptive, to say nothing of protective. He stopped you in your tracks this morning when you crept up on me.'

'He scared the heck out of me.'

Alexi chuckled. 'That's my clever boy!'

'Anyway, just for the record, I was not creeping; I was investigating. I do not creep.'

'If you say so,' Alexi replied with a knowing smile. 'You might want to change your technique in that case. It looked a lot like creeping to me.'

8

It was gone five in the afternoon by the time they left Natalie's cottage. What sunshine there had been had given up trying to compete with the heavy clouds, and a light drizzle fell on the Mini's windscreen.

While Alexi concentrated on the road, Jack used the opportunity to steal glances at her, noticing things that hadn't previously been apparent. The line of faint freckles across her nose. A tiny scar just below the hollow at the base of her neck. The cute way she mangled her lower lip between her teeth when she concentrated. A tough career lady who probably didn't realise she oozed femininity. She had worked her backside off to establish herself, only to have the rug pulled out from under her. She was feeling a little vulnerable because of it, and Jack could tell that annoyed her.

'I wish to god it would rain or not rain,' she muttered. 'I hate half-measures.'

'Want me to drive?'

'No one, but no one other than me, *ever* drives Fabio.'

Jack quirked a brow. 'Fabio?'

She patted the steering wheel. 'Fabio, meet Jack. Jack, Fabio.'

'Pleased to meet you, Fabio.' He grinned. 'What happens now? Is there a protocol? Should I shake his gearstick?'

'Absolutely not! You hardly know one another. Keep your hands to yourself, Maddox.'

Alexi continued to look at the road ahead as she fought a grin. He wanted to tell her to let it out. She had a lovely laugh, throaty and uncontrived. When she did let her guard down her smile was sincere, pushing up into her eyes and emphasising the silver flecks dancing in their depths. Jack had been told once by a doctor he'd briefly dated that the muscles needed to smile with one's eyes are involuntary, only becoming engaged in an authentic smile as opposed to the courtesy variety. Watching Alexi, he could well believe it.

'Should we have called ahead?' she asked. 'What if Walker isn't home?'

'Better to catch him off guard. If he's retired, it's a good bet he'll be home at this time of day.'

'I guess.'

Walker lived in a substantial house on a large plot. It was fronted by a pristine lawn, trimmed to within an inch of its life, not a flower or shrub in sight. The barren garden screamed of a man living alone. Jack wondered if garden-loving Natalie had seen it and, if so, what she'd made of it. Would it leave her feeling challenged or depressed?

'Stay, Cosmo,' Alexi said to the cat when Jack disentangled his feline neck-warmer and placed him on Alexi's vacated driving seat. 'We won't be long.'

'It's a tough life, mate,' Jack told the cat as he too exited the car.

They were encouraged to see a top of the range Audi parked in front of Walker's garage. Jack pressed the bell and waited. A short time later the door was opened by a short man wearing casual trousers with razor-sharp creases and a navy polo shirt. He didn't look as good in the flesh as he did in the picture they'd seen online, but there was a warmth and openness about the man that Jack thought women would find attractive. Far from seeming annoyed at being interrupted by strangers, he offered them a pleasant smile.

'Darren Walker?' Jack asked.

'Yes, what can I do for you?'

'We were hoping to have a word with you about Natalie Parker. I believe you know her.'

Walker's brows disappeared beneath his sparse hairline. 'Natalie – has something happened to her?'

'What makes you think that?' Alexi asked. So much for letting him do the talking, Jack thought. Still, it was probably unrealistic to expect a reporter to keep her mouth shut.

'Why else would you be asking about her?' His smile faded. 'Actually, do you mind telling me who you are?'

'I'm Jack Maddox, Private Investigator,' Jack said, holding out a hand which Walker instinctively grasped. 'And Ms Ellis is assisting me.'

Jack ignored Alexi's glare, aware that he'd hear about arbitrarily demoting her later. Walker released Jack's hand and offered his own to Alexi, eyeing her with evident appreciation. Not that many men with eyesight and a pulse could fail to be impressed by Alexi, he conceded, but Walker's approval was apparent in the not-so-subtle once-over he subjected her to. *In your dreams, mate.*

'A PI.' Walker took the card Jack handed him and studied it. 'I've never met one before. Never imagined that I would have reason to.'

'You haven't done anything,' Alexi said.

'That's reassuring. But if you're here about Natalie, I have to assume something *has* happened to her.'

'We just have a few questions.'

'Then you'd better come in.'

Walker opened the door wider and ushered them into a sterile hall. The walls were blindingly white, the carpet beige, the only piece of furniture – a teak hall stand with an ornate mirror above it – expensive but... well, unexciting. A set of golf clubs leaned against one wall but there were no coats occupying hooks, no discarded shoes or junk mail.

'This way.'

Walker opened the door to an equally unexciting living room that stretched the full width of the back of the house, also painted brilliant white. The beige carpet continued in here and was echoed in the colour of the leather furniture. The man was either addicted to beige or had employed an interior designer who lacked vision.

There were a couple of half-decent paintings on the walls to relieve all that white, a large TV in one corner, a few tables and lamps scattered about, and not much else. No plants, ornaments, books, framed family photos, or knick-knacks. The items that had made it through the door were in perfect alignment, not a speck of dust in sight. It was a bit like he'd just moved into a place that was already furnished and hadn't bothered to stamp his personality onto it.

'Please, sit down.' Walker addressed the comment to Alexi. Jack assumed he was included in the invitation and sank into a beige leather chair which was, he had to admit, sinfully comfortable. 'Can I get either of you anything to drink?'

'No, thanks,' Jack replied. 'We won't keep you for long.'

He took a seat across from them. 'Then how can I help you?'

'We've been asked by friends of Natalie's to see if we can find her,' Jack said, seeing no point in beating around the bush. 'She's been missing for four days and—'

'Four days. Oh dear.' Walker scratched his head. 'Still, that's not so very long.'

'It is when you have a business, obligations to fulfil, and you haven't made arrangements to cover them in your absence, or warned anyone that you would be away.'

'And you don't answer your mobile,' Alexi added.

'Oh yes, I see what you mean. How distressing. But I'm afraid I can't help you.' He paused. 'I assume you know I met Natalie through a dating agency.' Jack and Alexi both nodded. 'I'm a widower, recently retired and, to be frank, I'm finding retirement a bit lonely. Perhaps I should have remained in London. Not that I had any friends up there really, just colleagues and acquaintances, but still, it might have been easier than starting completely afresh.'

'Making new friends attracts fortune hunters,' Alexi suggested, casting her eyes around the room. Sterile it might be, but any female clapping eyes on the outside, on the neighbourhood generally, would know it had cost big bucks.

'Exactly.' Walker seemed relieved that she understood. 'One hears such terrible things nowadays, Jack. I know I'm not much to look at, or especially interesting, so when attractive women throw themselves at me, I'm not stupid enough to think it's my irresistible charm that draws them in.'

Jack felt sorry for the guy, but was glad he understood the score. Appearances mattered at any age. Unjust, but that was the way the world worked.

'So you joined a dating agency where the clientele have interests in common?' Alexi suggested.

'Quite. I was attracted to Natalie the moment I saw her

picture. She's elegant, educated, interesting, and very easy to talk to.'

'I understand,' Jack said aloud. 'How often did you date?'

'Three times.' His expression was self-effacing. 'We got along really well but, to be honest, I was surprised when she agreed to see me a second time, much less a third.'

'Why do you say that?' Alexi asked.

'Have you met her?'

Jack and Alexi both shook their heads.

'Ladies who look like Natalie don't choose men like me. I might have a few bob, but she doesn't know that. We chatted by email for a while before we dated, talked about our likes, our interests, but all she knows is that I retired early from the Civil Service. She doesn't know where I live, so she can't know about the house, or that I have no mortgage on it.'

Jack knew that wasn't true. If Natalie was aware of Walker's full name, finding his address would be child's play. Perhaps she really had meant to work a number on him. It was obvious that he was already smitten, so the hard graft had been put in. 'Anyway, we met twice more. I planned to ask her over here next week. It's time I was completely honest with her about my circumstances. I mean,' he added, sounding as though he was trying to convince himself, 'if she liked me before, all this can't hurt.' He waved his arms vaguely around. 'Although what she'll make of the garden, goodness only knows. I've been meaning to get someone in, landscapers or something, but I haven't got around to it. Natalie loves gardens and says she can make absolutely anything grow.'

'That's true,' Alexi replied. 'I've seen her garden. It's beautiful, but I'm like you, Mr Walker. I don't know a dandelion from a daffodil.'

'Please call me Darren.'

'Did she mention any friends or relations?' Jack asked. 'Anyone she was close to?'

He shook his head slowly, as though dredging his memory. 'No, she told me that she's divorced and has no contact with her ex. Her parents are dead and she has no siblings. I thought she was alone, like me.'

'So you can't think of anything that would have made her take off?'

Walker answered Jack's question with one of his own. 'Can't you put a trace on her car, or something?'

'Unless the car has a tracking device, it would be next to impossible. Besides,' Jack added softly, 'her car is still in her garage.'

Walker paled. 'Oh my god! This doesn't sound good.'

'It's certainly odd, but—'

'Can I ask how you knew Natalie and I dated?'

'We found your name on a piece of paper beside her phone,' Jack replied.

'Oh, right.' That appeared to satisfy him. 'What's being done to try and find her, apart from the two of you, I mean?'

'Her disappearance was reported by friends to the police,' Alexi said.

'I expect they'll come to see me as well.'

'Unfortunately, they aren't doing much to try and find her, because—'

'—because she's an adult, there's no obvious signs of an abduction, presumably, and no body.' He set his lips in a tight line. 'I do watch TV.'

'Which is where we come in,' Jack explained. 'The dating agency wants to keep their client base confidential, but they don't want to hamper efforts to find Natalie.'

'That's perfectly understandable. I imagine you'll be talking to all the men she met through the agency.'

'Yes, although you're the only one she saw more than once.'

'Am I really?' Walker seemed both surprised and pleased. 'Well then, you must let me know if there's anything I can do to help find her. It would be such a shame if anything's happened to her.'

'Quite.' Jack paused, legs stretched out in front of him, and crossed at the ankles. 'Did she happen to mention anything about the work she did before she moved to Lambourn?'

'She said that she worked in public relations and travelled a lot.'

Well, Jack thought, that would cover it. 'Not to worry,' he said aloud.

Jack nodded to Alexi and they both stood. It took a moment before Walker also found his feet and Jack could see he was genuinely distressed about Natalie's situation. They thanked him for his time and promised to let him know if they found her.

* * *

'Your assistant?' Alexi asked as she drove them off, conscious of Walker watching from his front window.

'People in your line of work get a bad press,' Jack replied, deadpan.

She shot him a sideways glance. 'Seriously?'

'Would I lie to you?'

Alexi harrumphed. 'What did you make of him?' she asked.

'I think he couldn't believe his luck when he linked up with Natalie and that he's genuinely upset about her disappearance.'

'Yeah, that's what I thought, too. He's lonely and regrets

leaving London.' She paused. 'Let that be a lesson to you, Alexi,' she added *sotto voce*.

Jack seemed surprised. 'I didn't know you had plans to leave the capital.'

'There's no reason why you should. Besides, I haven't made up my mind yet. Anyway, back to Darren Walker. Natalie might have been planning to work a number on him, but I'm convinced it wasn't the other way around.'

'I agree with you.'

'Okay, that leaves the other two guys.'

'I'll get Larry to check them out.'

'Larry?'

'He's an ex-cop who works for the agency from time to time.'

'Cassie won't like that.'

'I won't tell her if you don't.' He shot her a killer grin. 'And Larry sure as hell won't.'

'Old cops sticking together?'

'Hey, not so much of the old.'

She treated him to a seraphic smile. 'I speak as I find.'

Jack chuckled and shifted position. Cosmo shifted right along with him, while Jack absently scratched his ears. Alexi shook her head, astonished at her cat's total adoration of Jack.

'You two need to get a room,' she quipped.

'Is it my fault if your cat's a good judge of character?'

Alexi rolled her eyes as she stopped in a queue of traffic at a red light. 'You don't think it's worth paying the other two personal calls?' she asked.

'Nope. Time is of the essence, so we need to manage it well. I'm getting increasingly convinced that Natalie's disappearance has something to do with her previous occupation. We need to find out who Charles is, and if there's anyone else she's been seeing regularly. A jealous ex,' he said, fixing Alexi with a probing glance, 'or someone at the agency where she worked who feels they're being short-changed if she's branched out alone and taken their clients with her.'

'Is that likely?'

'Damned if I know, which is why we need to find out. In the meantime, Larry can look at the other two. I trust his judgement. If he thinks there's anything there, he'll sniff it out, then we'll go check on them.'

'Fair enough.'

Alexi pulled her car into the Hopgood Hall car park.

'I guess we'd better let Cheryl and Drew know what we've found out,' Alexi said as she climbed from the car. 'I wonder if they had any idea. About Natalie's secret life, I mean.'

'We'll soon know.' Jack placed his hand on the small of her back and guided her towards the door. It was an intuitively polite, albeit old-fashioned gesture that she couldn't object to without making a big deal of it. 'You go ahead. I'll give Larry a quick call, check in with Cassie, then join you.'

'Fine.'

* * *

Cosmo led the way to the kitchen, where Toby hurled himself at the cat in a frenzy of delight. Alexi smiled at the sight, threw her bag onto the table and looked up at...

'Patrick?' She stared at her ex, who'd made himself comfortable at the kitchen table, where he and Cheryl were sharing a pot of tea. Cheryl jumped up and threw Alexi an apologetic glance.

'He just turned up,' she whispered. 'Said you were expecting him.'

Alexi patted her friend's shoulder. 'It's okay.'

'Hey.'

Patrick stood up and tried to pull Alexi into an embrace, which she evaded. His lips landed fairly harmlessly in the vicinity of her left ear. Cosmo had just noticed Patrick. His back arched, his fur stood on end, and he emitted a series of angry hisses. Cheryl, who'd probably sensed the tension even before Cosmo's reaction, looked totally bemused.

'What are you doing here? How did you find me?' Alexi asked.

'I'm a reporter. It's what I do.'

'You'd damned well better not have tracked my phone,' she said, moving away from him with her arms folded.

'I'll leave you two to talk,' Cheryl said, beating a hasty retreat.

The door closed behind Cheryl, leaving Alexi trapped with her determined ex, an angry cat, and whimpering dog. The only sound in the room was Cosmo's hissing and Toby's confused yelps. Alexi, struggling to contain her anger, had absolutely no intention of relieving the tension with small talk.

'You haven't answered my calls,' he said.

'Any reason why I should?' Alexi looked away from him.

'Come on, Alexi, cut me some slack. I couldn't tell you what was going on ahead of time. It would have been more than my job was worth.'

'But not mine, apparently.'

He grasped her shoulders and turned her until she was compelled to look at him. Cosmo's hissing got louder. 'If there was something, anything, I could have done to secure your position on the paper, don't you think I would have done it?'

She shrugged. 'Does it matter?'

His sigh was deep and heartfelt. 'I love you, and want to spend the rest of my life with you. I thought you felt the same way about me.'

'I thought so, too.' She paused, looking up into his handsome face as she waited for regret to grip her and felt... nothing. It was liberating to have it confirmed that she really was over him. But it did make her wonder about her own constancy. She had really thought she was in love with him. She spent two whole days crying up a storm after she lost her job and then dumped him because she could no longer trust him. Perhaps he hadn't been the love of her life after all. 'Once,' she added.

'You know how the newspaper game's played, Alexi. It's all about the bottom line and cutting cloth accordingly. You were too good at what you did. You'd priced yourself out of the market.'

She arched a cynical brow. 'Nothing to do with the paper reducing its standards?'

'I had it all worked out. If you'd taken the position that was offered to you, I had plans to get you doing what you do best through the back door. Once management realised how badly the readers missed you, they would have had to let me.'

'Run the equivalent of a political gossip column and lose face in the eyes of the industry, to say nothing of readers?' She glowered at him. 'Is that the big master plan you've been at pains to talk to me about?'

He shook his head. 'You've changed.'

'Getting fired does that to a girl.'

'If you'd agreed to see me, or even taken my calls, I could have explained that you *would* get your job back. But you were so damned hot-headed, wouldn't listen to what anyone told you, and insisted on being paid off. You're angry, and you have every right to be,' he said, his voice softening. 'Now it will be harder for me to get you reinstated, but I can make it happen.'

'How do you plan to do that?'

Alexi expected more prevarication, empty promises. 'The Rachman feature.'

Her head shot up. That wasn't what she'd expected at all. Following the Morecombe Bay cockling disaster there had been an outcry about the exploitation of illegal immigrants forced to live in primitive conditions while worked, sometimes literally, to death. The apathetic public had been shocked into taking an interest in the problem. No one knew quite what to do about it, but everyone agreed someone had to be held to account.

Before she got fired, Alexi had been delving into a similar scandal in London, where illegal immigrants were housed like sardines in garden sheds, lacking even the most basic facilities, and charged a small fortune for the privilege by rich landlords. She'd given her project the code name 'Rachman' after the noto-rious Notting Hill landlord who had taken exploitation of tenants to new levels in the fifties and sixties. Alexi's story was potential dynamite, but everyone involved was too scared to talk on the record.

Alexi told herself Patrick was employing a few underhand tactics of his own to tempt her back into the fold and refused to show too much interest.

'What about it?' she asked, hating herself for asking. Once a reporter...

'Someone's come forward who's willing to talk.'

'Who? One of the people I'd been trying to cultivate? Why did they come to you?'

'Write that story and it will go a long way to getting your position reinstated.' He briefly removed his hands from her shoulders and spread them wide. 'Hell, you could probably take my job, to say nothing of all the awards you'd win.'

'Perhaps I've had enough of all the cut and thrust.'

Patrick laughed. 'You thrive on it.'

'I did once.'

'I called by your flat. Are you really letting it?'

'Yep.'

'Where will you live?'

She shrugged. 'The world's a big place. I can live or work just about anywhere I like. Here, for instance.'

Patrick's mouth fell open. 'You hate the country.'

'Well, you said it yourself just now. I've changed.'

'Cheryl said something about you looking for her missing friend.'

Alexi made a mental note to murder Cheryl later. She should know better than to mention something like that to a reporter, untrustworthy bunch that they were once they sniffed the possibility of a story!

'Promise me you'll think about it. The whistle-blower won't wait forever and I can't let the story slip through my fingers. If you don't want it, I'll have to give it to someone else.'

He was right and, damn it, she was salivating at the prospect of finally getting the story written. 'Yeah, okay, I'll give it some thought.'

His hands returned to her shoulders, his fingers digging almost painfully into them. Cosmo hissed louder. Patrick shot the cat a wary glance before dropping his hands to her waist and pulling her against him. 'Don't give up what we had together just because you're angry.' He whispered the words into the top of her head, while the fingers of one hand worked their way up her back and beneath her hair. 'We were good together and I miss you so damned much it hurts. Come back to London and we'll work this all out.'

'I've said I'll think about it. Don't push me, Patrick.'

'It's this guy you're working down here with, isn't it?' he said, his voice turning hard.

'What guy?'

'Aw, come on, Cheryl told me.'

'Cheryl talks too much.'

'She cares about you.'

'This has got nothing to do with anyone, other than me.'

'Your feelings are hurt. I get that part. And you deserve to be pissed off, but don't shoot the messenger. I have to deal with the owners *and* try to get the best deal for everyone on my staff, including you. I owe it to them all. The best way to fight fire isn't always with more fire.'

She nodded half-heartedly. Give him his due: Patrick always had played the game of office politics with the hand of a master. She, on the other hand, tended to speak her mind without first engaging her brain, especially when she was angry. Not a good idea but, hell, it had felt good to tell the owners of the *Sentinel* where to stick their job.

Alexi screwed up her features, angry, upset, and confused, wondering if Patrick knew how self-centred he sounded. 'You want me to feel sorry for you?' she asked. 'Okay, you have my sympathy. Now get out of here.'

'I thought I'd stay for a few days.'

'I don't want you here. Besides, you have a paper to run and Cheryl is full this weekend.'

'You think you don't want me, but I seem to remember when you couldn't get enough of this.'

Without warning, his lips covered hers, hard and demanding. Cosmo's hissing turned into indignant yowls and Alexi half feared for Patrick's calves. The other half of her befuddled brain was encouraging Cosmo to attack when the door behind her opened.

'Oh, sorry,' Jack's voice said. 'I didn't realise you had company.'

9

Larry was happy to fit the other two guys Natalie had dated into his schedule first thing the next day. Cassie was a harder nut to crack, proving resilient to Jack's most persuasive arguments, and blaming Alexi for his failure to return to the day job.

If Natalie was dead, Jack patiently explained to his recalcitrant partner, her body could turn up at any time. If that happened, damage control would be out of Jack's hands. He needed to find Natalie before anyone else did, preferably alive, and put his sister's mind at rest. Cassie didn't sound impressed but finally agreed to take a look at Natalie's phone records and get an identity for Charles.

Jack's disgruntled frame of mind didn't improve when he walked into the kitchen and found Alexi cosying up with some guy he'd never seen before. He apologised and turned to leave the room.

'Don't go, Jack.'

Her voice halted him at the door. Cosmo stopped making a god-almighty racket, blinked up at Jack, then stalked across to rub his big head against his calves. The man with Alexi – Patrick – looked on with open astonishment.

'Patrick Vaughan, Jack Maddox,' Alexi said curtly, walking away and half-turning her back on them both. She didn't embellish the introduction, but then she didn't need to. Vaughan was obviously her ex-boss, and ex-lover. It looked as though he wanted a reconciliation and Alexi didn't seem too averse to the idea. Vaughan extended his hand with obvious reluctance. Jack accepted it with an equal lack of enthusiasm.

'Patrick's just leaving,' Alexi said, breaking the brittle silence that prevailed as Jack and Vaughan continued to size one another up.

'Drive safely,' Jack said, heading for the door.

Drew and Cheryl were both already in the bar when Jack walked into it.

'What're you having?' Drew asked, beckoning Jack over.

'A beer would hit the spot.'

'I should have warned you Patrick was here,' Cheryl said, chewing her bottom lip, while Drew went to get Jack's drink. 'I should have warned Alexi, too, for that matter. He's definitely not her favourite person right now.'

'Could have fooled me,' Jack replied absently.

'He just turned up.' Cheryl looked conflicted. 'What was I supposed to do? Deny that Alexi was here?'

Jack allowed his surprise to show. 'He didn't know?'

'She hasn't been taking his calls.' Cheryl screwed up her features. 'I've never liked Patrick much, but it's not me he's trying to impress.'

'Yeah, well.'

Jack shrugged, unsure what else to say, or why he was so disgruntled. Drew placed a foaming pint in front of him before he'd reached any decisions. He took a long draught and felt himself beginning to unwind. He'd disliked Vaughan on sight, and had learned during his years on the force to trust his instincts, but it really wasn't his problem.

'How did you get on this afternoon?' Cheryl asked. 'Did you find out anything else about Natalie?'

'More than you could possibly imagine.'

Jack turned at the sound of Alexi's voice. She was alone. She pulled out the chair next to Jack and sat down.

'White wine, Alexi?' Drew asked.

'How large do your bar staff pour them?'

'That bad, huh?'

Drew laughed as he went off to get her drink.

'Sorry, Alexi,' Cheryl said. 'Did I screw up by letting on you were here?'

'It's okay.' She let out a long breath. 'He would have found me regardless. He's gone now.'

'He said he thought you'd be going back to the paper with him.'

'He was wrong,' Alexi replied succinctly.

The largest glass of chilled white wine Jack had ever seen materialised in front of Alexi. She took a healthy swig and sighed with pleasure.

'Is that a glass or a vase?' he asked, amused.

'Jack says you found out some stuff about Natalie,' Cheryl said, her expression grave.

Jack and Alexi exchanged a glance and prepared the Hopgoods for a shock before telling them just about everything they'd discovered.

'She was an escort?' Cheryl's mouth fell open.

'A high-class escort,' Jack amended.

'There's a difference?' Cheryl shook her head.

'A huge difference, not least in terms of earning power,' Drew replied.

Cheryl fixed her husband with a speculative look. 'And you'd know that because...'

Drew laughed. 'Not from personal experience.' He paused, his expression playfully regretful. 'I don't have that sort of money.'

Cheryl punched his arm. 'She's attractive enough to make a living that way. She has a way about her.' Cheryl frowned. 'I'm not sure how to describe it. A presence, an awareness? It's in the way she carries herself. The way she listens to what you have to say and appears fascinated. That's rare. People seldom want to talk about anything other than themselves but she never did.'

'Sensual is how Jack described her, and he's never seen her in person,' Alexi remarked, flashing an amused smile.

'What can I say?' Jack spread his hands. 'I'm a trained observer.'

'A tough job, but someone's got to do it,' Drew added with a boyish grin.

Their banter momentarily lightened the mood.

'So, let's see if I've got this right,' Cheryl said, her expression sobering. 'Natalie was born Natalie Seaton but used the name Natalie Dwight to ply her trade, then changed it to Parker when she moved here. She was adopted at birth, Seaton being the name of her adoptive parents, and her adoptive mother was keen on gardens and flower arranging.' Cheryl counted off the points on her fingers. 'Something happened. She ran away from home and was picked up for soliciting when she was... how old?'

'Fourteen,' Jack replied.

Drew winced. 'Bloody hell!'

'That's all we know, and we're lucky Jack's partner was able to find out that much,' Alexi said.

'Did she go back to her family?' Drew asked.

'We're still trying to find that out,' Jack replied, thinking it would take Cassie a long time to do the finding. She had a point to make. Like Jack didn't already get the message – loud and clear.

'My guess is probably not,' Cheryl said. 'I mean, she chose to enter the oldest profession there is. I'm betting she did that through necessity. If I was her adoptive mother, I wouldn't stand by and let her sell herself.'

A tall man wearing a flat cap, silver hair showing beneath it, entered the bar and nodded to Cheryl and Drew.

'Who's that?' Alexi asked.

'That's Graham Fuller, a local trainer.' Cheryl twitched her nose. 'It's his lads who occupy our annexe.'

'I recognise the name,' Jack said, watching as Fuller ordered a half with a whisky chaser and took a seat on a barstool. He kept glancing at his watch, as though waiting for someone.

'Yeah, he's a big shot around these parts,' Drew replied. 'Which is saying something because the place is riddled with training yards and locals aren't easily impressed by reputations. But his old man was a force to be reckoned with. Charming and charismatic, yet rumours abound still about his tough stance with his own family.'

'And yet Graham followed in the old man's footsteps,' Jack remarked.

Drew lifted a beefy shoulder. 'Word is, he never stopped trying to live up to his expectations. Graham's married to a rich American woman now and has a couple of grown kids.'

'He looks angry, or furtive. Not sure which,' Alexi remarked, watching him as he struck up a conversation with another barfly.

'He has a high opinion of himself,' Cheryl said.

'You don't like him?' Alexi asked.

She shrugged. 'I don't like his attitude. He thinks he walks on water.'

'He *is* royalty in this neck of the woods,' Drew pointed out.

'That doesn't mean he has to flaunt it, or use it as an excuse to be rude to people,' Cheryl replied. 'Just because he's had a few big winners. Not recently, mind.'

'Going back to Natalie and her chosen profession,' Jack said. 'Her adoptive mother may not have known what she got herself involved with since we have no idea what made her go that way so young.'

'She dated one guy three times,' Alexi said. 'We've just been to visit him and we're convinced he knows nothing about her disappearance.'

'What about her other dates?' Drew asked.

'One of my guys is looking into them,' Jack replied. 'But they don't look likely.'

'So, it all comes back to her mysterious past,' Drew said, leaning back in his chair. 'Do you think she moved to Lambourn at random? I mean, I know she's interested in horses—'

'Or claims to be,' Cheryl added. 'All the things we thought we knew about her are no longer set in stone.'

'Good point. But I still want to know, why Lambourn? Is there a reason for that choice? Some ulterior motive?'

'Hard to say until we know more about her,' Jack replied, drinking more of his beer.

'The problem,' Alexi added, 'is that the more we find out, the more complicated her background becomes.'

'Shame she isn't addicted to the internet, like everyone else nowadays,' Cheryl remarked.

'Being secretive goes with the territory if you're trying to hide your past,' Jack said. 'Quite a few people nowadays are shunning social media if they want absolute confidentiality.'

'Because the net is so easy to hack?' Drew asked.

Jack nodded. 'Any geeky teenager with a bedroom, computer literacy, and a grudge against the world in general—'

'Most of them, in other words,' Alexi said.

'Right, kids like that have a command over the net you can only dream about. They can't resist showing off and causing mayhem. So, it's safer to put nothing online unless you're prepared for the entire world to know about it.'

* * *

Jack noticed another man walk into the bar. He met Fuller's eye but didn't acknowledge him as he purchased a pint and took it to a corner table. Jack was unsure what it was about the newcomer that held his attention. He didn't look out of place and was unexceptional in every way. Even so, Jack noticed him get up after a few minutes and head for the gents. Fuller followed him almost immediately.

His curiosity piqued, Jack excused himself as well, convinced that the man had come with the specific intention of meeting Fuller. Jack wanted to know what was so private about their business that they felt the need to conduct it in the bathroom.

Fuller and the newcomer were huddled together beside the hand basins, talking in whispers. They both looked up when Jack walked in, frowned at him, and stopped their conversation. Jack nodded at them and headed for a cubicle. It had the desired effect. With a flimsy wooden door separating them from Jack, the two men continued their muted conversation.

Jack, with his ear pressed against the door, heard horses' names mentioned along with race meetings and, he was pretty sure, specific races. Shortly after that the two men left the facilities but Jack remained inside the cubicle, leaned against the door, and mulled things over. The newcomer had to be a bookie's scout and Fuller, the renowned trainer with his ear to the ground and a wealth of information inside his head, was giving him tips.

Either that or he was colluding in race-fixing.

Both activities were highly illegal, dangerous, and stupid things to do. Why would he take that chance? And why do so in the men's room in a Lambourn hotel? Jack had no idea how to answer his first question, but he figured the second was less of a conundrum. Jack knew next to nothing about the types who hung around the racing scene, but was pretty sure from what he'd overheard that he'd pegged Fuller's associate for what he was. Locals, who lived, worked and breathed horseracing, would have even less trouble identifying him if they were seen together in a public place, causing speculation about Fuller's association with the man. But who could possibly read anything into a chance meeting in a men's room?

'What are you up to, Fuller?' Jack muttered aloud as he washed his hands and returned to the bar. Fuller had struck up a conversation with a group of locals upon his return to the bar. The scout's empty glass sat on the table he had occupied and the man himself was nowhere in sight.

'Are you okay?' Alexi asked him. 'You look preoccupied.'

'Sure.' Jack wasn't ready to share what he thought he'd just witnessed. It didn't have any bearing on Natalie's disappearance and Jack didn't have time for distractions, even though the policeman in him still yearned to knock Fuller's game on the head. 'Where were we?'

'We were talking about Natalie's online presence,' Drew reminded him. 'We have to ask why she would be so cautious about her email and stuff like that, yet have a Facebook page and openly talk about buying a share in a racehorse?' He shook his head. 'It makes no sense.'

'That is a very good question,' Jack replied.

'What do you plan to do now?' Cheryl asked. 'Since you've satisfied yourself that your sister's clients aren't involved, will you keep on digging?'

'I don't think they're involved but I want to find an alternative reason for Natalie's disappearance that will point the police in a different direction, if it comes to that. Preferably one that will end with us finding her alive and well.'

'How?' Drew asked.

'The escort agency where she worked,' Jack replied. 'I'm hoping they will be able to enlighten us since I'm convinced her past life is the key to her disappearance.' He turned towards Alexi and grinned. 'Fancy a trip up to town tomorrow?'

* * *

Cosmo was confined to the kitchen while Alexi and Jack, at Cheryl's insistence, dined in their restaurant. They were shown to a round table in an intimate corner. There was an orchid in its centre, and a waiter lit a candle as he handed them menus. Alexi thanked him, then hid behind hers, pretending to study it as she tried to figure out why Jack was suddenly so distant.

She put her menu aside while Jack had a long discussion with the waiter about wines and selected a bottle. They ordered their food but before either of them had time to instigate a conversation, the waiter returned with their wine. Jack went through the ritual of tasting it and giving it the seal of approval. The waiter filled Alexi's glass and she took a sip. Water was poured, a basket of bread with olive oil dip placed between them and finally... finally, they were alone.

'What?' she asked crossly when she had absorbed the heavy

weight of Jack's gaze for several tension-filled minutes prior to the delivery of the bread.

'I can't help thinking it isn't me you really want to be having romantic dinners with.'

'What do you mean?'

'I obviously interrupted you and your boss at a vital point in your negotiations.' Sarcasm dripped from his voice and Jack knew he was behaving like a jerk. He just couldn't seem to help himself and dipped bread into the oil-balsamic mix as he tried to get himself together. 'Are you going back to London and your old job?' he asked.

'I haven't had a chance to think about it.'

'He offered you your position back?'

'Not exactly.'

'Then what?' Jack leaned back as the waiter placed their starters in front of them.

'There's a big exposé I put a lot of work in on,' she replied, piercing a seared prawn with her fork, lifting it to her mouth, and taking a bite.

'Tell me about it.'

Tight-lipped when it came to stories she was working on, Alexi surprised herself by opening up to Jack, telling him about the legwork she'd already put in and how much she wanted to see it through.

'Not just for personal glory, believe it or not,' she said. 'I really care about those poor people. One or two of them told me, off the record, that they would be better off returning to their home countries but can't afford the fare, or the shame they'd face once they got there. Their families scrimped and saved to send them to England, where they were promised a better life, unimaginable earnings... the usual hype those unscrupulous traffickers come up with to sell the dream.'

'They don't want to admit they were duped,' Jack said. 'I can understand how they feel, and why you're so obsessed with this story but, here's the thing – if you were the only one in direct contact with these people, how come the whistle-blower contacted Vaughan?'

'That's a very good question.' She paused while the waiter cleared their empty plates. 'He had my mobile number but... well, I hate to admit it, but I went into a bit of a downer when I left the paper and didn't answer my phone. Patrick had taken to calling me from numbers I didn't recognise and I didn't want to talk to him. Perhaps when he couldn't reach me, my contact rang the paper direct, trying to find me, and the call was diverted to Patrick.'

Jack fixed her with a probing gaze. 'Do you think he would have done that?'

'Why would Patrick lie?'

'Taking a wild guess, I'd say he's crazy about you, desperate to get you back to town, no matter what it takes.'

'But I would have found out he'd got me there under false pretences when my contact failed to deliver.'

Jack shrugged. 'But you'd be back where you feel most at home, and would have had time to calm down about the paper downsizing.'

'I don't think he seriously believed I'd leave London. He just thought I was avoiding his calls.' Alexi leaned her elbow on the table and her chin on her clenched fist, her gaze averted from Jack's to avoid watching him watching her with such unnerving stillness. 'He called at my apartment, saw I'd put it up for rent, and that spooked him.'

'The guy's in love with you,' Jack replied softly.

She finally met his gaze, the tension between them replaced

by something more fundamental. Something she preferred not to put a name to.

'Thank you.' She flashed a wan smile. 'I think.'

'What will you do?'

She sighed. 'I'm seeing a different side of Patrick now. A controlling, manipulative side, and I don't much like the view.' She shook her head. 'I want that story, I want my old job back, but I don't want Patrick.'

'You're not in love with him?'

'I don't think I ever was. Not really.'

His slow, somnolent smile tugged at Alexi on a level over which she had absolutely no control. The waiter appeared with their main courses, and Alexi was grateful for the interruption.

'Is Cassie working on Natalie's background?' she asked in a deliberate change of subject.

'Not exactly.' His knife slid through his locally-produced steak as though cutting through butter.

'What do you mean, *not exactly*?'

'Cassie has other priorities right now.'

'She's still annoyed with you.' Alexi shook her head. 'That's not helpful. We need to know about Natalie's arrest, who her adoptive parents were, and whether she went back to them after her arrest. If possible, we need to talk to them. We also need to know Charles's identity. If her activities are motivated by her past, then that information is essential.'

'That's why I'm hoping we'll learn more from the agency tomorrow.'

'I'm kinda looking forward to that. I'll be interested to see what it's like.'

They ate in thoughtful silence for a moment or two.

'Why would the agency tell us anything about Natalie's history?' Alexi asked. 'I should have thought their business relied upon absolute discretion.'

'I'm sure it does, at least in so far as the identity of their clients goes, but—'

'But if they think one of their own is in danger, perhaps at the hands of a client, they might be more forthcoming.'

'We can but hope.'

'I assume we're not going to ask for an appointment.'

Jack grinned. 'Absolutely not.'

'Do you have an address for it?'

'Yep. Cassie found it.'

'Of course, she did.' Alexi rolled her eyes. 'So, how do you want to play it when we get there?'

'I figured on the truth, but you'll have to let me think on my feet. It really depends upon who we see and how responsive they are. If they clam up, you might have to go from being my... *assistant*,' he said with a cocky grin, 'to your true self.'

'On the trail of a hot story?' She returned his grin. 'You'd be surprised what people tell me in confidence if I give them my word that I won't publish.'

The waiter cleared their empty plates and they both declined the dessert menu.

'I've been thinking,' Alexi said as they waited for their coffee. 'If Cassie's backed up, I might be able to get a line on Natalie's arrest, and her adoptive parents.'

Jack sat a little straighter. 'How?'

'I did an exposé once on the foster system.' He nodded. 'A lady high up in Social Services gave me a very frank interview highlighting the obstacles in the system that prevented them from doing their jobs as well as they would like. Most of it was off the record and she actually contacted me when the article was printed because she said that for once the argument was balanced. She reckoned I'd highlighted how her department was hampered and Social Services were shown as victims of... well, of government red tape and cut backs, which is true, by the way.'

'So, I take it you have the lady's contact details and think she owes you one.'

Alexi grinned. 'No harm in trying, especially since I have a valid reason to ask and she knows I won't reveal her involvement.'

'Worth a try, I guess.'

He drained his coffee cup and pushed his chair back. 'Come on, let's hit the computers for a while, see if anything new has come in.'

10

Jack and Alexi left Lambourn at ten the following morning. This time Jack insisted upon driving and Cosmo was bribed with a tin of organic tuna and a catnip mouse to stay at home.

On their way out, Jack hit the brakes and allowed a string of thoroughbreds returning from the gallops to cross the road in front of them.

'Aren't they magnificent?' Alexi eyed the spirited horses with appreciation.

'Makes you want to get your jodhpurs out again, does it?'

'Hardly,' she said. 'Hey, that's Tod, I think,' she added when the last jockey in line waved his thanks to Jack. 'It's hard to recognise him beneath that skullcap.'

'Who's Tod?'

'Tod Naismith. He's one of Graham Fuller's trainee jockeys. Lives in Cheryl's annexe.'

'Oh, right.' Jack moved the car forward once the horses were clear, thinking there was no getting away from Fuller. 'I haven't had a chance to ask. Did you manage to get through to your contact at Social Services this morning?'

'Yes. She was off to a meeting and couldn't talk for long, but I explained what we wanted to know about Natalie and she promised to get back to me later today.'

'Ah, the powers of the press.'

'Don't mock. I seem to be getting more co-operation out of my unpaid sources than you are from your business partner. Sorry,' Alexi added when Jack inhaled sharply. 'Sore subject?'

'Cassie has her... issues.'

'So I gathered.' Alexi sent him a look. 'Wanna talk about it?'

'Nothing to talk about. I don't like being at odds with her is all. I thought she'd understand my need to help my sister. Still, she'll get over it and come through with what we need.'

'Is it me that's caused her to get her knickers in a knot?'

'Hard to say.' He shrugged. 'Perhaps it's just that we're not getting paid. Cassie always has an eye for the bottom line. Cassie thinks that because we've excluded the men Natalie dated, my involvement is at an end. I don't agree. We argued about it.'

'I see.' Alexi changed the subject. 'So, where is this Mayfair Escort Agency? I'm betting it's not in the West End.'

Jack grinned. 'Clapham.'

'Clapham? That's not far from my old stomping ground. The property's expensive but it's not an exclusive address.'

'You seem to think we're going to a house of ill-repute.'

'Well, aren't we?'

'I doubt it. Interested parties in need of a *bona fide* escort sign up online and make their selection from pictures like the ones we saw on the site.'

'Not a website that anyone can access?'

'I'm guessing it's more exclusive than that nowadays. Anyway, they pay the agency for the escort's time and anything else that happens between them is, presumably, negotiated between the punter and the escort.'

'Is it an unwritten rule that the girls *must* give out?' Alexi snorted. 'That doesn't seem very fair.'

Jack pulled onto the slip road and filtered into the traffic on the motorway heading for London. 'You think they don't know what they're getting themselves into?'

'Damn sight better than standing around on street corners, I suppose.'

'These girls travel the world, first class, at their clients' expense. When it comes right down to it, what they do is not much different to being trophy wives. They have to look good, be inventive in the bedroom, and pander to the rich man's ego. Think about it that way, if it helps.'

She screwed up her nose. 'I'd rather not.' She sighed. 'Part of me can't help thinking the girls are being exploited, even though I can see that Natalie was canny and came out of it with enough money to set herself up for life.'

'Well, there you are then.'

The radio in Jack's car was tuned to a classical station. Presumably it was the motion of wheels on Tarmac and the soothing strains of Beethoven that caused Alexi to stifle a yawn. Her eyes fluttered to a close.

* * *

Alexi only stirred when Jack pulled off the motorway and slowed, snarled up in traffic as he hit the outskirts of London. She sat up, blinked, and then stretched her arms above her head.

'Sorry,' she said sheepishly. 'I'm not much company, am I? Where are we?'

'Getting close,' he said, checking his GPS as he waited at a red light.

Five minutes later, Jack was feeding a parking meter situated in a side street lined with elegantly restored Edwardian houses.

'This is as close as we're likely to get,' he said, placing a hand on Alexi's elbow and guiding her along the crowded pavement. 'The agency is in this side street.'

A discreet plaque situated in the centre of a black door confirmed they had found the right place. Alexi looked up at the rather grand, well-maintained exterior of the building and grinned.

'Can't judge a house by its façade,' she said flippantly.

Jack pressed the bell and the door swung open. They found themselves in an airy entrance hall with a tiled floor. There were open archways on either side of it, leading to sitting rooms. There wasn't a person in sight. Presumably the front door was covered by a camera, which accounted for its opening on its own.

'Not quite what you expected?' Jack asked.

Before she could respond, a young woman of no more than twenty appeared from the back of the house. She wore jeans and a sleeveless top, her hair pulled back into a ponytail, no make-up on her pretty face.

'Definitely not,' Alexi belatedly replied.

'Can I help you?' the girl asked pleasantly.

'We're here to see Athena De Bois.' Jack told her.

'Do you have an appointment?'

'No, but I'm hoping she can spare us a few moments. My name is Jack Maddox. I'm a private investigator.'

'Oh.' The girl lost a modicum of poise. 'I hope there isn't going to be any trouble.'

'I'm sure there won't be.' Jack handed her his card and treated her to a full wattage smile that made her blush. 'We just need to ask her a few questions about Natalie Dwight.'

'I see.' It was obvious the name meant nothing to the girl. 'If you'd like to take a seat in there,' she said, indicating one of the sitting rooms, 'I'll see if Athena's free.'

'Thanks.'

'Who's Athena De Bois?' Alexi asked as they sat.

'The woman who now runs this place.' Jack grinned at her. 'I did my homework.'

'Evidently.'

A short time later, the same girl returned.

'Athena will see you, if you'd like to come this way.'

* * *

The girl led them up a wide staircase and tapped at an open door at one end of the corridor. She ushered Jack and Alexi into the room and closed the door behind them. An elegant woman sat behind a marble desk in the tastefully appointed office. The walls were painted a soft shade of yellow. A large abstract painting dominated one of them and an equally large mirror reflected light projected through the full-length window directly behind the woman's chair.

A fig tree flourished in a ceramic pot in one corner of the room and a small, cream-coloured dog was fast asleep in a soft basket. The view looked over a decked garden with strategically placed tubs of flowering plants and expensive-looking outdoor furniture. The only indication of the nature of business carried out in the establishment was a statue of Aphrodite.

Athena De Bois was, Jack figured, probably pushing fifty but ageing gracefully, her poise and elegance immediately apparent as she stood to greet them. She wore tailored trousers, a fuchsia, silk blouse that clung to her slender body and her hair was swept back into a perfect chignon.

'Mr Maddox,' she said, extending a slim, manicured hand,

her nails varnished the exact same shade of pink as her blouse. Jack imagined such attention to detail was *de rigueur* in her line of work. 'I'm Athena De Bois.'

'Jack Maddox. Thank you for seeing us without an appointment.'

The hint of a smile flirted with her lips. 'A private investigator,' she said, picking up his card from her desk and twisting it between her fingers. 'My curiosity got the better of me.'

'This is my assistant, Alexi Ellis.'

The ladies shook hands.

'I know that name,' Athena said, a note of suspicion entering her voice as she subjected Alexi to an appraising glance. 'But not, I think, in the role of investigator. Help me out here, Alexi. Why do you look so familiar?'

'Jack's the investigator,' Alexi replied. 'You probably know me from the *Sentinel*.'

'Of course.' If Athena was discomposed to have a journalist in her office, she gave no sign and remained perfectly calm. 'I admire your work.'

'Thank you.'

'Please,' she said. 'Take a seat and tell me why an investigator and journalist are interested in my friend, Natalie Dwight.'

'She's gone missing,' Jack replied bluntly. 'And we're rather concerned about her.'

'Missing?' Athena raised a perfectly plucked eyebrow and appeared slightly less composed. 'How long for?'

'We're now into the fifth day.'

'Oh.'

'Do you know her?' Alexi asked. 'Well, presumably you do since you referred to her as your friend.'

'Excuse me, but before I answer you, I need to understand why you're here, Alexi, and in what capacity.'

'That's easily explained. I'm staying with a close friend in Lambourn at the moment. She and Natalie have become friendly. It's Cheryl who alerted me to Natalie going on the missing list. I agreed to take a look into it, and met Jack along the way. You have my assurance that I won't be writing about this, and if I ever do, I shall seek your permission before I say a word about your organisation.'

'Please don't take this the wrong way, but why should I believe you?'

Alexi flashed a wry smile. 'We're not all bad. I'm doing this as a favour to a friend, and because I feel as though I've come to know Natalie a little over the past day or so. I want to find her.' Alexi leaned forward. 'I can sense she's in danger and needs help rather badly.'

Athena leaned back in her chair, apparently satisfied. 'Very well, what do you need to know?'

'You said you and Natalie are friends,' Jack said.

'Oh yes. We worked here together for some years. I was coming to the end of my career as an escort. She was in training.'

Alexi frowned. 'Training?'

'There is a great deal more to this profession than you might think.' Athena appeared resigned to Alexi's misconception. 'How long do you think a person would last at your newspaper if they just assumed they knew how to be a reporter?'

Alexi conceded the point with a nod and a smile. 'I hear you.'

'Presumably you're aware that Natalie moved to Lambourn and set up a business in floral art,' Jack said.

'Yes, I did know that.'

'You keep in contact with her?'

'We're still friends.' Jack could tell from the slight tightening in her expression that he had offended her. 'It might surprise you to learn that escorts are capable of forming friendships, just like anyone else.'

'It doesn't surprise me in the slightest,' Jack replied composedly.

'Sorry.' Athena briefly lowered her head. 'Sore subject.'

'I can imagine.'

'Apart from my friend Cheryl Hopgood, who's a hotelier in Lambourn,' Alexi said, 'you're the only other friend of Natalie's we've come across, and we didn't actually know the two of you were friends when we came here today.'

'Natalie is a very private person.' Athena fiddled abstractedly with Jack's card. 'We *do* form friendships, but are cautious about whom we trust.'

'Which, presumably is why she changed her name when she stopped working and no one who knows her in Lambourn is aware of what she used to do for a living.'

'What conclusions do you think they would draw if they did?'

'Good point,' Jack acknowledged.

'If she wasn't driven out of town by jealous females, you can be sure those females would lock up their husbands.' Athena's smile became strained. 'Take it from me, it would be a waste of breath to tell them they had nothing to fear from her. Entertaining gentlemen professionally is one thing. When it comes to our private lives, we can enjoy the luxury of being considerably more selective.'

'I can understand that,' Alexi said.

'So, tell me how you think I can help,' Athena said.

'When did you last speak to Natalie?'

'About a month ago. She came up to town for a couple of days and we arranged to meet for lunch.'

'Did she tell you she planned to join a dating agency?'

'Yes, she wants to settle down, like a normal person,' she said quietly. 'She asked me if I thought she should do it and I told her to go for it.'

'It's a problem for her because if she finds someone she likes and tells him the truth about her background, he's unlikely to continue with the relationship,' Alexi said pensively. 'If she doesn't tell him, she'll be living a lie.'

Athena nodded. 'It's all right for men to have a chequered past but the same rules don't always apply to women.'

'We've investigated the three men she dated,' Jack said, 'and are satisfied that none of them know what's happened to her. So we decided to dig a little deeper and that's how we came across her past life.' Jack leaned back in his chair and hooked one foot over his opposite thigh. 'Our problem is that we can find out very little, other than that she worked here.'

'We know she was adopted,' Alexi said.

'And we also know she was arrested as a minor for soliciting.'

'She was.'

'But unfortunately we have no way of knowing if she returned to her adoptive parents, or how she became an escort,' Jack explained.

'I can't see how any of that information will help you. It's ancient history.'

'Perhaps, but I'll bet my pension on her disappearance not being random,' Jack said. 'She was targeted.'

'How can you be so sure?'

'There was no sign of a struggle in her home, her car is still in the garage, and she isn't answering her phone or email,' Alexi said. 'She's also missed one business commitment that we know of, which is totally out of character.'

'Yes, it is.' Athena frowned, looking genuinely concerned now. 'All right, I'll tell you what I know. She was arrested at the

Park Lane Hotel for trying to shake down a rich guest.' Athena's eyes were softened by a smile. 'It was obvious that she was under age and didn't have a clue what she was doing. Ordinarily girls like her wouldn't get through the front door of such establishments, but she must have slipped past the concierge when his back was turned.'

'You sound as though you witnessed the event,' Jack said.

'Oh, I did,' Athena replied calmly. 'I saw it all.'

* * *

Alexi blinked. 'You saw Natalie as a teenager trying to pick up a rich man in a five-star hotel?'

'I was there in the lobby, waiting for a client to finish a telephone call. Natalie was totally out of her depth, but even then she had a certain something about her that made her stand out,' Athena said with a sardonic smile. 'Natalie, I later learned, was adamant that she didn't intend to return to her adoptive parents but, of course, Social Services knew best and forced her to. I knew she would run away again, and they probably did too, but since she refused to tell them what had gone wrong, they had no choice.' Athena sighed. 'Suffice it to say, I told Bella—'

'Bella?' Alexi asked.

'The lady who ran this establishment when I was still an escort. I told her about Natalie and that I thought she had potential. When she ran away a second time and was picked up by vice, my contact tipped me the wink, we bent the rules by excluding Social Services, and I took responsibility for her.'

'Just like that?' Alexi asked, unable to keep a faint note of censure out of her voice. 'Without knowing why she was so determined to run from the only home she'd ever known?'

'I didn't need to know. I could see it in her eyes that she had her reasons. Compelling reasons that probably forced her to try and sell herself in the first place. I also knew that if she was sent back to the Seatons, she would run away again. Someone had to look out for her.'

'Weren't you asking her to sell herself by bringing her here?'

Athena sat a little straighter. 'Do you know how many beautiful young girls aspire to enter this profession?'

'Enlighten me.'

'As many as those who wish to become models or actresses and, believe me, as ambitions go, becoming a top escort is almost as unattainable. Take the girl that let you in just now, for example. What did you make of her?'

'She looked like the girl next door,' Alexi replied slowly. 'Fresh and young, and yet...' She glanced at Jack. 'She got your attention, even dressed casually as though not trying to make an impression.'

'Then we're doing something right.' Some of the tension left Athena's body. 'That's what we teach here. It's not all about sexy clothing and thick make-up. Just the opposite, in fact. The gentlemen on our books require understated sophistication. Look upon this place as an academy from which only one in ten ever graduates.'

'Blimey!' Alexi muttered.

'Natalie was fifteen by the time we took her in. She was angry with the world, with just cause, and didn't want to listen to anything we tried to tell her about the pitfalls of the occupation. She knew better, of course.' Athena's shrug was impossibly elegant. 'Well, what teenager doesn't? Most kids with that attitude refuse to toe the line and get shown the door, but Bella agreed with me about Natalie's potential and allowed her some leeway.'

'Please don't take this the wrong way,' Alexi said. 'But how do you learn to become an escort?'

'How much time have you got?' Athena smiled. 'Natalie was bright, so it was easy to get her to develop an interest in all the right things she'd need to keep herself informed about in order to make polite dinner conversation... politics, current affairs, stuff like that. She had to read the papers every day and answer questions intelligently upon a whole range of subjects. She learned to speak properly, to walk, to dress, to use make-up and style her hair. Trainees also get investment advice.' A ghost of a smile flirted with Athena's lips. 'We have an accountant on staff, believe it or not.' Alexi nodded. She believed it. 'Natalie's apprenticeship lasted two years.'

Alexi flexed both brows. 'That long?'

'We charge our clients a lot of money. In return, they expect the very best, which is what we pride ourselves upon giving them.'

'It sounds as though Natalie was your protégée,' Jack remarked.

'She was in many respects. I brought her in so felt responsible for her. We became friends, and I value that friendship. I hope you find her safe and well.'

'Can you think where she might have gone?' Alexi asked.

'No, I'm sorry, I can't. If I had any ideas, I'd tell you.'

'Please don't take this the wrong way,' Jack said. 'But it did cross our minds that she might have befriended a wealthy date with a view to exploiting that wealth.'

Shades of irritation clouded Athena's expression. 'Natalie was wealthy in her own right. Even if she was not, she wouldn't do that.'

'She purchased her house and paid for an extension from which to run her business. That made a big dent in her nest egg, but since then regular large amounts have gone into her account. You can see how it looks to an outsider.' Jack paused. 'Especially to the police, if they start digging.'

Athena shuddered. 'Let's hope it doesn't come to that.'

'We have managed to see her financial records through, shall we say, roundabout means. We've also alerted her bank manager to her disappearance. If he reports any financial discrepancies to the police, it will escalate their enquiry,' Jack explained. 'Which means her past will inevitably come to light.'

'We found out about it,' Alexi added. 'So they will too.'

'Yes, I see.' Athena turned her head to one side, as though she didn't want them to see her frown. 'I want her found, but I don't want any adverse publicity for this agency. We have a lot of high-profile clients who won't appreciate it.'

'Natalie used my sister's dating agency,' Jack said. 'Which is how I got involved, and my main concern is in protecting my sister's interests, just as yours is in protecting your own.'

'Do you know why Natalie ran away from home?' Alexi asked.

Athena pursed her glossed lips. 'Her father is a sports agent. Represents a number of top footballers, tennis players, people like that. He is well-known, very charming and highly respected.'

'Gerald Seaton?' Alexi said, frowning. 'Of course. I know that name. Who doesn't?'

Athena nodded. 'He took Natalie to some flashy awards ceremony when she was fourteen. Her mother, for some reason, wasn't there, so Natalie had a posh hotel room all to herself.'

Alexi shivered. 'Let me guess: the Park Lane Hotel.'

'Precisely. She told me how excited she'd been. How grown up she'd felt. She idolised her father, you see, and would do anything to please him. Well, anything except what it transpired he actually wanted from her.' Athena sighed. 'He told her afterwards when she went into meltdown that nobody would believe her if she talked about it. She owed him for taking her in and giving her such a luxurious lifestyle.' Athena frowned. 'All the usual garbage. But most worrying of all, he made it clear he didn't plan to stop. From that moment on, she was his whenever he wanted her.'

Alexi shuddered.

'He underestimated Natalie's strength of will, though. His actions shattered her hero worship and opened her eyes to the real world. She told me she grew up that day and accepted what she'd spent years trying to deny. There was obviously something fundamentally wrong with her. There must be or her birth mother wouldn't have given her up. And now, the man she looked upon as her father seemed to think he could use her as he pleased. Well, it didn't please Natalie, and she was determined it wouldn't happen again. She also decided that if she was attractive to older men she might as well make a living for herself on her own terms.'

'Hence her return visit to the scene of her worst nightmare,' Jack said softly.

'Quite.'

'Are her parents still alive?' Alexi asked.

'As far as I know. I would imagine her father has retired now. They live in Woldingham, Surrey.' Alexi knew of the village. Stockbroker central, with property prices to match. 'I'd love to see Seaton get his comeuppance, but I very much doubt there was anything Natalie could have done to get back at him after all this time. It would still be her word against his.'

'Was she bent on revenge?' Alexi asked. 'In her position, I suspect I would be.'

'She never really got past it. She told me more than once that it was like an obstacle, stopping her from being her own person.

I've often thought that's why so many people come out of the woodwork years later, accusing celebrities of nefarious wrong-doings, because finally the world is prepared to believe them.'

'Just a couple more questions,' Jack said when Athena took a glance at her watch. 'Natalie was exceedingly cautious about what she posted online.'

'In this line of work, caution becomes second nature.'

'I would imagine that carrying little physical baggage does as well.' Athena nodded. 'Which explains why there were so few papers, personal or otherwise, in Natalie's cottage. But she must have *some* things she needs to keep. Can you think where they might be?'

'Sorry, she didn't confide in me.'

'Did she make a will?'

'Most likely. We all use the same solicitor.' She rummaged in a drawer and produced a card. 'You can ask these people if they represent her interests.'

'Thanks,' Jack replied, smoothly pocketing the card. 'One last thing. Do you know if she had a client called Charles?'

Athena frowned and looked as though she wouldn't answer. But Jack could see that the name was familiar to her.

'He left a message on her answerphone, wanting to see her,' Alexi explained. 'He isn't a man she dated through Jack's sister's agency so we wondered—'

'Yes, I know who you're talking about. Occasionally clients form an attachment to a particular escort and continue to see her privately even after she leaves the business.'

'Don't you mind?' Alexi asked. 'I mean, you're cut out of the financial arrangements that way.'

Athena smiled. 'Not in the least. We have a business arrange-ment with our escorts while they are employed by us. They have a contractual obligation to work here for a specific time period that ensures we recoup the cost of their training and make a profit. When they leave, they are free to behave as they please.'

'But Charles is registered here?' Jack asked.

'Yes, he is.'

'Regular payments of a thousand pounds a time have gone into her bank account. Would Charles pay her that much?' Alexi asked.

Athena's lips twitched. 'She's selling herself short.'

Alexi's mouth fell open. 'She charged more than that when she worked here?'

'Considerably more.' Athena looked complacent. 'We're very good at what we do, and Charles does have very specific requirements.'

'Obviously.'

'I'm prepared to help you by contacting Charles, explaining the situation and asking if he's willing to speak with you. I know for a fact that he won't have seen Natalie over the past two weeks because he's been abroad on business.' Alexi and Jack exchanged a glance. 'One of our girls went to Paris to attend a party with him last week, which rather puts him in the clear in terms of being involved in Natalie's disappearance, doesn't it?'

Jack nodded. 'I guess it does.'

'Besides, they are very fond of one another and he has no reason to harm her.' Athena held up her hands. 'And before you ask, she would never even *think* of exploiting him, so don't go there.' She stood, indicating the interview was at an end. 'I assume it's all right to give Charles your number?'

'Of course.' Jack stood also and offered her his hand. 'And thank you for your time.'

'You're welcome. Please keep me informed, and let me know if there's anything else I can do to help you.'

'You'll be the first to know,' Alexi said.

'Oh, one more thing I've just thought of.' Alexi and Jack, on the point of walking through the door, turned to look at Athena. 'In her final year here, she started seeing a psychiatrist and talking her problems through. He encouraged Natalie to write it all down, get her feelings out on paper.'

Alexi and Jack exchanged a glance. 'We didn't find anything like that.'

'Well, she wouldn't leave it hanging around. It was way too sensitive.'

Especially if she planned to take her revenge, Alexi thought.

'Why did she decide to see a shrink?' Jack asked. 'What we have found out about her points to a private, self-contained person.'

'Absolutely, but when she told me she was thinking of giving up this work... well, let's just say that all our escorts are actively encouraged to talk the decision through with professionals. You'd be surprised how many of us got into the business for reasons similar to Natalie's, and how difficult it is for us to adjust to normality without help.'

'Yes,' Alexi said. 'I can imagine.'

'The doctor encouraged her to explore her feelings about being given up for adoption.'

'About her birth mother?' Alexi shared a glance with Jack. 'Did she try to find her?'

'Not to my knowledge. But there is something I've just remembered... I'm not sure if it's significant. She received some unexpected news that expedited her departure from this establishment.'

'Do you know who from?' Alexi asked.

'She said very little about it, but seemed profoundly affected by whatever it was. I tried to persuade her to postpone her decision to retire. I was running this place by then. Natalie was still only forty, but looked ten years younger and was in great demand. She could still have made a lot more money, but I could tell the mysterious communication had made up her mind so there seemed little point in trying to get her to change it.'

'Do you have the name of her shrink?' Jack asked. 'I know he won't tell me anything about their sessions but he might know something that will help.'

Athena smiled as she handed Jack another card. 'We have a resident psychiatrist on speed dial too,' she said.

11

'What did you make of that?' Jack asked as they left the house.

'That I'm in the wrong business. A thousand quid for...' She wrinkled her nose. 'On second thoughts, perhaps not.'

'Come on,' he said, grinning. 'I'll buy you some lunch while you reflect upon lost career opportunities. Then we can plot our next move.'

They made their way to the nearest pub. It was crowded with the lunchtime mob but Jack managed to nab a small corner table. Over sandwiches and soft drinks they reviewed all they'd learned.

'It sounds as though Natalie fell on her feet, at least initially, to be adopted by such a well-off family like the Seatons,' Jack said.

'She would have had the best of everything, I imagine, especially if she was an only child.'

'A good education and mixing with better off people would have been useful grounding for becoming an escort.'

Alexi nodded. 'It certainly made her self-assured. Perhaps

that's what Athena saw in her. I mean, how many fourteen-year-olds would have the confidence to walk into a five-star hotel and try to do what she did?'

'Fourteen-year-olds are very streetwise nowadays.' Jack took a bite of his ham sandwich.

'Natalie's safe, comfortable world had crumbled around her and she lost all self-worth.' Alexi ground her jaw. 'Bastard!'

'The one man she trusted above everyone exploited her. Of course she felt worthless. He would have told her it was her fault, and she probably half believed it. Her birth mother had given her up. Now the man she thought of as a father had abdicated that role because he didn't deem her a worthy daughter.' Jack shook his head. 'Poor kid!'

'Do you think it's true, though?' Alexi said reflectively. 'I was at a function once and Seaton was there. He has such presence, such charm. I never would have thought him capable of doing something so horrific.'

'The charmers, people in positions of authority, make vulnerable kids feel special when they're noticed by them. Look at all the high-profile cases that have come to light recently. Television celebrities abusing their positions for years and getting away with it – until now.' Jack abandoned his half-eaten sandwich. 'Still, we need to keep an open mind. Perhaps Natalie was a little princess, spoiled and indulged, and decided to rebel for no reason other than that she wanted some fun, which got out of hand.' Jack smiled across at her. 'There could be any number of other explanations.'

She folded her arms on the table and leaned towards him, her expression intent. 'Tell me you weren't thinking about your own trial by media when you recommended giving Seaton the benefit of the doubt.'

He flashed a sheepish grin. 'You've got me there, but still, it *does* pay to examine all the angles before passing judgement.'

'I keep thinking about her bank account. And those payments. I wonder if they're connected to the mysterious information she received. Do you think she blackmailed her father into paying up in exchange for her silence about what he put her through?'

'*If* he put her through it.'

'Well, even if he didn't, she could make up a convincing story that would see his reputation ruined.'

Jack nodded. 'The same thought had occurred to me.'

'Was Lambourn a random choice, or did that also have something to do with whatever news Natalie had received? As far as we know, she'd never been to Lambourn before she decided to settle there and you have to admit it's pretty quiet unless you're into horses. And, like me, she'd always lived in town before her move.' Alexi pursed her lips, frustrated. 'I know she wanted to make a fresh start, but still...'

'If we ever find the account of her life she's supposed to have written, we'll probably be able to nail the whole case. But, blackmailing her father?' Jack shrugged. 'I'd say it's a distinct possibility.' He paused. 'And a very good way to get herself killed.'

Alexi gasped. 'You're not saying—'

'It's just an observation.'

Alexi frowned into the distance and absently twisted the ends of her hair around her forefinger. 'I wonder if she tried to tell her adoptive mother what happened.'

'Why don't we go and ask her?'

'That was going to be my next suggestion.'

'The solicitors and the shrink definitely won't see us without appointments, and probably won't tell us anything we don't already know even if we do get past their gatekeepers. We need to prioritise and follow up the most promising clues first. If Natalie turns up alive and well, with some plausible explanation for her disappearance, we'll pack up shop and go back to our lives. If she doesn't...'

'If her body's found, you mean?'

'Yeah, if that happens the police will be all over this and we'll lose control, so let's leave the shrink and lawyer until later.'

Alexi was already Googling away on her iPhone. 'Gerry Seaton is a co-founder of Sporting Initiatives. He's now in his late sixties and retired as an active director five years ago, but retains a position on the board.'

'See if you can find an address for them.'

She shot Jack a grin. 'They still live in Woldingham. I'm wondering how much of an effort was put into finding Natalie when she took off for the second time. I dare say there's stuff online about it but that search will have to wait until later.'

'If Seaton *did* abuse her, he'd have been keen on covering his tracks, so I'm betting not much was done.'

Alexi grimaced. 'You're probably right.'

'Okay, let's go.'

They drained their glasses and left the pub.

'I've been to Woldingham a few times,' Alexi told Jack as he pointed his car in the direction of Croydon. 'It's on the North Downs. Very upper class. Has a thriving golf club, of which, I'll bet good money Seaton's a member.'

'Undoubtedly, especially if he's retired.' Jack slowed to thirty as they entered the village. He indicated left, past a row of shops that included a saddler's, a sporting goods store with a display of fishing rods, green wellies, and shooting sticks in its window, and the ubiquitous convenience store. Even posh people ran out of sugar, it seemed. 'This is the road,' he said, taking another left.

'And I'll bet that's the house.' Alexi pointed to a large pad in a good acre of ground, its front garden bursting with vibrant blooms.

Jack shrugged. 'All I see is lots of colour, so I'll take your word for it.'

'You haven't told me what you plan to say to them,' Alexi pointed out. 'You can hardly swan up to the door and ask Seaton if he would kindly 'fess up to abusing his daughter thirty years ago.'

Jack winked at her. 'I'll think of something.'

'Well, thanks for sharing,' she replied, sounding miffed.

'I'm not holding out on you. It's simply a situation that calls for improvisation. Until I gauge our reception, I've no idea which way to play it.'

'I suppose you think you can take one look at Seaton and decide if he's predator or victim?'

'All those years on the force did give me an edge, but I'm not always right.'

'Did I just hear you admit to having faults?' She offered him an incredulous look. 'You're fallible?'

Jack grinned. 'I didn't say I was often wrong.'

* * *

The house with all the flowers did indeed prove to be the Seaton residence. Jack drove his BMW through tall wrought iron gates that were wide open and followed a smooth, block-paved drive, halting the car in a turning circle at the front door.

'Nice,' he said to Alexi as they got out the vehicle and looked up at the modern, extensive, and immaculately maintained building.

Alexi merely grunted. Jack pressed the front door bell and it was opened by a short, plump woman with a pleasant, rather timid smile.

'Mrs Seaton?' Jack asked.

'Yes, can I help you?'

'My name's Maddox. I'm a private investigator.' He handed the bemused woman his card and turned on the charm. 'I'm sorry to call unannounced but I wondered if we could have a few moments of your time?'

'What's this about? Is it Na... have you news?'

'This is Alexi, my assistant. May we come in?'

'Yes, of course.'

She took them into a large lounge with full-length glazed doors leading onto a wide patio. A huge conservatory spanned one end of that patio and Jack could see the turquoise water of an indoor pool sparkling through the glass. The extensive back garden was also a riot of colour and didn't have a leaf out of place.

'You have a lovely home,' Jack told her.

'Thank you. Please sit down. May I offer you something to drink?'

'Tea, if it's not too much trouble,' Jack replied, flashing his most engaging smile.

'No trouble at all.' Mrs Seaton bustled towards what was obviously the kitchen. 'Make yourselves at home. I'll only be a moment.'

'Does that smile ever let you down?' Alexi demanded to know.

Jack turned the smile in question upon his partner-in-investigation. 'Not often,' he said. 'Don't judge. I'm betting you're not above using your own physical attributes to get interviewees to open up.'

She bit her lip. 'Why did you ask for tea?'

Without replying, Jack walked towards a sideboard crammed with family photographs. Almost all of them featured a girl – obviously Natalie – in various stages of adolescence, always smiling broadly. The photographs ended when she'd become a stunning teenager.

'Our daughter.'

Mrs Seaton had re-entered the room so quietly that the sound of her voice startled Jack. He almost dropped the picture of Natalie that he'd picked up to examine more closely. The child couldn't have been more than four years old. It made Jack feel indescribably sad to think how things had turned out for that little girl, innocent or otherwise.

'She's very pretty.'

'Thank you. Yes, she was.'

'*Was*?' Alexi asked as she helped clear a space on the coffee table for the tea tray.

'She disappeared, a long time ago now, but I still miss her every single day. I half-hoped, when you said you were an investigator, that you might have news of her. We did hire someone years ago but my husband dispensed with his services when he failed to find anything out. Even so...' Jack slowly shook his head, and saw the anticipation fade from Mrs Seaton's eyes. 'I've never given up wondering what happened to her. She's still alive somewhere; I'm absolutely sure of it. But what drove her away from home, I've never been able to fathom. She had everything she could possibly wish for, and two parents who loved her absolutely.'

Can she really have no idea, or is there nothing for her to know?

'It must be hard,' Alexi replied sympathetically, seating herself across from their hostess and nodding her thanks for the cup of tea, handed to her in a bone china cup and saucer.

'It is. I blame myself. I obviously did something wrong.'

'I doubt that,' Alexi replied.

'Would you like a biscuit?' Mrs Seaton proffered a plate. 'I baked them myself.'

'Well, in that case.'

Alexi selected a biscuit, took a bite, closed her eyes, and sighed.

'Delicious!' she said.

The older lady preened at the compliment. Based on what they knew of her husband's persona, Jack figured they had to be polar opposites, which didn't surprise him. He'd seen it more times than enough, and was already starting to understand why Natalie hadn't felt able to tell her mother what had been done to her, assuming something *had* been done and that she didn't actually try to talk about it. Mrs Seaton would have trouble believing the man she married capable of such depraved behaviour. She was devastated by the loss of her daughter, as evidenced by the photographic shrine in her living room, but if she'd had to choose between them, Jack wondered which way she would have jumped.

One of life's victims, was Fay Seaton. That's why they appealed to strong men like the one she'd married, who would find her easy to manipulate and control. Perhaps she even came from a moneyed background, giving Seaton the financial wherewithal to get his business off the ground. But Jack hadn't met Seaton yet and he might be jumping to erroneous conclusions.

But there again, he might not.

'We were just admiring your garden,' Alexi said.

'Why thank you.'

'It must be a lot of work.'

'It is, but I get help with the heavy stuff, which leaves me free to lose myself in the things I most enjoy doing. It's my passion, you know.'

'It shows.'

'I don't mean to be rude, but I don't have a lot of time. There's a gardening club meeting I need to attend very shortly.'

'Well then, I'd best come clean.' Jack flashed another of his winning smiles. 'I wasn't entirely honest with you earlier, Mrs Seaton, for which I apologise.'

'Oh,' she said, blinking in confusion. 'Then what—'

'I am an investigator, but Alexi isn't my assistant. She's a reporter with the *Sentinel*.'

Mrs Seaton cast Alexi a considering look. 'But, I don't understand—'

'Alexi is working on an article about children who go missing.' Mrs Seaton gasped. 'We don't mean to upset you, but your name came up during the course of her investigation and we wondered if you would be willing to talk about it.'

'Well, I...' Mrs Seaton fell into momentary contemplation but, fortunately, didn't ask how a PI came to be working with a reporter. 'I'm not sure what I can tell you after all this time. Besides, my husband says we shouldn't talk about Natalie. It upsets us both too much.'

Jack glanced at the gallery of pictures, suspecting that keeping them on display was one of the few areas in which Mrs Seaton had found the courage to defy her husband.

'From what our research threw up, it seems Natalie had the best of everything,' Alexi said softly. 'Did something change to make her want to leave home? Teenagers aren't always easy, are they?'

'Natalie never gave us a moment's bother.' Mrs Seaton frowned, suddenly looking decades older. 'That's why I've never been able to understand why she left.'

'Was she a good student?' Alexi asked.

'Oh yes, she was very diligent when it came to her studies.

She wanted to be a vet, specialising in horses, and she would have made it, too. Natalie could do whatever she set her mind to.'

'But she got herself arrested,' Alexi said, her voice soft and sympathetic, inviting Mrs Seaton's confidence.

'Oh, that was a misunderstanding. She was cross with us about something and tried to punish us by running off. She'd been to that hotel with her father a week or two before. It was familiar to her, which is why she must have gone back there, but the police jumped to the wrong conclusion.'

'Yes,' Alexi said gently. 'I expect they did.'

'I thought she'd got in with the wrong crowd at school and that they'd had a bad influence on her. It happens at that age, no matter how hard you try to steer them on the right path.' Yes, Jack thought, she would believe that. 'They have bad apples, even in good schools like the one we sent Natalie to. Anyway, we thought we'd set her straight. She promised us, but she hadn't been home for two days before she took off again, and this time she didn't come back.' She wiped a tear from her wrinkled cheek. 'I'm still hoping that one day she will.'

'What did she like to do?' Jack asked.

'Oh, she loved horses, just like most girls do.' Jack shot Alexi an *I-told-you-so* sideways glance. The admission also put Natalie's choice of Lambourn into perspective. If the love of horses had never left her, perhaps she genuinely wanted a share in a racehorse, explaining her need to shout about it on Facebook. 'She had her own pony, you know?' Mrs Seaton sighed. 'We eventually sold Dandy Kim, when it became apparent she would never return to ride him.'

'That must have been very hard for you.'

'For both of us. Natalie adored her father. They were so close I sometimes felt excluded.' She shook her head. 'That's ridiculous, I know, but we can't help the way we feel, can we?'

'No, we can't.'

Alexi leaned forward to touch Mrs Seaton's hand, her empathy for the woman's plight effortlessly seeming to communicate itself. Jack was starting to understand how she managed to get people to overcome their suspicion of reporters and open up to her. In this case it was the way she turned huge eyes, moist with sympathy, upon Fay Seaton and focused her complete attention on her.

'And then, of course, there was Perry.' Mrs Seaton reached across to the sideboard and picked up the picture of four-year-old Natalie with the puppy that Jack had examined earlier. 'It broke his heart almost as much as it did ours when Natalie disappeared. He sat at the gate every day waiting for her to come home from school but, of course, she never did.' Mrs Seaton sighed. 'I felt like giving up myself. I still don't know how I got through that terrible time.'

'You had your husband to lean on.'

'He was grieving too. It's funny, we ought to have been able to talk about it to each other, comfort one another, but we just seemed to skirt around the issue. Gerry buried himself in his work and I had... I wasn't very well. But I had my garden, which was a passion Natalie shared with me. It was unusual, I always thought, for a young girl but she had naturally green fingers and didn't mind getting them dirty.'

'She got that from you,' Jack said.

'Actually, no. Natalie was adopted. I wasn't able to have any of my own.'

'Oh, I see.'

'How thorough was the police investigation when Natalie went missing?' Jack asked.

Mrs Seaton shook her head. 'They were in and out of here for days, weeks... I don't really know. Like I said, I wasn't well. I had a bit of a breakdown, couldn't handle it, and my doctor kept me medicated. My husband handled it all and tried to protect me from it.'

The sound of a key in the front door had Mrs Seaton almost leaping from her chair. Her reaction confirmed Jack's suspicion that she was afraid of her husband, dominated by him, which is why the marriage had endured. 'And that will be my husband now. He's back from golf early.'

The man who strode into the room was tall, ramrod straight with not an ounce of spare flesh on his frame and a headful of silver hair. He wore expensive, casual clothes and the air of a man used to getting his own way. His gaze passed briefly over Jack and lingered a little too long on Alexi: a mixture of politeness, irritation, and very obvious appreciation of the female form. Definitely the sort arrogant enough to take what he wanted if it wasn't volunteered. He hadn't opened his mouth yet and Jack already disliked him. Mrs Seaton seemed too flustered to say anything so Jack took over, standing to introduce himself.

'Investigators,' he said jovially, turning on the charm. 'What have we done?'

'They were asking about Natalie, dear,' Mrs Seaton explained in a timid voice.

Seaton's smile faded. 'Do you have news of her?'

'Not exactly,' Jack replied, 'but there are a few—'

'Then why bring it up and upset my wife?'

'I'm not upset, dear. I like talking about Natalie. But I do need to leave now or I'll be late for my meeting. Perhaps you could answer any more questions our guests might have?'

'Of course.' He patted his wife's shoulder. 'You get along now.'

'Thank you for your time, Mrs Seaton,' Jack said, standing

and taking her hand in both of his. 'It was very nice to meet you and I hope you find out what happened to your daughter.'

'I doubt that we will ever know, not after all this time.' She shook her head in resignation. 'Still, it was nice talking about her again. I don't often get the chance.'

12

Left alone with Seaton, Alexi half-expected the charm to fade and his true character to show itself. If he was the reason for Natalie's disappearance and had kept it secret all these years, he had good reason to be worried, which would make him defensive. She was disappointed when instead of turning into a raging bull, he focused the full force of his smile upon her.

'Well now,' he said. 'Perhaps I can interest you in something stronger than tea.'

'Not for me, thanks,' Jack replied, even though the question had been directed to Alexi.

'Nor me,' she said.

'I hope you don't mind if I do.'

Without waiting for a response, he went to a well-stocked drinks cabinet and poured himself a substantial measure of single malt. With his back turned towards them, he took a long swig and then faced them.

'You didn't explain why you were asking about Natalie,' he said.

'You've seen what an effect your daughter's disappearance

has had on your wife,' Jack replied. 'Why haven't you done the decent thing and told her she's still alive and well?'

'I'm sorry.' Seaton blinked at Jack, his face a study of innocent bewilderment. 'I don't understand what you're getting at.'

He seemed so confused that Alexi was almost certain he must be innocent.

'We both know that isn't true,' Jack said, his voice tight with controlled anger.

'Look, we've tried to put this mess behind us. It was a terrible time when the child we both loved absconded but we've finally come to the conclusion that she must be dead. At least that gives us some sort of closure.'

'Dead?' Alexi asked. 'Why do you think she's dead?'

'It's the only explanation that makes any sense. She was a good kid, and we hadn't had any sort of falling out.' He shrugged. 'She had absolutely no reason to turn her back on all of this,' he added, gesturing around the opulent room. 'Besides, if she was still alive, she would have contacted us long before now. She knew how much we both adored her. Fay especially.'

'But there is another explanation, isn't there?' Jack said.

'What explanation?' he asked, deep grooves appearing in his forehead. 'Have you ever lost a child? No, I don't suppose you have, otherwise you wouldn't be asking such ridiculous questions.' He knocked back the remains of his drink and turned to refill his glass. 'Now, unless you have any specific knowledge of Natalie's last movements, I don't think there's anything else I can tell you, especially since you've avoided telling me why you're asking.'

'When did she first contact you again?' Jack asked, surprising Alexi probably as much as he shocked Seaton with the bluntness of the question.

'What the devil are you talking about?'

His bluster was almost convincing. Almost. A tic working beneath his left eye and the slightest of tremors in his hands gave him away. As did the fact that he glanced away to his left when he made his feeble attempt to deflect Jack's question.

'You raped her at the Park Lane hotel when she was fourteen.'

'What the devil do you think you're—'

'Pretty as a picture, wasn't she? All the laughter you shared, the come-ons she gave you, the way she idolised you. She was asking for it. Fourteen is the new twenty-five.'

Seaton's expression was set in granite. 'I don't have to listen to this slander.'

'You thought she'd be grateful,' Jack said, his voice silk on steel. 'Instead she ran, and tried for years to get over what you'd done to her. When she couldn't, she came back for her revenge and hit you where it hurt you the most. In your wallet.'

'You're deluded. Get out of my house!'

'Fine, but if we go, we'll be back, with the police.'

'And I'll sue for harassment.'

'Good,' Alexi said contemptuously. 'A courtroom is precisely where we want to get you. Even if you win, the publicity will ruin your reputation, to say nothing of your marriage. I'm betting your reputation, and appearances,' she added, taking her turn to spread her arms to embrace the elegant room, 'are all that really matter to you. You'll go to any lengths to protect them.'

'Even if Natalie did come back, making up some absurd story, why would I pay her to go away again?'

Alexi was wondering the exact same thing.

'Natalie was encouraged by a shrink to put down in writing what had happened to her.' Alexi watched Seaton carefully as Jack spoke. 'We've seen what she wrote and know what she had on you.'

Alexi crossed her fingers behind her back, praying he wouldn't ask what it was.

'She told you she wanted a one-off payment, but like all blackmailers, she came back again. And again. She was bleeding you dry, but part of you was willing to pay, if only for the pleasure of seeing her again. In spite of everything, you still wanted her. But it got too much. She became increasingly greedy. Threatened to tell your wife the truth, perhaps, even though you'd paid up.' Jack paused. 'Is that why you killed her?'

Seaton's head shot up. 'Now just a minute! One moment I'm a rapist, then a murderer. Make up your minds.'

'I think you're very likely both.'

Seaton remained silent, standing rooted to the spot like a deer blinded by headlights, his empty glass clutched in the slack fingers of one hand.

'You're deluded,' he eventually said with a negligent wave. 'If you really thought this was true and could prove it, the police *would* be here.'

'Oh, they will be, once Natalie's body is found. It's only a matter of time.'

'And even if it isn't,' Alexi added. 'We have her written account of what happened to her, as well as the diaries she wrote at the time of the rape.'

Jack shot Alexi a warning glance. They had no way of knowing if Natalie actually kept a diary, but Alexi thought it highly probable. Most girls of that age wrote down every single thought, feeling, and aspiration. Alexi certainly had.

'Natalie and her damned diaries.' Seaton fell into a chair, shared a glance between them, then shook his head and dropped it into his hands. Alexi sensed he was about to tell them the truth, or his version of it. 'Natalie, in spite of all we tried to do for her, had a genetic fault that meant she would never stay on the straight and narrow. It wasn't really her fault.'

Alexi's jaw dropped open.

'I warned Fay. I warned her.' He thumped his thigh with his clenched fist. 'You just don't know what you're getting when you adopt a child. But Fay stood her ground. She wanted a baby and wouldn't stop going on about it until I relented. Much good it did her. Bad genes will out, no matter how hard you try to instil your own standards and values into the child. Whatever happened to Natalie is down to genetics. How she can now cry rape is beyond me, especially given her chosen profession.'

'You have got to be kidding me,' Jack muttered.

Alexi was equally disgusted by his pathetic attempts to justify the unjustifiable. Even so, she wanted to punch the air in jubilation. By admitting he knew what his daughter had become, he had also admitted to having had contact with her since she became an escort.

'She'd been looking at me in a certain way for months,' Seaton sighed. 'Flaunting herself in a bikini as she climbed out the pool, knowing damned well what she was doing to me. I only gave her what she wanted.'

'Which will see you do jail time,' Jack snarled. 'She was underage.'

'She was looking at you, her daddy, for approval, not sex,' Alexi snapped. 'She trusted you.' She shook her head, feeling sick.

'I don't know how it all got so out of hand.' He looked up at them, as though expecting their understanding, sympathy even. 'It's not as though I planned it. Something inside of me just snapped. I guess I never was cut out to be a father. My own wasn't much of an example so I had to make it up as I went along. Kids don't come with instruction manuals.' He glared at them, a touch of his defiance in his eyes. 'But you have to believe I didn't mean to do what I did, and it never would have happened again.'

'Even though you told her she was yours whenever you wanted her?' Alexi asked.

Seaton's head shot up. 'Those words never passed my lips. I swear it.'

'And we should believe you because...' But oddly, Alexi did believe him, even as she voiced the question. It was impossible to fake such genuine surprise.

'When she came back, I tried to tell her how sorry I was, that I would make it up to her. I'd stolen her innocence and things could never be the way they once were. But at least I could make her see she had nothing more to fear from me. Or so I thought.' The brief defiance evaporated and he looked like a broken man. 'I knew when she went the second time that she wouldn't come back.'

'Why did you go to Lambourn?' Jack asked in an abrupt change of subject.

'Lambourn?' He appeared confused. 'Why would I go there?'

'To see your daughter. To persuade her to let up on the blackmail.'

'Is that where she lived? I've never been there. I've seen Natalie a few times, to hand over the money she demanded, but always in London, in public locations of her choosing.'

'How many times and how much did you pay her?'

'Three times. Ten grand each time.'

Jack let out a low whistle. 'How did she make contact with you?'

'The first time she was waiting for me when I left my office in London. I didn't recognise her at first. We went to a bar and I could feel all the pent up anger radiating off her.'

'I just bet you could,' Alexi muttered.

Jack touched her hand to stop her from interrupting.

'I tried to tell her again how sorry I was. She didn't want to know and laughed herself silly when I suggested she come back home. That her mother would have adored seeing her.' He sighed. 'Instead, she said she wanted a hundred grand. I said I couldn't get my hands on that sort of money. We settled on an initial payment of ten, but I knew she'd be back for more.'

'And you couldn't let her bleed you dry.'

'Actually, I felt kind of relieved in some respects.'

'To be blackmailed?' Alexi asked, frowning.

'To make amends in some small way. Not that I ever could. I don't expect you to believe this, but I'm not proud of what I did.' He dropped his head and rubbed his forehead with his thumbs, leaving white indentations in the tanned skin. 'If I could turn back the clock...'

'But you couldn't,' Jack pointed out. 'Natalie started taunting you, didn't she, even though you'd paid up? Extracting money from you was only part of her revenge. She wanted to spoil your peace of mind too. Keep you on the back foot by leaving you wondering what she intended to do next. She threatened to phone here and tell Fay what's you'd done. You couldn't take the risk. Natalie was the only aspect of your comfortable married life over which you couldn't control your wife's reaction. It all got too much, so off to Lambourn you went to put an end to it all.'

'I think you'd better go now,' he said. 'I've said all I have to say. I did pay Natalie to keep her mouth shut, but if she's dead, it's nothing to do with me. And don't try coming back with the police and shouting rape because I shall deny this conversation ever took place.'

13

'Jack, I don't believe he fell for that!' Alexi cried, bouncing up and down in her seat as they drove off. 'You were brilliant, making him admit to what he did.'

'I figured there had to be some sort of incontrovertible proof, otherwise, why pay up?'

'We didn't know for sure that he had.'

Jack grinned mirthlessly. 'We do now. I risked pushing it because he didn't throw us out the moment I mentioned rape. An innocent man would have been straight on the phone to his solicitor.'

'Very clever, but what if he'd just denied it, or asked us what the proof was?'

He paused at a T-junction. 'I assumed it has to be something super-personal, and embarrassing. Some habit he indulges in while having sex that no one other than his wife would know about—'

'Something he wouldn't admit to in front of strangers? He assumed Natalie had written about it and we've seen what she wrote.'

'Right.' Jack nodded, his expression grim. 'We caught him off guard and the bluff worked when I brought murder into the equation. But people like him don't go down without putting up one hell of a fight. He'll have explanations for the withdrawals from his account if the police get around to questioning him about them.'

Alexi was momentarily quiet. 'Do you think he did kill her?'

'He certainly had motive. But, if he told the truth about how often he saw Natalie and how much he paid her, then he probably wasn't the only person paying her to keep quiet.'

'Yes,' Alexi replied. 'The same thought had occurred to me. There are more large payments in her account, more recent too, than the ones Seaton made. But we do know he took her virginity and robbed her of her dreams. If Natalie had all that bottled up anger, I'm betting it was directed towards the man who set her on the road to ruin. I know mine would be. But if he did kill her and dumped her body anywhere near Lambourn, he won't go near the place again.'

'No.' Jack's smile was tight. 'But if he thinks there's anything in writing about what he did to her he might try to recover it, just to cover his back. If the police find her papers first, they'll be all over him. He knows that, especially since he'll assume we'll tell them about the conversation we just had. But, if we do go to the police with what we know, it means Mrs Seaton will learn how her daughter's been making her living all these years.'

'Ah.'

'Precisely. If she is still alive, I don't want to do that to Natalie, or her mum.'

'I agree, but it means that sick pervert continues to get away with it,' Alexi protested indignantly.

'I know, but even if he didn't kill her, he knows we know

about the blackmail and he *thinks* something exists in writing to incriminate him. That'll be enough to spoil his beauty sleep.'

Alexi screwed up her features. 'I really want to be there when they slap the cuffs on him. The way he looked at me made my skin crawl.'

'I wanted to push his teeth down his throat. I couldn't, so I hit him with words instead.' He winked at her.

'So, what do we do now?'

'We go back to Lambourn, I'll buy you dinner and we have another think about where Natalie might have hidden her papers. We now know that something definitely exists and it must be somewhere in that cottage of hers. We just didn't search thoroughly enough.'

* * *

Jack's phone rang just as he pulled off the motorway. Cassie. Again. They hadn't ended their conversation the previous evening on the best of terms and now wasn't really a good time to pick up. Not when he had Alexi sitting right next to him and Jack would have to use the hands-free facility because he was driving. There was no telling what Cassie might say and Alexi would hear every word. Still, she might have something for him relating to Natalie so he took the call.

'Hey, Cas. What's up?'

'Where are you? I've got some information on Natalie's phone records but, more to the point, there's some important stuff in the office on your *paying* investigations you need to see.' She placed heavy emphasis on the word *paying*.

'I'm ten minutes away. I'll stop by.'

'See you shortly.'

Jack disconnected. 'You don't mind, do you?' he asked Alexi.

'I don't mind, but I don't think your partner will be too happy to see me.'

'She'll get over it.'

'I'll wait in the car.'

'Not a chance.' Jack firmed his jaw. 'We're in this thing together. Besides,' he added flippantly, 'I'm not ashamed to be seen with you.'

'Good to know.'

He drove to his office, situated in a converted flat above a tobacconist's establishment on the outskirts of Newbury.

'Be it ever so humble,' he said, sliding his arm along the back of Alexi's seat as he reversed his car into the only available space. 'Come on, let's face the inquisition.'

'You are such a wuss, Maddox.'

He chuckled. 'I prefer to think of myself as a pacifist.'

Jack opened the outside door with a key and led Alexi up a narrow staircase. Cassie was on the phone when he ushered her into their two-roomed office suite. She smiled when she saw Jack. Then her eyes fell upon Alexi and that smile faded. She finished her call and stood up. Jack made the introduction and sensed the two women sizing one another up as they shook hands.

'I didn't realise you weren't alone, Jack,' Cassie said, making it sound like an accusation.

He told Cassie where they'd been and what they'd discovered.

'You think the father killed her to stop the blackmail?'

'We think someone did,' Alexi replied. 'We don't think her father was the only one she was blackmailing but don't know who the other person was yet.'

'Not anyone connected to your sister's agency,' Cassie said pointedly to Jack.

'What do you have on Natalie's phone records?' Jack asked.

Cassie handed over a sheaf of papers. 'I haven't had a chance to check them all out, but two numbers that she called regularly stand out. One is to a floral supplier. Another is a local trainer, Graham Fuller.'

Fuller again, Jack thought, recalling the incident in the cloakroom the previous night.

'Fuller.' Alexi's head jerked up. 'A lot of the people working for him live in Cheryl's annexe.'

'It might be worth having a word with them when we get back to Lambourn,' Jack said. 'If she was interested in buying a share in one of his racehorses they'll know about it, and it will explain the calls.'

'You're going back?' Cassie asked. 'Is that really necessary? All the stuff you were waiting for on the credit fraud case has come in.' She indicated a pile of paper on Jack's desk. 'The client's been on the phone several times. He wants to meet with you tomorrow.'

Jack knew she had a point. Still, Lambourn and Newbury weren't far apart. 'I'll be back tomorrow to take care of it,' he said, scooping up the papers. 'I'll look at them tonight and call him.'

Cassie pursed her lips. 'Fine,' she said shortly, returning to her desk and immersing herself in whatever was on her computer screen.

'Nice meeting you,' Alexi said as she walked through the door Jack held open for her.

Cassie mumbled something unintelligible in response.

'That went well,' Alexi said with a wry smile as she slid into Jack's car.

'Sorry she was so rude. There was no call for that.'

'She's under pressure. I recognise the signs.'

'Sometimes Cassie makes her own pressure. We're busy, but not *that* busy.'

'She likes to control things,' Alexi replied. 'Especially you.'

'She's certainly welcome to try.'

* * *

They remained silent for the short drive back to Lambourn. When they got close, Jack pulled his car into a space outside The George.

'This place was built in the eighteenth century, apparently,' he said, cutting the engine. 'It's the oldest licensed pub in Lambourn.'

Alexi smiled. 'You sound like a tour guide.'

'I am *such* good value.'

She laughed. 'Keep thinking that way, Maddox.'

'You ever been here?' He clutched both hands over his heart. 'They do real ale from Arkell's Brewery.'

'O... kay, just so long as you don't expect me to drink any.'

'Leave that to the experts,' he replied, chuckling as he opened the door to the bar.

A short time later Jack had a pint of the desired ale, Alexi a large glass of wine.

'So,' she said, once they'd ordered their food. 'I think we need to go back to that cottage, tear it apart, and find Natalie's private papers. The longer she remains missing, the more convinced I become that she's dead. The police could pile in at any time and if we don't find her documents, they sure as hell will.'

'The police won't take too much interest unless there's a body.'

'So you keep reminding me,' Alexi said, shuddering.

'Got to hand it to the girl, she was clever. We know Seaton paid her three lots of ten grand but she didn't bank all of it.'

'Different amounts each time to avoid raising suspicion, *and* keeping it below the level that would have the bank's regulators asking questions about its origins.'

Jack took a swig of beer and wiped the foam from his mouth with the back of his hand. 'I can see why the police wouldn't take our concerns seriously without anything to back them up. Now, if we find her papers, it would be a whole new ball game. We'll have to hand them over, of course.'

Alexi grinned. 'Only after we've read them.'

'Talking of which...' Jack pulled Natalie's phone records from his inside jacket pocket and checked them against the list of numbers his sister had given him for her three dates. 'She didn't call any of them,' he said, feeling relieved. 'They must have communicated only by email.'

'That looks good for your sister. Natalie was being cautious and hadn't got close enough to give any of them her phone number.'

'Unless she had a pay-as-you-go we know nothing about. One she used for her blackmail business.'

'You have a suspicious mind, Mr Maddox.'

He fixed her with an unrepentant grin. 'Goes with the terri-tory, Ms Ellis.'

Their food was placed in front of them, bringing a temporary halt to their conversation.

'Okay, so how do find out what Natalie discovered?' Alexi asked musingly. 'Whatever it was that made her decide to retire. I have a feeling that's the key to everything.'

'Her papers,' Jack said. 'Everything comes back to her papers.'

'I know she didn't want to trace her birth mother, but

supposing she changed her mind and actually did. She probably wouldn't want anyone to know, just in case she was rejected again.'

'But why would she, after so many years?'

'Good question, but *if* she did, it would be easily done. At age eighteen, she would be entitled to apply for a copy of her original birth certificate, and details of her adoption, wouldn't she?'

'The law changed to allow that, but only for people born after '72. She would have just missed the boat, which means she would have had to see a shrink appointed by the state and explain her reasons for wanting to see the records after all this time.'

'Ah.'

'Besides, she'd disappeared, remember, changed her name. She didn't want her adoptive father to find her and, presumably, didn't want to upset her adoptive mother. There would be a risk of them discovering she'd been asking questions and then Fay Seaton might find out what she did for a living.'

'I thought all these things were confidential.'

'They are, and the risk of the Seatons finding out would be slim, but don't forget how obsessive Natalie is about her privacy.'

'Do you think she was ashamed of what she'd become?'

Jack shrugged. 'As the years went by, I'm guessing she became increasingly determined to have her revenge. You have no idea the extreme sorts of crimes committed in the name of revenge.'

'You don't need to tell me. I'm a journalist, remember?'

'Yeah, you are.' He sighed. 'Anyway, we'll ask Natalie all those questions if we find her.'

'Athena said it was her shrink who wanted her to trace her birth mother but the only way to do that was to talk to another shrink, one not of her choosing. How's that for irony?'

'Maybe her own shrink will tell us why he thought she should go down that route.'

Alexi laughed. 'Maybe the moon's made out of cheese.'

He affected surprise. 'You don't have a high opinion of shrinks?'

'They have their place, but I sometimes think they do more harm than good. People bury bad memories for a reason and being forced to confront them often backfires.' She pushed her empty plate aside and leaned towards him. 'You agree with my assessment of the psychiatric profession, don't you? Come on, Maddox, 'fess up. What turned you against such a fine body of professionals?'

'Working as a policeman requires a cynical mind-set, but that's a discussion for another day. Back to business. Did you know there're over fifteen hundred racehorses in training in this valley?'

'No, but it doesn't surprise me. There seem to be way more horses than people.'

'Right, and it costs a small fortune to keep them in training, which is why a lot of people sell shares. Doesn't it strike you as odd that Natalie only negotiated with one trainer that we know of?'

Alexi wrinkled her brow as she pondered the question. 'Perhaps a particular horse had taken her fancy.'

'Possibly, but it doesn't fit with what we know of her character. Any sentimentality she might have had in her dissipated the night her father raped her.'

'You can't know that for sure.'

'I can make an educated guess, based on what I've seen of her cottage and what we've learned from people who know her.' Jack leaned back and fixed Alexi with an intense look. 'When she ran away from home the second time, according to Fay

Seaton, she took nothing with her except a few clothes and the contents of her father's wallet. She loved her dog and her horse but didn't take any snapshots of them, nothing. It was as though she pulled a curtain across that part of her life and started afresh which, in my opinion, shows the makings of one very single-minded, strong-willed teenager.'

Alexi tilted her head to acknowledge his conjecture. 'That's a good point.'

'Right, so why only enquire about the share in one horse? She was in a strong negotiating position because she had the cash to make it happen. Why didn't she capitalise on that?'

'I wish I knew.'

The waitress cleared their plates, they both declined coffee, and Jack asked for the bill.

'Cosmo will think you've been unfaithful,' Jack quipped.

'He knows better than that. I'm a one-cat woman.'

Jack chucked. 'Right.'

'Tell me about you and Cassie,' she said. 'Why is she so possessive?'

'We've never discussed it.'

'Come on, Maddox!'

'Okay, I suppose you could say she picked up the slack when I got divorced.'

'You dated?'

'I wouldn't call them dates exactly.' Jack waggled one hand from side to side in a considering gesture. 'More soul-searching conversations during which I did most of the talking and she just listened. There was nothing more to it from my perspective, but I sometimes wonder if I gave out the wrong signals.'

'Which is why you tread on eggshells around her?'

'Is that what I do?' Jack was genuinely surprised by the

suggestion. 'I was distracted by the divorce, blamed myself for putting too much time into the job and neglecting my wife.'

'You didn't want to divorce?'

'I think I knew it was inevitable, and I was upset rather than heartbroken. I just didn't want to feel it was all my fault. Cassie was a good sounding board because she knew us both and could be objective.'

Alexi turned sideways on her chair and looked at him more closely. 'You ended up in bed with her?'

'No, but it got close. I was drinking too much, drowning my sorrows, she was there, available and... well, you know.'

'Going into business together has reinforced her belief that you're interested in her.'

'I don't see how.'

Alexi sent him a droll look, accompanied by an impatient huff. 'Of course you don't. You're a man and haven't taken the time to think it through. You told Cassie you felt your work had driven a wedge between you and your wife, then agreed to work with Cassie. What message do you think that sent?'

'You're saying Cassie imagines I've partnered with her with a view to having a relationship that work can't interfere with.'

'Give the man a prize.' Alexi's smile faded. 'If you don't want her that way, you need to straighten it out with her. It's not fair to leave her hanging.'

He sighed. 'You're right. I hadn't thought it through in that way.'

The bill arrived and Jack picked it up. 'Let me get this.'

'An old-fashioned gentleman. How refreshing.' She leaned across the table and planted a kiss on his cheek. 'Thank you.'

'My pleasure.' He placed his credit card on the plate and waited for the waitress to come back with the necessary machine. 'Consider it payment for the soul-searching.' Jack treated her to a languid smile. 'So, your turn. What do you plan to do about Patrick?'

'Unlike you, Maddox, I know my own mind. Patrick and I are history.'

Jack knew she meant it, but wondered if she realised just how deeply Vaughan was hooked on her. The man wouldn't go quietly.

'What about his offer of work?'

She shook her head. 'I can't work with him. I haven't had much time to think about it, but I'm already starting to like the idea of going freelance.' Her eyes sparkled. 'Just think of the story I could write about Natalie's life. Don't worry, I won't,' she assured him, presumably in response to his horrified expression. 'I can't as things stand, but it's made me realise how much freedom there is in having the luxury of pleasing myself rather than an editor.'

'If you don't mind not eating.'

'I'm okay financially, for a while anyway.'

'Good.' He inserted his pin number into the machine, thanked the waitress when she handed him his copy, and then stood to pull the table out so Alexi could get up. 'Come on then, let's go and put your cat out of his misery.'

* * *

They drove the short distance back to Hopgood Hall in companionable silence. Alexi had enjoyed the intimate dinner with Jack. If she was honest with herself, she'd also enjoyed having the complete attention of a man who made female heads turn. But she had no intention of becoming another Cassie. He'd be gone in another day or two, once they got the business of Natalie sorted, and she could get on with her life, free from distractions.

'Here we are,' he said, breaking the silence as he pulled his car up next to her Mini.

They walked through the hall, directly into Cheryl's kitchen. It was empty, but for Cosmo and Toby, curled up together in Toby's basket.

'Hey, Cosmo, we're home,' Alexi said, dumping her bag on the table.

Cosmo lifted his head and blinked at them like an outraged parent demanding to know why they'd stayed out so late. Then he stood up, pointedly turned his back on them and curled back up again with his face to the wall. Jack laughed aloud.

'He's sulking.'

'Women don't have a monopoly on that particular trait.'

Cheryl pushed through the door, her hands full of menus, looking distracted. 'Oh, you're back. Have you eaten?'

'Yes thanks,' Jack replied. 'We grabbed a bite on the way.'

'Are you okay?' Alexi asked, concerned. 'You seem a little stressed.'

'Bloody Marcel,' she replied, tossing her head. 'We just got the weekend's menus printed up, then he throws a wobbly over the signature dish *he* insisted upon including. Something about consistency of the sauce that made the entire dish inedible.' She shrugged. 'I tasted it and thought it was divine. Honestly—'

'You should stand up to him,' Jack said, relieving her of the menus and placing them on the kitchen table. 'Let him know who's boss.'

'In *his* kitchen he reigns supreme, and don't we all know it.'

Alexi nodded sympathetically. She'd heard more than one verbal eruption coming from the vicinity of the kitchen since her arrival. 'Why are chefs such prima donnas?' she asked.

'Because we let them be, I suppose,' Cheryl replied. 'But we can't risk upsetting Marcel. He's part of what keeps this place afloat. He's too good for us, and we all know it. I think he only stays because he likes the gee-gees and gets a few tips from the guys who come in here. But still, it's only a matter of time before he packs up his knives and legs it.'

'Just so long as he doesn't do any back-stabbing with them before he departs,' Jack remarked.

'This is *not* funny, Jack,' Alexi said crossly.

'But probably accurate.' Cheryl threw herself into a chair. 'Tell me what you found out. Anything to take my mind off domestic royalty.'

Before Alexi could reply they were joined by Drew. Also muttering a few choice words about stroppy chefs, he made a beeline for the corkscrew. Seated around the table, Alexi and the guys shared a bottle of wine.

* * *

'Let's get this straight,' Cheryl said, looking a little taken aback when Jack and Alexi had filled them in. 'You found Natalie's adoptive parents, went to see them, accused her father of rape and he admitted it. Phew!' She fanned her face with her hand. 'You guys don't take any prisoners.'

'The man's a total creep,' Alexi replied, wrinkling her nose. 'But so charismatic that, at first, I was inclined to believe he was innocent.' She shrugged. 'It just goes to show how much stock we put on appearances. If he'd been a grumpy old bastard with bad breath and yellowing teeth, I probably would have automatically assumed his guilt. No wonder Natalie didn't speak out. No one would have believed her, not back then.'

'You weren't taken in by him?' Drew asked, addressing the question to Jack.

'There were a few things about his reaction that didn't add up, despite the fact that Fay Seaton told us Natalie was a happy, well-adjusted child and had no reason to run away.'

'Seaton loves the limelight, is always ready to be the mouthpiece for the athletes he represents, and doesn't shy away from the camera,' Drew said, screwing up his features in disgust. 'He thinks on his feet and knows how to play his audience.'

'Right,' Jack agreed.

'But would he really harm Natalie?' Cheryl asked.

'He seemed genuinely surprised when we suggested that he might have done away with her to put a stop to the blackmail,' Alexi replied. 'But, like I say, his performance almost fooled me. He certainly had a motive, but none of that gets us any closer to finding Natalie. Unless she turns up and wants to press charges there's sod all we can do to make him pay. And probably not even then, given that she's blackmailed him over it.'

'So, what next?' Cheryl asked.

'Jack has some stuff to do for his day job before the morning,' Alexi replied. 'I thought I'd go through Natalie's phone records, see if I can identify any of the numbers she called less frequently.'

'I'll look at them with you,' Cheryl volunteered. 'If they're local numbers, I might recognise them.'

'Thanks.'

'In that case, ladies, I'll leave you to it.' Jack patted the wedge of papers Cassie had given him and pulled a face. 'I have homework and my teacher is likely to test me on it. Catch you in the morning, Alexi.'

'Okay, good night.'

'And I'm needed back in the bar,' Drew said, bending to kiss his wife's head. 'There's no rest for the wicked.'

Laughter sounded from the annexe. 'That'll be the grooms

returning from the pub,' Cheryl said. 'One day, they'll remember to do it quietly.'

Alexi grabbed the printed picture of Natalie she'd been carrying about in her bag and went to the back door. 'I need to ask Tod if he remembers seeing Natalie at Fuller's yard and, if so, what she was doing there.'

Cosmo stirred and deigned to follow her from the room with Toby tagging along. Alexi met the returning revellers before they reached their accommodation.

'Hey,' Tod said, his eyes lighting up at the sight of her. 'Sorry. Were we too noisy?'

'Actually, I wanted a quick word with you.'

He offered her a sweeping bow. 'I am entirely at your service.'

Alexi laughed as she unfolded Natalie's picture. 'Do you recognise this lady?' she asked.

Tod took the picture from Alexi and held it beneath one of the outdoor lights. 'Sure, that's Natalie. She's a local florist. Why do you ask?'

'Has she ever been up to your yard?'

'Yeah, frequently as it happens. She's interested in taking a share in Super Nova. He's a promising two-year-old Graham's just taken into training.'

'You say frequently. How often has she been to see the horse?'

'Dunno. But I've seen her hanging around at least three times. Maybe more.'

'Is that normal?'

Tod smiled. 'It's a big investment she's considering, so I guess she needs to be sure.'

'Why big? Surely a lot of people take shares in horses?'

'Yeah, you've no idea how many pieces a horse can be chopped into, figuratively speaking. Up to twenty isn't unusual.

But Natalie is considering a quarter share so Graham's job is to convince her the horse has real promise, which he does. It's a big deal.' Tod shrugged. 'There again, perhaps she just likes hanging about the yard and soaking up the atmosphere. Some people are like that.'

'Who dealt with her enquiries about Super Nova?'

'The guv'nor.'

'What, every visit? Is that normal?'

Tod grinned. 'She's very attractive.'

Alexi laughed, but when it became apparent Tod couldn't tell her anything more, she thanked him and said good night.

'Hey.' His voice caused her to turn back. 'Why are you asking me these things? Why not ask Natalie herself?'

'I would if I could find her.'

'She's probably gone off with some bloke somewhere,' Tod replied. 'I bet she gets plenty of offers. Do you want me to ask the boss if he knows anything?'

'No, it's okay, thanks Tod.'

Alexi planned to visit Graham Fuller and do the asking herself.

She returned to the kitchen, poured the remainder of the wine into her glass, and told Cheryl what she'd learned from Tod.

'I suspect Jack will need to go to his office tomorrow, at least temporarily, so I'll go and see Fuller on my own.'

'I hope we're not going to lose the pleasure of Jack's company.' Cheryl grinned. 'He certainly makes the place look pretty.'

Alexi conceded the point with a wry twist of her lips. Cosmo, having forgiven her for abandoning him all day, leapt gracefully from the floor and landed on her lap. She smoothed his big head and the cat responded with a thundering purr.

'He likes you, Alexi.'

'Cosmo? Of course he does. I feed him, don't I?'

Cheryl tutted. 'You know very well I'm talking about Jack.'

'Even if that's true, I'm not in the market for romance. Besides, he already has a very overprotective partner lusting after him.'

'I get the impression your Mr Maddox doesn't allow anyone else to tell him who he should or should not date.' Cheryl grinned. 'Besides, Cosmo likes him. That has to count in his favour.'

'I wish I knew what made Cosmo decide if a person is worthy of his notice. His instincts are almost human... no, better than human when it comes to judging character. I thought he just liked people who were no threat to me, but he disliked Patrick from the word go.'

'There you are. He *is* a good judge of character.'

Alexi smiled. 'He's a very unusual feline.'

Cosmo purred louder, obviously aware that he was being admired. 'Come on then, help me plough through these phone numbers.'

'Slave driver.'

14

Alexi and Jack were both up early the following morning and encountered one another in the upstairs residents' lounge. Jack had his car keys in his hand, about to leave.

'Hi,' he said. 'I missed you last night.'

'You were on a long phone call when I came up. I didn't want to disturb you. Thought you might be whispering sweet nothings to a girlfriend.'

'If only. What did you get from Tod? I saw you talking to him through the window.'

Alexi told him. 'Sounds genuine enough, but I'm planning to go up there now and see if I can talk with Fuller myself.'

'Be careful.'

Alexi blinked at him. 'Why?'

'I'm not sure.' Jack scratched his neck. 'There's something about him that doesn't add up.'

Alexi was surprised when Jack told her what he'd overheard in the men's room.

'Blimey, you think he's hard up? I find that difficult to believe. He's a famous trainer. Even I've heard of him. I'd have thought owners would be clamouring to have him take their horses. Why would he risk it all?'

'He might have expensive habits. Don't forget his staff accommodation burned down in mysterious circumstances, which probably resulted in an insurance claim. And Drew says he's always having to chase him for outstanding rent.'

'True, but I don't see how he can have anything to do with Natalie's disappearance. If she was thinking of taking a share in that horse, it would be in his best interests to have her alive and well. Anyway, we haven't unearthed any connection between them.'

'Just take care, that's all I'm saying.'

'I'll do that. Then I'll go on to Natalie's cottage and see if I can find her hiding place.'

'Don't pull up all the floorboards,' he said with a grin. 'Oh, and there's no point in going to see Fuller yet. He'll be up on the gallops, watching his horses being put through their paces at the crack of dawn.' He consulted his watch. 'Leave it another couple of hours.'

'I knew that.'

His grin widened. 'Course you did.'

Alexi actually didn't have the first idea how the racing world worked and evidently it showed.

'You going into Newbury?' she asked.

'Yeah, I have a meeting scheduled with a client, but I should get that cleared up this morning. I need to put some time in at the office after that but I'll be back this evening. If you find anything significant, or need me in the meantime, call my mobile.'

'I *can* manage without you.'

'I'm just saying. We don't know what we're dealing with, so tread carefully and trust no one.'

'Have you heard back from the guy you had checking out Natalie's other two dates?'

'Actually, yes. Both guys seemed surprised and genuinely concerned about Natalie's disappearance. They confirmed individually that they'd only dated once, communicating by email. They admitted they couldn't believe their luck when they saw Natalie and weren't surprised when she didn't want to hook up for a second time. Anyway, Larry's pretty sure they're not hiding anything, which is good enough for me.'

'Okay, we'll put them to the bottom of the suspect list.'

'We don't really have any suspects, other than Seaton.'

'How many more do we need? He has motive, means and opportunity. Isn't that the yardstick you cops measure these things by?'

'It's hard to apply those criteria when we don't have a crime to apply them to.'

Alexi folded her arms defensively. 'We ought to bear Walker's name in mind. I don't think he had anything to do with her disappearance, but she *did* date him three times and we haven't found anyone else she allowed to get that close. He planned to move their relationship on by inviting her to his house. Maybe she refused.' She shrugged. 'People have killed for less.'

'That's a reach. But I agree, we should keep him in mind.'

'Okay, so we have a suspect list of two. That makes me feel as though we've achieved something. Now, what about her solicitor and shrink? Are you going to try and get appointments with them?'

'I'll put calls into them when I get to the office, but unless they're willing to reveal anything significant, which I doubt, there's not much point in going up to town again.'

'Oh, I don't know. I can be quite persuasive, given the right motivation.'

Cosmo stalked up to them and wrapped himself around Jack's legs, purring.

'Take this guy with you today,' Jack said, bending to scratch his ears. 'It'll make me feel better.'

'I will, but only because I can't deal with another of his strops if I leave him behind.'

The corners of his lips lifted. 'Good enough. Right, I'm out of here. Take care.'

He grabbed his iPad and phone and waved over his shoulder as he flew down the stairs, taking them two at a time. Alexi shook her head at his retreating figure. He was incorrigible. Dressed in a long-sleeved shirt that hung loose outside his jeans, his hair still damp from the shower and flopping over his eyes, she had to agree with Cheryl's assessment of him. But she'd cut her tongue out before she admitted it.

'Okay, Cosmo,' Alexi said. 'You ready for another day's hard sleuthing?' She stroked her cat's sleek back. 'I'm determined to show Newbury's answer to Dick Tracy that he's not the only one who knows how to get results. Natalie's hidden her personal stuff somewhere. I'm a woman. I ought to be able to think like she does and figure out where.'

* * *

Alexi had been unsure what to expect from Fuller's venture when she arrived there much earlier than Jack had suggested. She was a reporter, on the trail of a story, and always concerned about being scooped, she didn't do waiting under such circumstances. She looked about the trainer's pristine establishment with a combination of surprise and interest. Spick and span, everything was neatly in place, not so much as a blade of hay littering the cobbled yard and barns beyond. There were several rows of loose boxes set around a quadrangle. Some, but not all, were occupied by leggy horses munching away at hay nets. One or two of them glanced at her as she walked past, displaying refined heads with widely spaced, intelligent eyes, and long, arched necks.

She had left Cosmo in the car, thinking there would probably be dogs around and not wanting him to take them on. Having Fuller's dogs coming out on the losing end of a fight with her cat, or having him traumatise one of the horses, wouldn't be the best way to encourage his cooperation. Alexi chuckled as she considered the possibility of threatening Fuller with letting her cat loose in his yard if that cooperation wasn't forthcoming.

She wondered what Cosmo would make of these noble creatures. For her part she was starting to appreciate why it was known as the sport of kings. Just standing there, she felt a sense of history and tradition permeate her soul. She allowed the smell of warm horseflesh and sweet molasses, the sound of contented munching, and the tranquillity of her surroundings to soothe her.

'I feel a feature coming on,' she muttered to herself. 'Why would such strong, noble creatures allow themselves to be dominated by considerably weaker men?' She thought of *Animal Farm* and conceded that Orwell had probably been onto something.

'Can I help you?'

Alexi turned at the sound of a voice. The voice in question belonged to a girl of no more than twenty wearing muddy boots, jodhpurs, and a body warmer over a polo shirt, her long hair pulled, appropriately enough, into a ponytail. Alexi wondered if she was one of the residents of the annexe. She was very slight of build. Perhaps a trainee jockey – or were they apprentices? Whatever, women rode right alongside their male counterparts nowadays, didn't they? It was one of the few sports where they supposedly competed on equal terms.

'I'm looking for Graham Fuller.'

'Do you have an appointment?'

'Do I need one? It'll only take a minute.'

'He doesn't usually see people without appointments. Can I tell him what it's about?'

'Super Nova.'

'Oh, are you a prospective owner?'

'Something like that.'

The girl's attitude became less guarded as she led Alexi to one of the boxes. Its inhabitant was a rich bay colour, indistinguishable to Alexi's untrained eye from all the other horses she'd seen, most of whom were also brown. But there was no question that he was handsome. He looked up and whinnied when he saw the two of them looking at him over his half-door. The girl produced something from her pocket and offered it to the horse on the flat of her hand. He snuffled and crunched on whatever she'd given him.

'What was that?'

The girl looked at her askance. 'A mint. Horses love them. If you're thinking of becoming an owner, I should have thought you'd know at least that much.'

'I have a lot to learn.'

'Evidently. Hang on a minute. I'll go and see if the guv'nor's about. They came back from the gallops a while ago and are at breakfast. Won't keep you a moment.'

Super Nova discovered Alexi had no supply of mints of her own, lost interest in her, and returned to his hay. She seemed to be kept waiting for ages and was on the point of giving up when a slim, muscular man strode across the yard in her direction, two spaniels at his heels. The same man who had been in the bar the other night, only Alexi had barely spared him a glance on that occasion.

Fuller looked to be in his late sixties, with a weathered face and a smile that didn't trouble his eyes. He'd probably once been a handsome man, but time and the ravages of the outdoor life had left their mark. As he got closer, she noticed a network of fine broken blood vessels decorating his face and nose. A drinker, she thought. Wisps of grey hair poked out from beneath the brim of a flat cap that appeared to be surgically attached to his head. She was repulsed by the traces of grease creeping up the outside where it clung to his scalp.

'I'm Graham Fuller,' he said without preamble. 'I gather you are interested in Super Nova.'

'Alexi Ellis.' She shook his proffered hand, waiting for him to recognise her name. When it became apparent that he didn't know who she was, Alexi was relieved. If he had any useful information to impart, he was less likely to tell a reporter for fear of adverse publicity. 'Thanks for seeing me without an appointment.'

'Not a problem. What do you need to know about Nova?'

Breakfast was obviously over and the yard gradually filled with knots of people, chatting and laughing. They noticed Fuller and the huddles dispersed with lightning speed. Alexi thought it interesting that all his workers appeared frightened of him.

She watched the grooms go about their business. Horses with coats that already shone brightly enough for a person to see their own face in them were being vigorously brushed. She noticed a groom doing something clever with a piece of plastic that left the horse he was working on with diamond shapes on its quarters. A couple more wore rugs and things to protect their legs and were being loaded into a lorry. One of them didn't want to go up the ramp and it took two grooms, with a rope around its backside, to persuade it. Was there a race meeting today? She didn't even know if Fuller trained chasers or flat racers. Face it: she barely knew the difference between the two except, obviously, one lot had to jump over obstacles and the others just ran like hell.

'Is there somewhere we can talk?' Alexi asked.

'You don't want to look at the horse?' The friendliness in Fuller's smile, such as it was, evaporated. 'I'm a busy man.'

'Okay then, I'll try not to waste your time. What can you tell me about Natalie Parker?'

She watched him carefully and was convinced there was a momentary shift in his expression when she mentioned Natalie's name. It was gone before she could be sure, leaving her with no opportunity to decide if it was guilt, fear, or merely recognition.

'She's thinking of taking the remaining share in Super Nova. I guess the two of you must be friends, which is what brought you here.' He leaned closer and Alexi caught a whiff of alcohol on his breath. It was only ten in the morning. She knew these people got up at some ungodly hour, so probably worked on a different time clock to everyone else, but still... 'What I don't understand is why. Oh, and in case you're wondering about the horse, I haven't heard from her for a while, so I don't know what she's decided.'

'She's gone missing. I'm trying to find out what's happened to her and your name appeared a lot on her phone records.'

'So you're not interested in Super Nova?'

Thanks for your concern about Natalie. 'I didn't say I was interested in a share. Your girl just assumed. Anyway, I should have thought you'd be keen to help me find Natalie, seeing as you appear to have so much invested in... well, her potential investment.'

It was true. Fuller seemed awfully keen to shift the

remaining share, reinforcing Jack's impression that he was strapped for cash. Then again, there could be a perfectly innocent explanation. Perhaps the principal owner was a personal friend, or someone who couldn't afford to keep the horse in training with Fuller unless another investor took up some of the slack. Part-owners were responsible for a share of the training fees, she thought. If the horse had the potential Tod implied, Fuller would be keen to hang onto it.

Perhaps he actually owned the horse himself, as opposed to simply training it. If he did, and needed others to take up shares, he must definitely be harder up than this top-notch set-up implied. Appearances, Alexi knew full well, could be misleading. Were trainers allowed to be owners? What Alexi knew about the rules and regulations pertaining to horseracing was woefully negligible. She was usually far more diligent about her research and blamed Jack for distracting her. Even so, her journalist's nose seldom let her down when something wasn't quite right, and at that precise moment it was twitching like she was in danger of developing serious allergies.

She knew next to nothing about racehorse syndicates. She knew next to nothing about a lot of the stories she'd worked on in the past, but that hadn't stopped her from sticking her oar in. The only difference this time was that she hadn't made sure of her basic facts before piling in. Hitting the ground running on a live investigation changed all the rules.

'Aren't racehorse syndicates managed through an agency of some sort?' Alexi vaguely recalled reading an article in the *Telegraph* a while back.

'Usually, but Nova's owner doesn't want a ton of people muscling in on the act.'

'Who owns him?'

Fuller shrugged, evasive. 'What's that got to do with anything?'

'I can find out easily enough.'

'Then that's what I suggest you do.' He scowled off into the distance, but continued to stroke Nova's sleek neck. 'Look, syndicates can work, but just as often they don't. People disagree. They know sod all about training but if their horse wins a couple of races, they get flushed with success and think they're experts all of a sudden, entitled to interfere. If an owner wants to keep a majority share in a horse, but doesn't want the hassle of a load of armchair experts looking over his shoulder, he might seek a private investor. Someone who has some spare cash, enjoys the sport, but who's content to take a back seat.'

Someone like Natalie, who wouldn't want to put herself into partnership with a load of strangers asking questions about her background. 'I see,' Alexi replied pensively. 'How much does it cost to train a decent horse?'

'After the initial cost of purchase?' She nodded. 'Well, buying a horse as good as Nova could cost anything up to a hundred thou. Then training fees add up to a good thirty K a year, and that's without entry fees, veterinary costs, insurance...'

'Blimey,' Alexi said faintly. 'You really do have to want to do it, don't you?'

He actually smiled. 'You really do.'

'What if a horse breaks a leg?'

Fuller said nothing. He appeared to be deep in thought and she wasn't sure if he'd even heard her speak. She would give a lot to know what was going through his mind.

'I'm sorry,' Fuller said after a prolonged silence that was in danger of becoming embarrassing. 'Of course I'm concerned about Natalie. It certainly explains why she hasn't returned any of my calls. I was annoyed with her, if you want the truth. She'd all but committed to the horse, then gave me the silent treatment. If she'd had a change of heart, it wouldn't have killed her to let me know.'

Unfortunate choice of words. 'When did you last see her?'

'Not sure.' He paused to think about it, but something told Alexi he didn't really need to. 'I suppose a couple of weeks ago. She was very keen on Nova and said she'd be in touch again in a few days, once she'd organised the necessary funds. I'm still waiting to hear from her.'

'Did she ever bring anyone with her when she came here?'

'Not that I recall.'

'How often did she come?'

He shrugged. 'A few times.'

'Did you always deal with her?'

'No, I think I only saw her the last time, or maybe twice.'

Which didn't jibe with what Tod had told her. He'd implied the two of them always seemed to have a lot to say to one another. Alexi's list of suspects had just gained another name. Why Fuller would want to murder an investor was less clear and would require more research. Perhaps she'd actually told him that she'd had a last minute change of heart. But she couldn't imagine Fuller resorting to murder because of it.

'Okay, Mr Fuller.' Alexi extended her hand. 'Thanks for your time. If you think of anything else that might help, perhaps you'd give me a call.'

She handed him a card with just her name and mobile number printed on it. It gave no indication as to her profession. He pocketed the card without looking at it.

'When you find Natalie, ask her to call me about Nova, will you?'

'I'll do that. Presumably you've left messages for her.'

'Several, but she's not answering.'

'Where did you leave them?'

'Excuse me?'

'On her mobile, or landline?'

'Oh, both.'

Unless he'd left a message on Natalie's landline before she went missing and she'd deleted it, then that was the first lie she could call him on, Alexi thought. Whether it was the only lie he'd told her was another matter, but Alexi's mild suspicions about Fuller had just gone up several notches. Interviewees who had something to hide often embellished the truth in an effort to appear helpful. It was the small details that caught a person out and Fuller had just stumbled over a tripwire.

'Right, thanks then.'

'Er, sure I can't interest you in Nova? He's going to make quite an impression on the racing world, you just mark my words.'

So why are you having so much trouble getting backers? 'Sorry,' Alexi replied, shaking her head. 'I don't have that sort of money.'

He continued to stand by Super Nova's door as she walked away, still absently stroking the horse's neck. Tod waved to her from across the yard. She waved back as she climbed into her car and drove away.

'Well, Cosmo,' she said. 'That was interesting. Two things stood out. First off, he didn't once ask me why I was investigating, or what my connection was to Natalie. Odd, don't you think? And secondly, he used the phrase "to tell you the truth". And what do we know about people who talk like that? That's right, baby: it's a pretty safe bet they're lying through their pointy little teeth. And he didn't ask if the police were involved, or any of the questions you'd expect from a concerned friend, or even a decent person. Not that he's decent. And he was far too full of himself, but still...'

* * *

Alexi was still chatting aloud when she pulled up at the side of Natalie's cottage, cut the engine, and rummaged in her bag for the key.

'Okay, Cosmo,' she said, releasing his leash and leaning across to open the passenger door for him. 'You and I are not leaving here until we find Natalie's hiding place. It's a small cottage. How hard can it be?'

Cosmo streaked from the car, hissing and growling like the panther he sometimes pretended to be. Alexi tensed. He only ever got like that when he sensed the presence of someone he *especially* didn't like. Alexi was unsure what to do. Stay in the car and call for help, or go and investigate? Who could she call, and what could she tell them? *My cat thinks there's someone here who shouldn't be?*

That settled it. Apart from not wanting to be sectioned, passivity didn't sit well with Alexi. Besides, Cosmo hadn't attacked anyone for several days – not since that little game he'd played with the postman back in Battersea – and was probably getting withdrawal symptoms. She grabbed a spanner from the glove box of her car, just in case Cosmo needed any help. She slid her phone into the front pocket of her jeans and found a travel-size can of hairspray at the bottom of her bag which went into the other pocket. Carrying pepper spray in England was against the law, but there was nothing that said a girl shouldn't be prepared for a bad-hair day.

She tucked her bag beneath the seat and climbed from the car, clicking the doors locked and pocketing the key. Then she walked around to the front of the cottage, following the racket Cosmo was making.

Gerry Seaton leaned against the bonnet of a shiny Mercedes

C Class, casting wary glances at Cosmo, who attempted to take nips out of his ankles in between hissing at him like a snake on steroids.

* * *

Jack met his client in the lobby of a Newbury hotel and imparted the good tidings. His investigations had uncovered the name of the employee who was using customers' credit card details for his own purposes. It happened more frequently than Joe Average realised, but no one got away with it for long. Jack didn't see any need to point out to his client that he could easily have discovered the employee's identity without expensive help from the Fenton-Maddox Investigation Agency. Everyone has to eat.

He returned to the office by late morning, glad that Cassie was out on a case of her own. Alexi had identified what he should have seen for himself long before now. By letting Cassie get too close at the time of his divorce, then going into a business partnership with her, he'd given the impression that he wanted more from her than that. He slapped his forehead with the heel of his hand. He was an idiot! He'd talk to her about it today, if she came back before he needed to leave for Lambourn again, and clear the air. It was sometimes necessary to be cruel to be kind. Worse-case scenario, if their partnership became untenable, he'd just have to re-establish himself – again – but this time on his own.

He completed the paperwork on the case he'd just cleared up and emailed the client his final account. He checked the progress on a few other on-going enquiries, made phone calls relating to them, and updated his notes. Then he called Natalie's shrink. He was with a client but called Jack back half-an-hour later.

'Obviously, I can't tell you anything about the sessions I had with my client, Mr Maddox, but I do share your concern as to her whereabouts. Disappearing doesn't sound like something she would do.'

'Did she mention anyone she was particularly close to? Someone she might have run off to see if they were in trouble.'

It was a forlorn hope, and Jack knew it. She wouldn't have gone without her car. Unless she'd been picked up, of course.

'Even if she did... I'm sorry, but—'

'I'm not asking you to name names, doctor. It was a non-specific question.'

The shrink's prevarication confirmed Jack's feelings about the uselessness of his profession and he hung up, none the wiser. The solicitor's office was another matter. He was put straight through to the guy who handled Natalie's affairs. Apparently he'd been warned by the concerned Athena at Mayfair Escorts to expect his call. Since that establishment provided him with a lot of work, it stood to reason that he would be as helpful as possible.

'Still no news of Natalie?' he asked.

'Unfortunately not. Is there anything you can tell me that might help?'

Jack was leaning precariously back in his swivel chair, feet propped on his desk, thinking he was chasing another dead end. He was stunned out of his lethargy when the solicitor replied in the affirmative.

'I've been thinking about that since receiving Athena's call, and actually there is one thing that isn't bound by confidentiality,' he said.

Jack sat bolt upright and his feet hit the floor with a resounding thud. 'Tell me.'

'It happened a few months before Natalie retired from the agency. I received a call from another solicitor asking me if I represented Natalie. He knew her date of birth, national insurance number, and a few other official details that enabled me to confirm we were talking about the same person.' Jack felt his blood pressure spike, the way it always did when he caught a break in a case. 'It transpired this other solicitor represented the estate of a woman who'd just died. She had left Natalie a bequest, which he wanted me to pass on to my client.'

'Are you able to tell me what the bequest was?'

'No, unfortunately not.' Jack's blood pressure returned to normal. Another brick wall. 'Because I don't know. It was a thick bundle of papers. Natalie opened them in my office. She only glanced at them but became very agitated and, as I say, shortly after that, she gave up working for the agency.'

'Do you know the name of the person the other solicitor represented?'

'Oh yes.' He paused. 'The dead woman was Laura Brooks, Natalie's natural mother.'

15

'Miss Ellis,' Seaton said with a flash of even white teeth. This time Alexi wasn't taken in by the charisma and stood facing him, the spanner concealed in the sleeve of her sweater. 'Fancy seeing you here.'

Cosmo arched his back and his caterwauling got louder: a cross between a growl and an angry mewl. Alexi had never seen him react quite so aggressively but, then again, she'd never found herself in such a potentially threatening situation before. Beneath all that glossy charm, Seaton definitely had a dark side to his character.

'I thought you'd never been to Lambourn and didn't know where Natalie lived?' Alexi said scathingly.

'Can we talk inside? Since you're here, I assume you have keys. I can't think straight with that racket going on.' He nodded towards Cosmo who obligingly growled a little louder.

Alexi shook her head. 'I don't think so.'

'I'm no danger to anyone. Besides, you have a pretty ferocious guard cat there.'

'Shame Natalie didn't have him around when you killed her.'

Seaton expelled a long sigh. 'I. Did. Not. Kill. My. Daughter.' He enunciated each word, slowly.

'Just like you didn't know where she lives?'

Alexi was no longer frightened, but mad as hell that Seaton had turned up, presumably to look for whatever it was that Natalie had on him. She had to admire his nerve, doing so in broad daylight. Nerve or desperation? She ought to call the police and she ought to do it now, but she'd never been big on taking the sensible course of action. Besides, Seaton was right about one thing. Having a pissed-off feline on the prowl was a good way to persuade Seaton to explain himself. Not that she had the slightest idea how to make Cosmo attack on command, or if he even would, but Seaton didn't know that.

'Hey, Cosmo,' she said, snapping her fingers.

The cat gave one final warning hiss and, to her astonishment, retreated. He walked over to Alexi and bumped and twined around her legs, purring as he rubbed his head against her calves.

'A most unusual feline,' Seaton said, nodding towards Cosmo. It wasn't a warm day but Alexi noticed the sweat on his brow. Yeah, good cat, she thought, making a mental note to reward Cosmo with extra tuna that evening. 'Where's your partner?'

'On his way.'

But she could tell he didn't believe her. She should ring Jack now. He was only twenty-odd miles away and never paid much attention to speed cameras. If he thought it was an emergency, he'd probably get to her in ten minutes or less. But if she rang him, Seaton would know for sure that he *wasn't* actually on his way. He probably wouldn't be caught unawares by Cosmo for a second time. Besides, if he had a weapon – a knife, or even a gun – she couldn't see him hesitating to use it on Cosmo.

'Can we talk inside?' he asked for a second time.

Alexi folded her arms, still clutching the spanner firmly in one hand. 'How did you know where Natalie lived?'

'The last time I met her to hand over money, it was in a pub in Clapham. Presumably it was familiar territory for her, what with the agency she worked for being based there. Anyway, I left first, then doubled back, followed her to her car and took the registration number.'

That was careless of Natalie. In her shoes, Alexi would have made sure she didn't park anywhere near their meeting place. Presumably she thought she had Seaton where she wanted him, too scared of the hold she had over him to fight back.

'And you had a friend somewhere, probably a policeman at your swanky golf club, run the number for you?'

'I just wanted it to stop, and make it up to Natalie in some way if I possibly could. Make her understand that I was ashamed and genuinely sorry.' He paused. 'I wanted to tell her she's the sole beneficiary of our will and that nothing would give my wife greater pleasure than to see her again, if we could just find a way to put the past behind us.' He dropped his head and kicked at the gravel beneath his feet. 'I know what you think of me, and I don't expect you to believe me, but it's true.'

The media's darling putting on a convincing show, a brutal rapist trying to cover his tracks, or genuine contrition? Probably a combination of all three, Alexi decided.

'You imagined Natalie would return home and not tell your wife the truth about why she ran?' Alexi opened her eyes wide in disbelief, unsure if the man was naïve or too used to getting his own way to see the bigger picture. 'How do you imagine Fay would have felt when she learned how Natalie had been making her living?'

'Perhaps Natalie would have spared her that knowledge. And

all the other stuff, too. She could have made something up about why she ran, for Fay's sake. After all, it was me she wanted to punish, and she sure as hell achieved that ambition.'

Alexi didn't think anything the self-centred bastard said could have surprised her, but he'd just managed it. She rolled her eyes. All that twaddle about his wife's feelings and she had almost... almost fallen for it. 'Why are you here? Come to revisit the scene of the crime?'

'I wanted to see where she lives, and if there was any sign of her.'

Alexi rolled her eyes. 'Of course you did.'

'She never lost her love of flowers.' He glanced at the lovely garden. 'She got that passion from Fay.'

Alexi didn't respond. Had he really thought she'd be won over by a little nostalgia and a sad smile? And yet, part of her still wanted to believe he regretted what he'd done, the damage he'd caused to two lives – Natalie's and his wife's. Damn, he was good! She reminded herself he would only tell her what he wanted her to hear, and that certainly wouldn't be the truth. She neither liked nor trusted him, but if they'd met under different circumstances, she would probably have been charmed by him.

'I suppose you were hoping to get into her cottage and find all the incriminating stuff she has on you,' Alexi said, finding her voice.

'In broad daylight?'

His reasonable tone only made him seem more dangerous. She felt vulnerable and exposed but knew better than to show it. Not a single car had passed the cottage during the time they'd been having their confrontation. No one had passed it on foot or horseback, either. Natalie had chosen her secluded hideaway a little too well.

'Unless you can tell me anything useful about what

happened to Natalie, then I think you'd better go. My partner and I haven't told the police about Natalie blackmailing you. Yet. So they don't know you paid her to keep silent, but I figure they will take an active interest in her disappearance if they ever learn of it.'

It was a hollow threat and they both knew it. 'How would that make Natalie look?'

'More to the point, what would they say at the golf club?' Alexi shot back. 'I doubt your police contacts will stand by you if there's a whiff of *that* sort of scandal attaching to your name. Murder and rape trumps blackmail in the high-stakes crime game.'

'Please let me know if you discover what's happened to Natalie,' he said politely as he opened his car door. 'And if I can help you in any way... well, I don't suppose you would want my help.' He offered her one of his charming smiles and slid into the driving seat. 'I hope to hear from you soon with good news.'

'Don't hold your breath,' Alexi muttered as he reversed into the lane and drove away.

No matter how genuine his contrition seemed, it didn't alter the fact that Natalie had to have something that would incriminate him if it ever came to light. She watched his car disappear around the corner. Only when it was out of sight did she release the breath she'd been holding and uncross her arms, which were shaking.

'That went well, baby,' she said aloud, bending to stroke Cosmo's head. 'Come on. We're not scared of that big bully, are we? And we're not going to let him upset us. Let's get this search on the road.'

Alexi returned to her car to grab her bag. She then approached the cottage's front door and fiddled with the strange locks, hampered by her shaking fingers. She dropped the keys and some colourful language but finally managed to get the door open. She went straight to the kitchen, poured a glass of water from the tap, and downed it in two gulps. Gradually her heartbeat returned to a more normal rate and she was able to think about her confrontation with Seaton without trembling.

'Bullies hate being confronted,' she told Cosmo, who was stalking along the work surfaces. The cottage smelt musty so Alexi opened the back door to let in some fresh air.

'Now, Cosmo,' she said, staring speculatively around the pristine kitchen. 'Where do you think she hid her papers? In the cottage, or in her workroom out the back?' Cosmo rubbed his head beneath her hand. 'Hmm, that's what I think, too. She had customers in and out of the workroom, but this was her private space, so we should concentrate on the cottage.'

Alexi shoved the spanner into the back pocket of her jeans before putting the kettle on and making herself a mug of instant coffee, needing the caffeine hit. She found a tin of pilchards in a cupboard. Figuring that Cosmo would need to recharge his batteries following his busy morning, she peeled back the lid and decanted the contents into a bowl which she placed on the floor. Cosmo stalked across to it, sniffed suspiciously, then settled down to consume his snack.

While Cosmo cleared the bowl and then set about fastidiously washing his face, Alexi investigated every nook and cranny in the kitchen. She reasoned that if Natalie was hiding a lot of papers, they couldn't be jammed into... well, into a jam jar. If, on the other hand, everything had been put onto a memory stick, it could be hidden just about anywhere and she might never find it.

* * *

A half-hour later, Alexi stood back with her hands on her hips, convinced the kitchen hid nothing more incriminating that a few cans of food past their sell-by date. She moved on to the lounge, which took considerably longer to search, mainly because there were so many books lining the walls. She removed each of them and flipped through the pages to see if anything had been slipped between them and also felt along the shelving for any hidden nooks, feeling as though she was featuring in an old-fashioned spy film.

Nothing.

The floor and the rest of the walls were solid and there was nothing hidden beneath the seat cushions or stuck to the bottom of the sideboard. She even checked inside the chimney, disturbed an old bird's nest when she poked upwards with a stick and received a face full of soot for her trouble.

She made her way to the cloakroom and washed her sooty hands and face.

'This is disheartening,' she told Cosmo. 'Perhaps I should have let Cheryl come along and help me. Besides, I could use the company. No offence, babe, but our conversations sometimes get a bit one-sided.'

Cosmo blinked his hazel eyes twice and preceded her towards the staircase, knowing without needing to be told that their next port of call would be Natalie's bedroom. By then it was mid-afternoon and Alexi's stomach growled, reminding her she'd forgotten to bring anything with her for lunch.

'It won't kill me to skip a meal,' she muttered, standing on the threshold to the bedroom and looking around her, wondering where to start.

This sleuthing business wasn't as easy, or as glamorous, as they made it out to be on the telly. Alexi chided herself to get on with it with a reminder that as things stood, no one would take

Natalie's disappearance seriously, especially when her previous line of work came to light, along with the fact that she was a blackmailer. It was down to Alexi to come up with irrefutable proof that something bad had happened to her.

Alexi had been able to remain detached while searching the other rooms, but pawing through another woman's personal apparel somehow seemed like an invasion of privacy. Cosmo felt no such qualms and stalked into Natalie's dressing room, where he leapt onto the shelf full of sweaters and curled up on one.

'Cosmo! You'll leave hairs everywhere. Come on now, I need your help. I know this is the shelf where we found Natalie's bank statements and it's very clever of you to remember that, but...' Alexi clapped a hand over her mouth. 'Oh my god! Cosmo, you're a genius!' She grabbed his face between her hands and plastered kisses over it. 'I'd been wondering why we found those statements in such an odd place. She was about to file them away, wasn't she? But she didn't because... because the phone rang, the doorbell disturbed her... something. She put them down, they got buried beneath her sweaters somehow, and she forgot about them. Which means we're getting warm, baby boy. Jump down, I need to check this out.'

Cosmo sent Alexi an appraising look, then leapt down from the high shelf and stalked from the room. Alexi lost no time in removing everything, which is when she noticed that the shelf wasn't as deep as the ones above it, but the lower ones were equally shallow. Euphoria swept through her. She was definitely onto something. The hiding place was ingenious. She doubted whether the police would have found it, even if they did a systematic search of the premises. She tapped the back wall, producing a hollow sound to confirm her suspicions. But there was no obvious way to remove the panel and get to the goods behind it.

'I'm not giving up now,' she said aloud, feeling carefully for any hidden catches. She removed the spanner from her back pocket, thought for a minute, then put it aside. 'Don't be stupid,' she muttered. 'This calls for something a little more subtle.'

Alexi slipped back down to the kitchen and rummaged in a drawer, looking for something flat to slip between the panel and the wall that would enable her to prise the panel away. Natalie obviously had a clever way of separating the two but Alexi was too impatient to try and figure it out. Instead, she found a small, flat-headed screwdriver which would do the job nicely, causing minimal damage.

She ran back up to the dressing room, carefully applied the tip of the screwdriver to the slight gap between panel and wall, and put pressure on it. The panel came loose with a loud cracking noise and fell away. Her heart thumping, Alexi slid her hand into the deep space that opened up to her, and pulled out an old-fashioned concertina file bursting at the seams with papers.

'Yes!'

Alexi punched the air with a clenched fist before placing the file on the floor and returning her hand to the gap. There were more files that looked as though they contained official papers. There was also a heavy bag that she struggled to bring through the gap. Eventually doing so, she placed it on the floor and unzipped it. Bundles of banknotes spilled onto the floor: all used, all twenties and fifties.

'My god!' Alexi covered her gaping mouth with her hand. 'Who the hell was she blackmailing?'

Whoever it was, she'd obviously only banked a fraction of her ill-gotten gains. Alexi was now more curious than ever to get to the bottom of things. A cursory glance at Natalie's bank papers convinced her that the answers lay not there but in the concertina file.

She left everything else where it was and carried the file to Natalie's bed. It was meticulously organised, just like everything else about Natalie's life appeared to be. Alexi removed the contents one section at a time and placed each one on a different part of the bed. Then she went through them, forcing herself to be methodical. There wasn't room for all the papers and her, so she sat cross-legged on the carpeted floor and started to read. She was tempted to ring Jack and tell him what she'd found but since she wasn't yet sure what she *had* found, she restrained herself, not wanting to appear needy.

The oldest section of the file contained diaries, written in the round hand of a teenager. A veritable treasure trove which would undoubtedly lend a clue as to what Natalie had over her adoptive father. It would take ages to read through them and Alexi wanted to get a snapshot of what else was hidden away before she started on them.

She gasped when she came across a letter from a solicitor, and a bequest from Natalie's birth mother, a lady called Laura Brooks.

'So, she found you,' Alexi muttered aloud, reading through the letter. 'Oh my god!'

Its contents made spine-chilling sense. Everything fell into place and she knew now what must have happened to Natalie.

And why.

* * *

Jack glanced at his watch, saw that it was after 3 p.m. and thought about checking in with Alexi. Then he heard the downstairs door open, which meant Cassie was back. He put his phone down. It could wait. If Alexi had found anything important, she'd have called him.

Wouldn't she?

Jack still didn't like or trust reporters, in general, but there were exceptions to every rule.

'Hey, Cas,' he said when she walked in. 'How's it going?'

'I'm working a new case,' she replied, dumping her bag on her desk and fixing him with a considering look.

'Anything I should know about?'

'It's more my area than yours.'

'Okay. Coffee's just made.'

'Thanks.' She went into the alcove that served as a kitchen and poured herself a cup. 'How about your credit card business?'

'Done and dusted. I've even invoiced the client.'

'I'm impressed.'

'Because I solved the case?'

'No, stupid. Because you sent the invoice.'

She perched a buttock on the edge of her desk and sat facing him, sipping at her coffee, the underlying tension impossible to ignore.

'I'm surprised to see you here,' she said.

'I work here.'

'I know that, but I was starting to wonder if you'd forgotten.'

'My sister needed my help.' When she sent him a cynical look, Jack almost lost it. 'You think I should have left her hanging?'

She planted a fisted hand on her hip. 'Your sister?' she asked with attitude.

'Stop it, Cas. I pull my weight around here. What I do in my own time is down to me.'

'It's not what you do, but who, that bothers me.'

'It's never been that way between us,' he said, addressing the elephant in the room.

'It would have been, eventually.' Her belligerence gave way to pathos. 'We're a great team. I understand what makes you tick *and* I lent a shoulder when you needed one.'

'Christ, Cas, don't do this!' Jack ran a hand through his hair. 'If I've given you the wrong signals then I'm sorry. I'm not in the market for a serious relationship. Not now, perhaps not ever again. Besides, you can do a damned sight better than me.'

'Oh, please!' She threw her hands in the air. 'It's not you, it's me. Is that the best you can do?'

'I don't know what—'

'It's the reporter woman.'

'She's got a name.'

Cassie appraised him through narrowed eyes. 'Yeah, she does, and it's spelt Trouble.'

Jack held on to his temper by the sheer force of his will. 'You and I work well together, but my private life's my own. If you can't accept that then—'

'I hear you,' she said sullenly. 'It's not that I'm begging, or asking you for anything you're not prepared to give. It's just that I hate to see you making a fool of yourself, but I guess that's your call.'

'Right.' He treated her to an economical smile. 'Are we good to keep working together?'

She returned his smile, but he could see it took her a lot of effort. 'Sure. I get the message.'

Tension still fogged the atmosphere, but at least Jack had made his position clear. He was dying to get back to Lambourn and see what Alexi was up to, but figured that would be a bad move so soon after their frank exchange of views. He'd stay another hour, do some internet surfing and see what he could find out about Natalie's mother, Laura Brooks. Cassie immersed herself in her own work and the only sound was the clacking of fingers on keyboards. Until Jack found something that caused him to elevate from his chair.

'Oh my god!' he yelled, picking up the phone and dialling Alexi's number.

'What's wrong?' Cassie asked, looking up.

'I know what happened to Natalie, and Alexi's just put herself directly in the firing line.'

* * *

'Jack needs to know about this.'

Alexi spoke aloud, her voice barely audible above the sound of her disjointed breathing. Drawn by a stronger force than the need to communicate with Jack, she didn't reach for her phone. Instead her attention remained focused on the damning letter from Natalie's mother that made such chilling sense of everything Natalie had done since reading it herself. A simple document that had dramatically changed the course of Laura's child's life in ways she couldn't possibly have anticipated or intended. Unwittingly, Laura had provided Natalie with an outlet for all that pent up anger and resentment, with catastrophic consequences.

Alexi read the letter again, more slowly, allowing sufficient time for her addled brain to absorb the implications. She wanted to be sure she hadn't misunderstood anything the first time because a compelling need to know had made her read the next paragraph before she'd properly digested the contents of its predecessor.

She came to the end and lowered the letter onto her lap, tears stinging her eyes at this poignant message from beyond the grave. The icy chill freezing her bloodstream gave her some idea of just how profoundly affected Natalie must have been by the brutal reality of a past she wasn't supposed to know anything about.

The way she had so patiently and meticulously planned her revenge made perfect sense to Alexi who, now that she knew Natalie's secret, herself felt exposed and vulnerable. She was surrounded by Natalie's papers and money, there was a killer on the loose, and she was very much alone.

Self-preservation kicked in. She'd give Jack a quick call, tell him what she'd discovered, then pack all this stuff into her car and hotfoot it back to Hopgood Hall. There was safety in numbers. She'd share it all with Jack and between them they would decide what to do about it. Not that there was any real question about their next move. Natalie was dead. Any lingering hopes to the contrary dissipated the moment she started reading that letter. A letter that would give the police more reason than enough to launch a murder enquiry, even without a body, and arrest the man who must be the murderer.

She pulled the phone from her pocket and nearly jumped out of her skin when it rang in her hand. She saw Jack's name on the screen and almost laughed with relief. Talk about telepathy.

But before she could take the call, the phone was wrenched from her fingers and thrown across the room. She looked up, her heart pounding, directly into the cold eyes of a killer.

She screamed but there was no one to hear her.

16

'A reporter?' Graham Fuller growled. 'I should have made the connection.'

He towered over her, his features twisted into an impenetrable mask of resentment. Anger radiated from him, competing with the smell of alcohol on his breath. She sent him a defiant look but refrained from comment.

'You looked familiar.' Fuller's aggrieved voice filled the silence. 'But all those questions about Natalie distracted me, just like they were supposed to.'

'But then you remembered.' Alexi's own voice sounded commendably calm. 'I had no idea I had such a diverse readership.'

'I saw Tod wave to you. When he told me who you were, I knew you'd do my work for me. People like you never can mind their own bloody business.' His gaze briefly encompassed the mess surrounding Alexi. Before she could take advantage of his momentary distraction, he fixed her with an icy glare, his lips stretching into what could either have been a smile or a grimace.

'Don't even think about it,' he said, speaking softly but sounding infinitely more threatening than if he'd been ranting.

'What are you doing here?'

'What do you think?'

Alexi didn't see much point in beating around the bush. 'You want your daughter's papers.'

'That interfering bitch wasn't my daughter.'

'Actually, she was.'

'I knew you'd come around here snooping once you left the yard. Snooping is what you lot do the best. I think this proves my point.' He encompassed Alexi's find with a wide sweep of one hand. 'I wondered where her stuff was but when she refused to tell me and I couldn't find anything here myself, I thought she might have invented it all.'

Alexi stared up into the dead eyes of the man who had undoubtedly killed his own daughter. She hadn't known Natalie personally, but had lived her life vicariously for the past few days, which made her loss feel personal.

Just her luck that her phone had rung at the exact time Fuller came up the stairs. The noise of the ringtone and the hammering of Alexi's heart when she discovered the horrifying truth had masked the sound of his footsteps. He'd caught her unawares and Alexi knew with absolute clarity that he couldn't afford to let her live.

Fuller would have come in through the open back door. How stupid of her not to have locked herself in. Not that that would have kept him out for long, but at least his breaking in would have given her advance warning.

'Natalie *was* your daughter,' Alexi replied, swallowing her fear and meeting Fuller's gaze head on. 'Your father ordered her mother to abort, and gave her the money to pay for the procedure. He told you to walk away, which is what you did. After all, impressing the man so you could take over his empire was all that mattered to you. If you thought about Laura at all after your fling, you simply assumed that she'd followed orders, just like everyone in your dysfunctional family always has. But she wasn't a member of your family and couldn't bring herself to kill her baby. So she had the child and put her up for adoption.'

'Evidently,' he said, sounding disinterested. His gaze focused upon the bundles of money spilling across the carpet. 'Glad to see she didn't get to spend my money.'

'You're a callous bastard!' Alexi knew it was a mistake to let her emotions show but couldn't seem to help herself. 'You impregnated a fifteen-year-old girl who would do absolutely anything for you because she was horse mad, and a promising rider, hoping to become a three-day eventer. You were the son of an influential trainer and promised to help Laura kick-start her career. She was flattered, but too young to understand that all you really wanted to do was get into her knickers...'

Alexi was too choked up to continue. Talk about history repeating itself. Natalie's mother must have been scared and confused, and needed him more than ever at that difficult time. Laura was only fifteen when Fuller had impregnated her, just as Natalie had only been fourteen when her adoptive father had raped her. No wonder Natalie acted in the way that she had when she discovered the truth. She still hadn't got past what Seaton had done to her, and then she found out her birth mother's tragic story. It would be enough to tip anyone over the edge.

That would be why she gave up on being an escort, moved here, and methodically put her plan into action. Seaton first, then her father.

'You own Super Nova.' Alexi said and Fuller simply nodded. 'You noticed the chance to own a really good horse but by then your daughter was blackmailing you to the extent that you needed a partner to take some of the strain. Natalie pretended that was why she kept coming to your yard and you hated not being able to control her. She wanted to flaunt her hold over you, rub your nose in it and watch you squirm. That must have hurt.'

'She was a vindictive little bitch.' His upper lip curled back into a disdainful sneer. 'She had no idea what she was getting herself into.'

Alexi flexed a brow. 'Was? Where is she now?'

'Somewhere you'll never find her.'

'I found *you* and put two and two together. It's taken me two days.'

'Congratulations.'

'That must be why she spread the word about buying a share of a racehorse on Facebook. A public declaration only she could enjoy that told the world she fully intended to screw her miserable father for every penny she could get.'

He made a scoffing sound at the back of his throat. 'Don't worry about Natalie. She's beyond help. It's your own skin you should be worrying about.' He snorted. 'I've had just about all I can take from interfering females.'

A chill crept down Alexi's spine. She had been counting on Cosmo to distract him but there was no sign of him, and she had nothing to fight back against Fuller with. He was older than her, but taller and considerably stronger, and the alcohol didn't seem to have dulled his reactions. She wouldn't get to stand up before he overpowered her. She had that mini-sized can of hairspray in her pocket still, but she probably wouldn't be able to get to it because he was watching her intently. She'd left her spanner on a shelf in the dressing room. She could see it: so near yet so far. It was her only hope. She had to get to it.

Somehow.

'You couldn't let Natalie live,' Alexi said, playing for time.

'Having an illegitimate child was no big deal, not even back in the seventies, but Laura was underage. If that could be proved, then not only would your precious reputation be in tatters but you could also do jail time.' She sent him a snide smile. 'So you had to silence her for good.'

'What's the game?' he replied, sneering. 'Keep him talking until reinforcements arrive? That old ploy?' Well yes, actually. Alexi had hoped that by not answering Jack's call, it would bring him running. Or else Cosmo would give up his pursuit of the rodent population in Natalie's garden and realise she needed his help. 'Forget it!'

'You have a wife and family, don't you? Grown kids and, didn't I hear somewhere that you married into money?' Alexi expelled a hollow laugh. 'Bet your wife didn't realise what she was getting herself into.'

'Shut up!'

Alexi locked gazes with him, refusing to back down. 'Truth hurts, does it? She probably doesn't know that you pass inside information to racing scouts, either.'

He glared at her, his mouth literally falling open. 'How—'

'You should choose your meeting places more carefully.'

'And you should worry about yourself.' He recovered quickly and took control of the situation. 'Collect all this stuff up and put it in the bag with the money. Quickly.'

Alexi moved slowly, taking every opportunity to glower at him. In actual fact, it was the moment she'd been waiting for. She didn't think he'd seen the spanner. His attention was all on the money. Greed would hopefully be his downfall.

'You won't get away with this. Killing Natalie is one thing. She had a chequered past and no one to miss her.' Alexi moved closer than necessary to the dressing room as she scooped up the piles of cash. 'I, on the other hand, have a whole newsroom of people waiting to hear from me, to say nothing of my friends here. *And* an editor who already knows I suspect you.'

'You only just found all this stuff. If you'd known before now you would have turned it over to the police.'

'Journalists guard their stories more closely than you look after your pampered horses. And when I'm missed, this place will be swarming with police.'

'Who said anything about killing you? If I can destroy what Natalie had on me, no one will believe your wild story, nor will they care, and I'll sue your paper for a large fortune if it prints one unsubstantiated word.'

Alexi wasn't buying it. She knew very well that he couldn't risk letting her live. The moment she was free of him, she would get a copy of Natalie's birth certificate and go to the authorities with what she knew. If he'd heard of her reputation as a journalist then he would be aware that once she got her teeth into a juicy story she never let it go. Alexi cocked her head to one side, hope igniting. She'd just heard something. It sounded like a battering ram hitting a solid wooden door.

Cosmo, please!

It must have been the wind because the sound didn't come again and Alexi's hope died with it. Fuller obviously heard the noise, too. He took his eyes from her for a second and moved a step closer to the open door, peering around it. Alexi didn't hesitate. She leapt to her feet, lunged for the spanner and raised it above her head, ready to strike him with all the force she could muster.

He must have sensed her presence because he turned with lightning speed and aimed a vicious blow to her stomach. She deflated like a burst balloon, clutching her mid-section with one hand as she crumpled to her knees, having the presence of mind to keep hold of the spanner.

'Pass it over.'

He grinned as he extended a hand, clearly enjoying himself, and Alexi had no choice. She reluctantly gave him the spanner and he threw it onto the bed.

'I don't have any particular argument with you and don't want to cause you unnecessary pain.' His expression hardened. 'But I will if you try anything like that again.'

'You expect me to do as I'm told and simply let you kill me? The world has moved on since the days when you compromised a fifteen-year-old and then walked away without a backward glance.' She summoned up a defiant look. 'Women fight back when they're cornered nowadays.'

'It takes two.'

'Oh, please! You were eighteen, she was a star-struck kid.' Alexi sent him a disgusted look. 'Just as a matter of interest, how much did Natalie take you for?'

At first, Alexi thought he wouldn't tell her. That would mean admitting a woman had got the better of him and this guy was definitely a misogynist. 'A hundred grand,' he said shortly. 'She found out that's how much I'd paid for Nova and said a daughter ought to be worth as much as a horse.' He screwed up his features. 'She was wrong. The horse would have given me a decent return on my investment.'

She shot him a withering look. 'You're despicable.'

'And you're trying your transparent distraction tactics again.' He smirked. 'Get this stuff into the bag. Now!'

Alexi was still bent over, nursing her stomach, not having to feign light-headedness. The guy certainly packed a punch. But she couldn't give way to the pain. She was on her own, needed to get the better of the man who stood between her and the door, and needed to do it now. He'd run out of patience. Chances were he intended to kill her here and dump her body elsewhere. He was definitely in self-preservation mode and she was collateral damage.

She lurched towards the bed, grabbed the spanner and ran at Fuller with the determination of a woman fighting for her life. She felt his fetid breath peppering her face as he laughed and lashed at her with a thumping right hook, connecting severely with her temple. Her world span. She saw stars but refused to let go of the spanner. She raised it, unsure how much strength she could put behind the blow.

'You're quite a spirited little thing, aren't you?'

He laughed again, enjoying himself as he reached for the spanner. This situation was manna from heaven for a bully of Fuller's ilk. But that was okay. For once, he was doing precisely what she wanted him to. Mentally thanking Patrick for insisting she find the time for self-defence classes, she whirled in a semi-circular motion and her foot connected hard with the side of Fuller's face.

'What the—'

He shook his head, dazed, taken completely by surprise. But her satisfaction was short-lived when he surprised her with the speed of his retaliation, chopping viciously at the back of her knee with his booted foot. She cried out and fell to the ground. He followed her down, seeming to forget about the spanner. Her heart sank. She hadn't even slowed him down.

He grabbed one of her wrists and held it above her head, half-covering her body with his own, making sure he kept his groin clear of her one working knee and both of her feet. Hold the spanner, or let it go and try to jab a finger into his eye?

Before he could grab her other hand, she twisted her body sideways and bit down as hard as she could on the fleshy part of the arm pinning her wrist. He howled and slapped her face so hard that her head snapped back and made painful contact with the leg of the iron bedstead. Alexi felt her strength sap as more of his body weight pinned her down, forcing the air from her lungs, making it a struggle to breathe. This was it. She'd enraged him and he really was going to kill her.

His hands circled her neck and slowly squeezed. She saw stars and all the fight drained out of her. It would be easier to close her eyes, surrender to the inevitable and wait for the end to come.

'That's it, honey,' her aggressor said in a sing-song voice. 'Now you're getting it. When it comes right down to it, women are no different to horses. They just need a firm controlling hand to remind them who's boss.'

The pressure on her neck gradually increased. Very gradually, like he got a kick out of this and wanted to make it last. Images of Natalie filled her head, urging her to fight, always to fight. She saw Fay Seaton's face, too. She would never know peace if she didn't learn the truth about Natalie's struggles.

More banging from downstairs spurred her on. She was sure now that it must be Cosmo. He'd been shut out but hadn't given up on her so she wouldn't give up on herself. Using every vestige of her rapidly dwindling strength, Alexi lifted her free hand. Fuller noticed but had obviously forgotten about the spanner and simply laughed at her. Infuriated when she caught a glimpse of his smug smile, Alexi bashed the spanner against the side of his skull, surprised at how much strength she was able to put behind the blow. Even more surprised when she heard the sound of splintering bone.

Fuller cried out, a combination of surprise and pain, but the pressure on her neck didn't ease.

* * *

Jack floored the accelerator as he drove back to Lambourn, his gut telling him Alexi was in trouble. He'd checked with Cheryl, who confirmed she hadn't returned to Hopgood Hall.

Jack squealed to a halt in front of Natalie's cottage. Alexi's car was parked where she usually left it. Everything seemed tranquil. Perhaps he'd over-reacted.

His concerns returned when he rang the front doorbell and no one answered. Because Alexi wasn't in the house, or because something was preventing her from getting to the door? Perhaps she was in the workshop. Jack went around the back and his concerns multiplied when he encountered a snarling Cosmo hurling his body repeatedly against the kitchen door. He saw Jack and let out a blood-curdling yowl.

The moment Jack opened the door, the cat streaked through it and bounded up the stairs. Jack followed right behind him and burst into Natalie's bedroom, his worst fears realised. Fuller was on top of Alexi, his hands around her throat. She was motionless. There was blood pouring from a crack on the side of Fuller's head and a manic look in his eyes. Cosmo hurled himself onto the man's back and scratched at his eyes from behind, making the most terrifying noise.

Fuller's hands had left Alexi's neck, but she still wasn't moving. Fuller got up and stumbled around the room, blood now pouring from scratches to his face as well as his skull. There were papers everywhere, as well as loads of cash, and Fuller was disturbing it all with his blind blundering. Jack solved the problem by planting his fist squarely in the centre of the man's face and knocking him out cold. Satisfied that he wouldn't be going anywhere any time soon, he crouched beside Alexi and felt for a pulse, terrified there wouldn't be one to find. Cosmo sat on her opposite side, making piteous, human-like sounds as he stroked her face with a paw.

'Alexi,' he said softly, touching her forehead, willing her to open her eyes.

He tried to get his phone out of his pocket and call the emergency services with one hand and continue holding hers with the other. He could already see dark bruising forming around her neck, another bruise on her cheek and a cut to her temple. But at least she was breathing, albeit shallowly and unevenly. He put his call through to 999 and told them to hurry.

'Fuller.'

* * *

Jack almost jumped out of his skin. He'd looked away from her at the exact moment she'd opened her eyes and her voice, shallow and croaky, was the most welcome sound he'd ever heard.

She blinked up at him. 'The bastard was going to kill me,' she rasped.

'It's okay. You and Cosmo got him first.'

At the sound of his name and Alexi's voice, Cosmo purred loudly and rubbed his head gently against Alexi's uninjured cheek.

'He's saying sorry for not getting to you sooner. So am I.' Jack ran his free hand through his hair. 'Christ, Alexi, I never should have left you alone.'

'I can... can—' She burst into tears.

'Shush. An ambulance is on its way, and so are the police.'

'Before the police... there's some stuff here we need to hold on to.'

The effort it took for her to talk was obviously taxing her strength. 'Don't worry about that.'

'You don't understand...'

His reassurances only appeared to make her more agitated. 'What is it?'

'There's Natalie's diaries from when Seaton raped her... and Jack, she was writing a manuscript. Must keep them.'

'Okay, I'll get them.'

'Copy all the stuff from her mother.'

Jack didn't know what she'd found, but was rapidly piecing it together. He needed to work quickly, remove the stuff the police didn't need to know about, and copy the stuff that would enable them to prosecute Fuller.

'I'm on it.'

Jack didn't want to leave her side, but the papers clearly mattered to her more. He was distracted by the sound of Fuller regaining consciousness. Cosmo prowled across to sit over him and gave a warning growl.

'Don't even think about it,' Jack told him as he gathered up the scattered papers and quickly sorted out the ones that he thought would need to be copied. 'Scratch his eyes out if he moves a muscle, Cosmo.'

Half-an-hour later, Natalie's photocopier had been pressed into service, the papers Alexi wanted were safely stowed in Jack's car, and the cottage was crawling with police and paramedics. One of the latter dealt with Alexi's head wound.

'Probably won't need stitching,' he told her. 'Head wounds always bleed a lot, but the cut's not deep. However, that bang on the head might have left you with a concussion and you've got a bruised larynx. Best come back in the ambulance with us. We'll get you checked out in casualty. You'll need an X-ray.'

She closed her eyes and nodded once, like she was too tired to argue.

17

Alexi felt as though she was floating on a chemically induced high. If this was death, it wasn't so very bad. Then voices that were very much of this world broke through the misty fog inside her brain, causing anxiety to nag her back to consciousness. There was something important she had to finish. She reluctantly forced her eyelids open and had absolutely no idea where she was. Everything was white: white walls, white ceiling, white bedcovers, and an antiseptic smell that made her want to gag. Except she couldn't because her throat hurt like hell.

So did all the rest of her.

Then it all came crashing back. She was in hospital. But she had no idea how long she'd been there or if anything was seriously wrong with her. Fuller. What had happened to him? Thinking made her head ache. She wanted to close her eyes again and find a way back to that fluctuating sleep that had ended far too soon. But she couldn't do that. Now that she'd remembered her ordeal, each time she closed her eyes she could feel Fuller's hands around her neck, the pressure on lungs that felt as though they would burst like over-inflated balloons, the cold determination in his hard, flat eyes as he slowly choked the life out of her. The overwhelming temptation she had felt to let her life slide away because the effort to fight back was beyond her.

In a panic, she turned her head to one side and saw a large male figure sprawled in the chair beside her bed, engrossed in whatever he was reading.

'Jack,' she whispered.

'Hey, you're awake.' He sent her a megawatt smile. 'How do you feel?'

'What time is it? How long have I been here?'

'It's early morning. They gave you something to make you sleep. You were getting agitated, trying to talk. The nurse just came in and said you should be awake soon.'

'Have you been here all night?' she asked, her voice croaky and raw.

'Where else would I be?'

She tried to sit up. Every bone in her body protested but Jack helped her, then bolstered the pillows behind her. He handed her a cup with a drinking straw and she greedily allowed water to trickle down her bruised throat. Never had water tasted sweeter.

'You're going to be fine,' he said. 'A lot of bruises and a swollen knee—'

'Fuller kicked it from beneath me when I tried to attack him.'

'I should have been there!' He grasped her hand and gave it a gentle squeeze. 'I'd like to see him try and kick me around.'

'Why? You didn't know he was—'

'I knew there was something off about him when I overheard his conversation in the men's room, and we knew Natalie had had a lot of contact with him. I should have put it together sooner. If I'd got to you just a minute or two later, I...'

'How did you know?'

'Once I got the name of Natalie's birth mother from her solicitors and did some digging, I found a few old articles about Laura Brooks online. She had a promising career as a junior three-day eventer. When I made the connection to horses and Fuller's father's yard, it all fell into place.'

She thought about that for a moment but was distracted when Jack moved. 'What are you doing?'

'Ringing for the nurse. She told me to let her know if you woke up.'

The nurse responded to the bell, checked Alexi's vital signs, and nodded her satisfaction.

'Would you like a cup of tea and something light to eat?' she asked.

'What I'd like is to go home,' she said, not very graciously.

'The doctor will have to discharge you and he won't do that until you've had something to eat and drink.'

'Okay then, tea would be good. Thanks.'

'I'll be right back,' she said, to Jack, not to her.

'You didn't need to stay. That chair looks uncomfortable,'

'I've slept in worse places.' He winked at her. 'Besides, you're getting VIP treatment. A private room with a police guard outside the door, no less. I had to lie and say I was your significant other.'

On the evidence she'd seen so far, Alexi figured he could probably have charmed the nurses into letting him do anything he wanted to.

'Tell me what happened after they brought me here.'

'It was pandemonium. At first the plod were a bit overawed by Fuller, what with him being akin to a local god. They seemed to think I was the aggressor and wanted to slap the cuffs on me.'

Alexi spontaneously laughed, but regretted it. 'Don't say

anything amusing,' she said, choking and reaching for the water. 'It hurts.'

The nurse interrupted them and placed a tray over Alexi's knees. Rather anaemic-looking scrambled eggs and tea.

'Eat up,' Jack said, holding a forkful of the unappetising eggs to her lips, 'and I'll tell you some more.'

The eggs tasted as cardboardy as they looked but the warm tea soothed her throat and made her feel a little better.

'It took me a while to make the uniforms understand what they were dealing with. Cosmo didn't help, of course. When they took you off, he created merry hell because he couldn't go with you. No one could get near him, except me, so I put him in my car—'

'Did your upholstery survive?'

'Of course. Cosmo and I understand one another completely. Anyway, I put him in the car, safe in the knowledge that no one would get near the papers I'd copied, or the diaries and stuff I'd already taken from the cottage, with Cosmo standing guard over them. Then I went back inside and patiently explained it all. Eventually... eventually,' he said with an exaggerated sigh, 'they realised what they were dealing with, got their act together, and a murder squad came out from Reading nick. They read Natalie's mother's letter, I then told them who you were and what Fuller had tried to do, and he was taken away in handcuffs.'

'Damn, I wish I'd seen that.'

'Sorry sweetheart, but at least he's under lock and key. He was swearing blue murder when they took him away, asking all and sundry if they knew who he was, threatening to sue for wrongful arrest... all the usual. Then he demanded a lawyer.'

'He hasn't admitted anything?'

'Not yet.'

'Damn!' Alexi shook her head, close to tears of frustration.

'Unless he tells them where he hid Natalie's body, it might never be found.'

'Shush, don't get worked up. We'll find her.'

'I hope we do.' She sighed. 'Is that Natalie's manuscript?'

'Yes. Very poignant stuff.'

'We need to get out of here. Cheryl and Drew—'

'I went back there first and dropped Cosmo off. They know you're all right.'

They were interrupted by the doctor. He examined Alexi and wanted her to stay with them another day. She refused and so by mid-morning she was in Jack's car, on the way back to Hopgood Hall. The swelling in her knee had subsided sufficiently for her to be able to hobble under her own steam. She didn't want to think about the bruises to her face and neck, or the bash she'd taken to the head, to say nothing of the bruise forming on her belly where Fuller had punched her.

'The police will want to talk to you once we get back,' Jack warned her as he drove.

'That's okay. I have a few things to say to them.'

The moment Jack pulled his car into the forecourt at Hopgood Hall, Cheryl and Drew, along with Cosmo and Toby, came bounding out to meet them.

'We've been beside ourselves.' Cheryl engulfed Alexi in a cautious hug.

'You should see the other guy,' she replied, giving Drew a kiss on the cheek and slowly bending to greet Cosmo.

'Let's get you inside,' Jack said, sliding an arm around her waist and helping her to walk the short distance.

* * *

'So Fuller had no idea he actually had a daughter,' Cheryl said when they were all seated around the kitchen table drinking tea. 'Well, not Natalie, anyway. He has other kids with his American wife.'

'Did Natalie's mother pursue her dream and make it in three-day eventing?' Drew asked.

Alexi shook her head. 'According to the letter she left for Natalie, her heart went out of it after the way she was treated at the hands of the Fullers and she saw a very different, ugly side to the equestrian world.'

'I'll just bet she did,' Cheryl said, grinding her jaw.

'Just like Natalie's career choices were derailed after what Seaton did to her,' Drew added. 'No wonder Natalie was so determined to get her revenge.'

'Fatal revenge,' Alexi said softly. 'Laura took an office job and finished up marrying her boss, a widower old enough to be her father.'

'She probably felt comfortable with an older man who was willing to look after her,' Drew said pensively. 'More in control. Natalie's life was all about being in control as well. Two abused women doing what they could to protect themselves, and then fighting back.'

'Yes,' Alexi agreed, her voice hoarse, raspy. 'They didn't have any children of their own and her husband died ten years ago. Then, a year before Natalie moved here, her mother discovered she had terminal cancer. She'd never forgotten her only child, and set about trying to find her. She got investigators onto it, and they probably found out all the stuff that Jack and I did.'

'Did they ever meet?' Cheryl asked, her eyes filling with tears.

'No,' Alexi replied. 'I guess Laura figured it was too late to mend that particular fence.'

'But she left that letter,' Cheryl pointed out, 'to be given to Natalie upon her death. She assumed Natalie would want to know about her start in life and the reasons why her mother couldn't keep her.'

Cheryl made it sound as though she desperately wanted to believe Natalie died fighting for justice for two generations. Alexi couldn't fault her friend's reasoning.

Except that she could.

Instead of blackmail, Natalie could have gone to the police, or better yet, to the media with all the information she'd gathered on Seaton and Fuller. Trial by media was way more effective nowadays. By going to the papers, Natalie would have been viewed as the victim that she was. So too would the mother whom she'd never met, and Seaton and Fuller would both have done jail time. But because she turned to blackmail, she would be seen as a manipulative woman with a grudge to bear.

'Do you think her mother's soul-cleansing was the right way to set the record straight?' Drew asked, standing behind Cheryl and absently massaging her shoulders with one large hand. 'She was no longer around to answer Natalie's questions, and couldn't have known what the consequences would be.'

'Having read the letter several times, I'd say she was conflicted,' Jack replied.

'Don't the police have the letter?' Cheryl asked.

Jack winked at her. 'We might have kept a copy.'

'And all of Natalie's childhood diaries, as well as the manuscript she was writing,' Alexi added.

'Best not to mention that to the police,' Jack warned. 'There's nothing there that impinges upon Fuller's culpability and we don't want Fay Seaton to learn about her husband's perversions from Natalie's diaries. If she has to hear it at all, it would be better coming from us.'

'Did Fuller admit to murdering Natalie?' Cheryl asked.

'He did to me,' Alexi replied. 'But Jack says when the police took him away, he was denying everything.'

Cheryl rolled her eyes. 'Of course he was.'

'And he's probably got a fancy lawyer who will try and muddy the waters,' Drew said, curling his lip in disgust. 'If they find out Natalie was an escort, that will open a whole new can of worms.'

'That's another reason why it's better not to let the police see Natalie's diaries and manuscript,' Jack replied. 'It would cast Seaton in the role of alternative suspect. Especially if they delve into his financials and discover she blackmailed him, too.'

'Fuller's lawyer will have his work cut out to cast doubt on his guilt,' Alexi rasped, 'because Natalie was very thorough. She'd managed to get a sample of Fuller's DNA and paid a private lab to compare it to her own. There's a ninety-nine point seven per cent chance that Fuller's her biological father. Her mother also included a sample of her own DNA with the letter she left for Natalie. He won't be able to talk his way out of that one.'

'Where are those samples now?' Jack asked.

'Being held by the lab that ran the tests, along with the original results.'

'She really wasn't taking any chances,' Cheryl said. 'Good for her.'

'There was a ton of cash hidden in the house,' Jack said, yawning. 'The police have all that.'

'Natalie took Fuller for a hundred grand.' Alexi said. 'The same amount as he paid for Super Nova.'

'Kind of poetic justice, when you think about it,' Drew mused, turning to the stove to heat up some soup for their lunch.

'Yeah, she only banked small parts of it and, I'm guessing here, laundered the rest through her business. That would be one of the reasons why she set it up, and explains why it was already in the black.'

Drew served them with Marcel's homemade soup and Alexi surprised herself by feeling hungry again.

Jack's phone rang.

'That was the lead detective in the murder squad,' he told Alexi. 'He needs to come and talk to you. Might as well get it out the way. They'll be here in an hour, which gives you time for that bath you said you wanted.'

'Sure.'

'I'd best hide this evidence,' he said, pointing to the diaries and manuscript he'd brought back from the hospital. 'And I have a few bases to cover. I'll be a few minutes.'

'Jack,' Alexi said, her croaking voice halting him before he was halfway across the room.

'Yes.' He turned to look at her, his eyes dark and intense. 'What is it?'

'Thanks.'

He looked surprised. 'For what?'

'Oh, I don't know.' She cautiously shrugged. Even that small gesture caused half the nerve endings in her battered body to protest. 'Let me see. Saving my life is probably worth acknowledging.'

He swallowed and took a step towards her, as though he wanted to say more. Then he appeared to remember Cheryl and Drew were both there and the moment of mutual awareness passed.

'Any time,' he said flippantly.

"You'll have one hell of an inside story to write when this is all over,' Cheryl remarked as she and Alexi watched Jack leave the room.

Astonishingly, that thought hadn't even occurred to Alexi.

Well, maybe not so astonishing, given that she'd just narrowly escaped being Fuller's second victim. She held that thought as she turned to the kitchen mirror, wincing as she assessed her appearance. A dressing on her temple covered the gash where she'd hit her head on the bedstead. There was already a dark reddish tinge surrounding it. The same was true of her cheek, where Fuller's hand had struck it so violently.

She instinctively touched the dark marks ringing her neck like an ugly collar and closed her eyes for an expressive moment, waiting for the nausea caused by delayed shock and visual realisation to dissipate.

'Come on,' Cheryl said softly from behind her. 'I'll help you with that bath.'

18

Jack ran up to his room, phoned Cassie, gave her an abbreviated version of events and told her she'd have to cope without him for a day or two. He'd been in no mood to handle her tantrum the previous day and was surprised when she accepted what he told her now with calm resignation.

Next Jack called his sister, told her the same story and warned her to expect a visit from the police.

'They'll check into Natalie's background and will want to know why I got involved,' he told her. 'It's best they hear the truth from me.'

'Of course you need to be straight with them. Don't worry about me. I'm just so glad your friend survived.'

Jack phoned Reading nick next. As luck would have it, there was a uniformed sergeant on desk duty, one who'd been there forever and owed Jack a favour from the days when Jack had been seconded to Reading as part of a fraud investigation. Technically, Jack was a person of interest, as they say, in a murder case. Make that a potential murder case. Still no body. Even so, the sergeant shouldn't tell him anything.

'Fuller's being interviewed now,' the sergeant said. 'He's lawyered up and so far hasn't said much. How's the woman he tried to throttle?'

'Recovering, but it was a close call.'

'I dunno.' Jack could imagine the sergeant scratching his balding head. 'You think you've seen it all when you've been in this game as long as I have, but I never would have pegged Fuller for a villain.'

'Can't trust anyone these days.'

Jack told the sergeant he owed him a drink and hung up. Then he sat back and had a good think about their conversation, more convinced than ever that if Fuller didn't confess and tell them where he'd hidden the body, he might well get away with murder. He would go down for rape of a minor and for attempted murder, but how long for? His brief would dig up all the sordid details of Natalie's past. How she blackmailed her biological father until he was in danger of going under financially. Everything would get spun, glossed over, and Fuller might not pay the ultimate price.

'Not on my watch,' Jack said aloud, grimly determined.

His next call was to Athena at Mayfair Escorts, warning her that Natalie was dead and she would undoubtedly receive a visit from the police.

'I'm glad Alexi's okay,' she said, her voice low and full of melancholy at the sad news she had just learned.

'I'll send her your regards. Thanks for thinking of her.'

'She made quite an impression upon me.'

Me too.

Jack had some time to kill before the police arrived so decided to dig a little deeper into Fuller's background. Jack thought about talking to Fuller's lads living in Drew's annexe but decided against it. Fuller's place would be buzzing with rumour and speculation about the future of the yard. The lads wouldn't be human if they didn't worry about indiscretion costing them their jobs. Besides, if the police discovered Jack had interfered in the investigation by talking to the lads before they could, he would only piss them off unnecessarily.

Jack absorbed himself in some of the endless articles he found online about Fuller. And very interesting reading they made too.

'Well, well,' he muttered, reaching for his phone and calling Cassie again. 'Hey,' he said when she answered. 'If you were serious in your offer of help, can you do some digging for me?'

'Sure. What do you need?'

Jack told her.

* * *

When Alexi, dressed in a simple sheath dress and flat shoes, re-entered the kitchen, Jack was the only person in it. He had Cosmo on his lap and was stroking his back with smooth swoops of his large hand.

'Hey,' he said, looking up and smiling at her. 'Feel better?'

'A little.' She poured herself a coffee from the pot sitting on the counter.

'He was trying to open the kitchen door when I got there,' Jack said, nodding in Cosmo's direction.

'I left it open. Fuller must have come in that way and closed it behind him.'

'Right. It's one of those handles that you push down. Cosmo was leaping up at it. I figure he was trying to land on the handle and force it down.'

'I think he must have been a human in a previous life. He certainly thinks like one.'

'He loves you. Wants to protect you.'

Alexi took a sip of her coffee. The warm, rich liquid trickling down her throat was soothing. 'You've read Natalie's diaries and I haven't,' she said, taking the chair next to his. 'Are you going to make me guess what Natalie had on Seaton?'

He grimaced. 'Her diaries were touchingly naïve, up until the day that changed her life. She was excited about going to that do with her dad and critical of her mum for not attending . Natalie couldn't understand how anything could be more important than a glamorous awards event in a posh hotel but was really stoked about taking her mum's place. She had a new dress and all her friends were envious.'

'Poor kid.'

'Right. Her description of what happened that night is as harrowing as it is detailed including, significantly, details of a birthmark on Seaton's privates.'

'Ah,' Alexi replied, nodding slowly. 'The smoking gun.'

'Quite. Anyway, she really was an innocent and believed Seaton when he told her afterwards that she'd brought it on herself. She hated herself after that and I don't think she ever really got to like who she became. Well, perhaps not until recently and then, as we know, her every action was guided by the DNA of human motivation—'

'Otherwise known as revenge,' Alexi said softly.

'Right. If she hadn't gone to that damned navel-gazer and if he hadn't encouraged her to explore her past, things might have turned out very differently.'

'I agree Natalie's past would have been better left alone. But don't lose sight of the fact that Seaton did ruin her life and she didn't want to let go of her anger. Something had to give. I'm just glad she had the stamina to run away when she was still a teenager, even if she did finish up doing what she did. At least that was on her own terms.' Alexi placed an elbow on the table and leaned the uninjured side of her face in her cupped hand. 'I keep worrying that Fuller will use his influence to wheedle his way out of this.'

'The same thought occurred to me, so I did a little digging. I found some interesting stuff, so I got Cassie to dig deeper still.'

'I know that look.' Alexi smiled. 'I take it all is not what it seems in the Fuller household.'

'When are things ever what they seem? Okay, here's the short version. Fuller's father—'

'The one who wanted Laura to abort her baby?'

'Yeah, that charmer. He was a very successful trainer back in his day and ruled his yard with a crop of iron. He was a bully who had no time for personal weaknesses and everyone was scared of him, including his kids.'

'Which is why Graham Fuller walked away from Laura and toed the parental line.'

'That's the way I see it. Anyway, the prodigal son obviously redeemed himself because Daddy dearest passed his business over to Graham. But Graham has slowly run it into the ground because—'

'Because he has a drinking problem. I smelled it on his breath when I saw him... blimey, was it only yesterday morning? Anyway, it was early and he'd already had a fortifier or six.'

'There've been some problems. Horses not being entered in races, or being entered in the wrong ones. Owners stuck with him because of his reputation but talk has spread about booze, a short fuse, and some fairly public rows. Quite a few of them have now taken their horses away.'

'I noticed a few of the boxes in his yard were empty. I assumed the horses were out... wherever it is that they go.'

Jack grinned, presumably at her ignorance.

'Fuller married a rich American, and they have two grown kids. A daughter who works in Newbury as a management consultant. Doesn't want anything to do with horses and seldom returns home. The son is following the family tradition and being groomed to take over the training yard... if it survives.'

'They have financial problems, don't they?'

'Yeah. Fuller was asked to look at Super Nova on behalf of his then owner. Fuller knew a good thing when he saw it, talked the horse down, persuaded the owner to sell at a bargain price and used his wife's money to buy the colt for himself.'

'Very ethical.'

'Quite. The owner in question got into a big bust-up with Fuller over it when he found out Fuller had done the dirty on him.'

'Fuller didn't care because Super Nova would restore his fortune and his reputation. Then Natalie came along and demanded money with menaces, as they say in your old profession. She left him with no choice but to try and sell a share or two in his talented horse so that his wife didn't have to find out about the blackmail.'

Jack nodded. 'That's my take. Cassie took a peep at his bank accounts. He's up to his eyes in debt. Overdrawn to the limit, blah, blah. And he had no idea how often Natalie would come back for more, or if she would decide to go public with what he'd done once she'd bled him dry. He couldn't let it go on.'

'Oh, Natalie!' Alexi sighed. 'She should have come to me. I'd have got justice for her.'

'I suspect Fuller's wife knows he's been arrested by now, and probably some of the details. Whether or not she chooses to stand by him is another matter. She might stick it out for the sake of her kids, or she might cut and run. If she runs, without her money Fuller can kiss bye-bye to his expensive lawyer.'

'Let's hope that happens then. If it does, there's more chance of him pleading guilty and telling the police where he's hidden the body.'

'With what they have against him, his best bet is to cut a deal in return for a lighter sentence. At least that would avoid the additional embarrassment of a trial.'

Cheryl and Drew joined them and Jack updated them on his findings.

'There was a lot of talk when his stable lads' accommodation mysteriously burned down and the fire didn't touch anything else,' Cheryl told them.

'The fire investigators were all over it but couldn't prove anything, especially because they knew about a very public argument with an unhappy owner and his threats to take revenge. In the end, the insurers had to pay out.'

'Fuller is always behind in paying us for the accommodation we now provide for his lot,' Drew added. 'If we didn't need the dosh so badly, I'd tell him to take a hike. I'm sick of constantly chasing him for it.'

'We're gonna have to think of an easier way for you to make ends meet when this is all over,' Alexi said.

'Believe me,' Cheryl replied with feeling. 'If you can do that, you can live here rent free forever.'

Alexi laughed. 'Beware what you wish for.' She fiddled with her empty cup. 'Oh, by the way, with all the excitement, I forget to mention that Seaton turned up at Natalie's cottage yesterday.'

Jack gaped at her. 'You have got to be kidding me.'

'He claimed concern about Natalie—'

'And you fell for that?' Jack looked horrified.

'Of course not, but subsequent events have convinced me he didn't kill Natalie. All he wanted was to recover any incriminating evidence she had against him.'

'I think our visit must have prompted Seaton to act,' Jack said. 'He started to wonder if Natalie was actually dead, which is what we implied. If so, the police would get involved eventually and might find that evidence, which would put his name squarely in the frame. He had to get it back to keep himself in the clear and to stop his wife from finding out.'

Alexi nodded. 'I think you're right.'

'That'll be the police,' Drew said, standing to answer the front door bell. 'Use the upstairs lounge to talk to them, Alexi. You won't be disturbed there.'

'They might want to talk to you two as well,' Jack warned. 'You reported Natalie's disappearance and they'll want you to confirm you asked Alexi to look into it.'

'No problem,' Cheryl replied. 'But I can't guarantee I won't tear them off a strip for not taking us seriously.' Her expression sobered. 'If they had, Natalie might still be alive.'

Alexi knew that wasn't the case, but understood her friend's frustration, her need to blame someone else as well as Fuller.

* * *

'Are you feeling better, Ms Ellis?' the inspector asked, giving Cosmo a wide berth and wincing when he caught sight of her necklace of bruises. 'I hear you had a lucky escape.'

'I feel okay,' she replied cautiously, shaking the man's outstretched hand.

The detective constable produced a digital camera and with Alexi's permission took close-ups of her neck, and then the interview started. They didn't separate Jack and Alexi, treating them as victims and would-be witnesses. They went over everything several times, recording the conversation. They weren't aggressive, and implied the case was all but wrapped up.

'What's Fuller's reaction?' Jack asked when the tape was switched off. 'Off the record.'

The inspector shrugged. 'He's lawyered up and isn't talking. The arrogant sod seems to think he can walk away from all this.'

'Ain't gonna happen,' Jack replied, flexing his jaw.

'Count on it.' The inspector stood and shook each of their hands. 'I'll call and arrange for you to come in and sign your statements. But it can wait until Ms Ellis is properly back on her feet.'

The moment the detectives went downstairs to speak with Cheryl and Drew, Cosmo came out from beneath his chair and jumped onto Alexi's lap.

'What now?' Alexi asked, absently stroking him.

'How about a drive to Woldingham?'

'I like the way you think,' Alexi flashed a slow smile. 'It's not a journey I relish the thought of, but I think we should be the ones to break the news to Fay Seaton before the police get around to her.'

'Right.'

'Okay, but how much are we going to tell her?'

'All of it,' Jack replied, with a grimace. 'We owe it to Natalie.'

They waited for the police to leave. Then they went back downstairs and told Cheryl and Drew what they planned to do.

They walked outside and Jack opened the passenger door of his car for Alexi. Then he opened the rear door for Cosmo, who had made it crystal clear he had no intention of being left behind again.

19

Jack pulled his car up in front of the Seaton residence and cut the engine. Seaton's car was nowhere in sight.

'Ready?' he asked, reaching across to squeeze Alexi's hand.

'As I ever will be.'

They rang the bell but no one answered.

'Don't say she's out, too.' Alexi had psyched herself up for the interview and wanted to get it over with.

'Let's go round the back.'

Fay was down the end of the large garden, pruning something. She looked up when she heard them approach and smiled.

'Oh, hello again.' Alexi noticed hope flare in her eyes and hated what they were about to do to her. 'Do you have more news? About Natalie, I mean. Let's go into the house. It will be more comfortable talking there... oh my goodness!' Fay clasped a hand over her mouth. 'Whatever happened to you?'

'I had an accident, but I'm okay.'

'Goodness,' Fay muttered in a bewildered tone as she led them through the patio doors directly into the lounge and asked them if they would like tea. They declined. Fay sat upright in an armchair, her expression a combination of anticipation and resignation, as though a part of her sensed what she was about to hear but the rest of her wasn't ready to deal with it.

'It's bad news, isn't it?' she said softly. 'I can tell from your expression.'

'The very worst, I'm afraid.' Alexi crouched beside her, ignoring the protest from her injured knee as she took the older lady's hand. 'I'm so very sorry.'

'I think I've always known she must be dead.' Tears flowed freely down Fay's cheeks. 'It's a relief to know, in a way. How, when, did she die?'

'She was murdered.'

Fay lifted a trembling hand to her mouth. 'You hear about child abductions but you never think—'

'This didn't happen when she was a child, Fay. It was just a few days ago.'

Fay shook her head, looking lost and bewildered. 'I don't understand.'

'Up until a week ago Natalie was living in Lambourn.'

'Lambourn? Why does that sound... just a minute, that famous trainer? It was all over the news this morning. My husband was quite put out about it, which struck me as odd. He's never taken an interest in horseracing. He was arrested in connection with the disappearance of a local woman; the trainer, that is. Was the woman... was she my Natalie?'

Alexi squeezed her hand and nodded. 'I'm so very sorry.'

'But she might not actually be dead.' Hope flared in her eyes. 'They said they haven't found a body.'

'She's dead, I'm afraid,' Alexi replied. 'Fuller tried to kill me yesterday. I was in Natalie's cottage, looking for more clues about her disappearance, and he caught me there.'

'What did Natalie get caught up in?' Fay looked as though she was holding on by a whisker. But she had hidden depths, as evidenced in her determination to adopt a child against the wishes of a strong-willed husband. She was going to need all that strength of character to see her through this nightmare. 'Please tell me.'

Alexi did, explaining about Natalie's birth mother and the actions Natalie had subsequently taken.

'She must have been devastated, but blackmail...' Fay produced a handkerchief and mopped her eyes. 'And that doesn't explain why she left here when she was fourteen. I need to know what I did to drive her away.'

It was typical of the woman's self-effacing attitude that she automatically assumed the blame was hers.

'About that, Fay. Do you remember that award do Natalie went to with your husband?'

'Of course. She was so excited. She had a new dress. She was very off with me because she thought I should have put Gerry's interests ahead of my own and gone as well. She was too young to understand... I wasn't good in those sorts of situations. Gerry was better off without me cramping his style.'

Ah, Alexi thought, so she knew, or suspected, that her husband played away from home and tried not to mind. As gently as she could, Alexi explained what had happened.

'No!' All colour drained from Fay's face and she looked on the point of passing out. 'Don't say such things. I refuse to listen. I don't believe a word of it.'

'Get her some water, Jack.'

He returned from the kitchen with a glass and Alexi held it to Fay's lips. 'Take deep breaths and try to stay calm. Drink some water, it will help.'

'My husband is far from perfect,' she managed to splutter,

anger overcoming shock. 'But he loved Natalie and would *never* do something so terrible.'

'We can prove it,' Alexi said softly.

'See for yourself.' Jack handed her the incriminating diary, opened to the appropriate page.

She gasped when she saw the pink cover decorated with pictures of ponies. 'That's Natalie's! Where did you get it?'

'I found it in her cottage in Lambourn,' Alexi replied. 'Read those pages and tell me if you think a fourteen-year-old could possibly make something like that up.'

Fay reached for a pair of glasses and started to read. Sobs racked her body before she was halfway down the page. The diary fell from her fingers. Alexi enfolded the older woman in her arms and simply let her cry.

'I've lived with that monster all these years and didn't have a clue. How could I not have known? How could Natalie not have told me? Surely she knew I would do anything for her.'

They allowed Fay to rant and ask questions to which they had no answers. Eventually she asked one they could reply to, one which they would much prefer not to answer since it would cause Fay more pain.

'I can understand now why she ran away again, after they brought her back that first time. What I don't know is how she managed to support herself. She was only just fifteen.'

Alexi told her the brutal truth. Fay had stopped crying and took it with surprising calm.

'She lost all respect for herself, I suppose, discovered that men liked her and so used that to her advantage.' She sighed. 'She was the sweetest little girl, but Gerry's actions made her grow up overnight.'

'It is *not* your fault,' Alexi replied. 'Never think that.'

'We needed to tell you all this,' Jack said, 'because the police will discover who she was sooner or later and will want to talk to you. We didn't want it to come as a complete shock.'

'Thank you for that, anyway.' She straightened her spine, a determined expression pushing aside her bewilderment. 'I know now what I must do.'

Before Alexi could ask what she meant by that, Jack spoke. 'Natalie contacted your husband a while back and extracted money from him as well, just after she gave up working at the agency and moved to Lambourn.'

'I hope she took the bastard for every spare penny he had,' she replied aggressively, her jaw trembling with emotion.

'Will you be all right?' Alexi asked. 'Is there anyone we can call to be with you?'

She looked at Alexi as though she'd grown a second head. 'Do you honestly think I intend to spend another moment beneath this roof with that pervert?'

'But your life, your garden—'

'Is just a garden. I want to see where Natalie lived these past few years, and what sort of a life she'd made for herself. I... I also want to be close by if her body's found. I failed her in life. I don't aim to fail her in death as well. Will you take me back with you?'

'Of course,' Alexi replied, giving her shoulders a gentle squeeze, 'if that's what you'd like. You can stay in my friends' hotel. It was Cheryl who asked me to look for Natalie. She was Natalie's friend and will be able to tell you a lot more about her than I can.'

'Thank you.'

'Shall I help you pack?' Alexi asked. 'We need to do it now. We don't want your husband to come home and find us here.'

'Whereas I would welcome the confrontation,' Fay replied

* * *

Twenty minutes later, Jack carried a suitcase down the stairs for Fay and Alexi toted the only other bag she intended to take.

Fay scribbled a note, placed in the centre of the kitchen table, that said:

gone away for a few days F

'That'll shake him,' she said, a flash of defiance temporarily pushing aside the despair in her eyes.

'He'll suspect you know about Natalie,' Jack warned her. 'Because, excuse me for saying so, but as far as I can tell, Natalie is the only thing you've ever defied him over.'

'So far.'

They went out to the car, which is when Alexi remembered Cosmo. Before she could remind Jack, he'd unlocked the car and opened the rear door for Fay. Cosmo, curled up asleep, opened his eyes wide as Fay slid onto the seat beside him. He blinked at her in his customary lazy, contemplative fashion, as though sizing her up.

'Oh, a cat. How nice. I love cats but Gerry would never let me have one. He's allergic.'

'Be careful,' Alexi warned, smiling when she thought about Seaton's confrontation with Cosmo the previous day. He would be even more allergic now. 'He's not very sociable.'

'Of course he is.'

Cosmo proved her point by climbing onto her lap and purring up a storm.

'Remarkable,' Alexi muttered, sharing a glance with Jack.

'Do you think Natalie was Gerry's only victim or does he make a habit out of underage girls?' Fay asked pensively, speaking for the first time as they reached the outskirts of Lambourn.

'Men with those sorts of persuasions seldom stop at one,' Jack replied.

'Then we must make the police aware of what he did to our daughter. That might encourage others to come forward.'

'I wouldn't recommend it,' Jack said. 'Quite apart from anything else, the CPS would be reluctant to prosecute because, unfortunately, Natalie is no longer alive to accuse him. Her written word wouldn't be enough to secure a prosecution.'

'And besides,' Alexi added. 'If Fuller doesn't confess to killing Natalie, his lawyer will try and find another person with a reason to silence her. She did blackmail your husband and threaten to tell the world what he did to her. That's a pretty powerful motive and might fill a jury's mind with enough doubt to acquit Fuller.'

'Possibly, but it infuriates me that Gerry should continue to get away with it.'

'We'll find another way to make him pay,' Jack assured her.

'Natalie's cottage is down that lane,' Alexi said, indicating the turning as they passed it. 'We'll show you it as soon as we can. At the moment it's still a crime scene and we wouldn't be allowed inside.'

'Thank you. You're being very kind.'

Jack's mobile rang. He used the hands-free device to take the call. 'Fuller's talking,' a voice said.

'A sergeant friend of mine at Reading nick,' Jack mouthed to Alexi. 'Right,' he said in a normal voice into the phone, 'is he putting his hand up?'

Alexi sensed Fay's tension and reached between the seats to take her hand as they both listened.

'There's been a right to-do,' the sergeant replied, chuckling. 'His wife's disowned him and is legging it back to the States, refusing to foot his legal bills. His brief heard that and disappeared faster than a fiver staked on a hundred-to-one outsider.

Our boys took the opportunity to explain a few facts of life to Fuller while he was between lawyers and made him understand he's going down for a long stretch, even if we never find Natalie's body. We've got him banged to rights for trying to throttle Ms Ellis and having underage sex with Natalie's mum. The media would crucify him.'

'Count on it,' Alexi muttered.

'Anyway, he's admitted to killing her.' There was a collective release of breath within the car. 'He says it was an accident. They were talking, got into an argument, he struck her, she fell and hit her head and... well, you know the score.'

'Did he say where she is?'

'Yeah, he says he panicked, like they all do, and instead of calling us to the scene of a fatal accident, he put her on his quad bike and took her up to Membury Woods. She's in a shallow grave. There's a team up there now.'

'Thanks,' Jack said grimly, cutting the connection.

'It's over, Fay,' Alexi said softly as they turned into Hopgood Hall's driveway.

20

There was a media frenzy in Lambourn once Natalie's body was found and identified. Fuller was charged with murder, rape of a minor, and the attempted murder of Alexi, although her name as the victim hadn't yet been released. All the hotels within a ten-mile radius were booked out and the pubs struggled to keep up with demand. Television trucks blocked the lanes and locals brave enough to venture out of doors had microphones shoved beneath their noses. If you were a villager, it followed you had to know something newsworthy. A sound bite for the six-o'clock bulletin. How hard could it be to get one?

Hopgood Hall was under siege. Drew could have let all his rooms ten times over but refrained out of respect for Fay, whom he and Cheryl had taken under their wing. The bar was packed with hacks eager for the inside story, aware it was Drew who had identified Natalie's body. Drew employed extra help to keep up with the demand for alcoholic beverages.

Some of Fuller's lads were giving interviews, seeming to think their jobs were a thing of the past so they might as well cash in somehow. Tod was amongst them but he didn't tell them much, promising to give Alexi the true insider's story of life in the Fuller concentration camp, as he called it, once the dust had settled. Part of Alexi didn't want the story. Being on the receiving end of mob-journalism had given her a very different perspective of her chosen profession and she didn't much like what she saw. Bribery, bully-boy tactics, ridiculous speculation based on the flimsiest, unsubstantiated rumours were methods used to fill airtime and column inches. It was tacky, sensationalist, and about as reliable as a politician's promise.

Alexi recognised some of her former colleagues and kept out of sight. She and Jack took refuge in the kitchen, unable to let Fay see Natalie's cottage until the media storm blew over.

Alexi's phone rang. Patrick. With a sigh of resignation, she accepted he wouldn't give up until she spoke to him, so she took the call.

'At last,' he said.

'Patrick, what can I do for you?'

'Come on! You're sitting on the story of the decade. Murder, underage sex, and...' His breathing echoed down the line. 'Is it you, the attempted murder? You were looking for a friend of Cheryl's, Drew identified the body... it all fits.'

'I'm fine.'

'The hell you are! I'm coming down.'

'No!' She swallowed. 'No, Patrick, you're not. You have a paper to run and it's a jungle down here. Hopefully the mob will move on before my name gets leaked.'

'You think that's important? About the paper, I mean. I know you don't have a high opinion of me right now, but...' He paused and she could imagine his agitated expression as he ran fingers through his hair and juggled commitments in his mind. 'Nothing matters more than you,' he said softly.

Other than scooping the opposition. Alexi chased the thought away. It was what he did. And what she would have done too not so long ago. His first thought would be for the story. Of course it would. But she knew he felt something for her as well, otherwise why pursue her? She would have to find a way to tell him that she no longer returned those feelings. Right now it didn't rank high on her list of priorities because it would be the start of a battle she didn't have the energy to fight.

'I'm fine. Really. But there's no point in coming down. All the hotels are full anyway.'

'Will you at least file your story with us? I have people down there, but you have your finger on the pulse. No one can eclipse your version of events.'

'I can't talk about most of what I know until after Fuller's been sentenced.'

'I hear he's due before Magistrates today.'

'Yes. He's going to plead guilty.'

'I'm sorry this has happened to you, Alexi, and I know this isn't the right time to ask but have you thought more about my proposition?'

'You're right, Patrick. This isn't the time.' *Coward!*

She hung up, aware of Jack's gaze fixed on her profile.

He smiled at her. 'How's Fay doing?'

'She's read all of Natalie's diaries and they've made her cry. A lot.'

'That's to be expected. Has she got the strength to tackle her manuscript?'

'She's on it now.'

Jack nodded but before he could say anything more, their conversation was interrupted by Fay herself.

'How are you doing?' Jack asked, standing to pour coffee for them all.

'I'm finding the manuscript easier because it's written with such clinical detachment,' Fay replied, sighing. 'It's almost as though she's talking about someone else's life.'

'Yes,' Alexi agreed. 'She held back on describing her feelings and stuck to the facts.'

'Which means it lacks heart. We all want to know what was going on inside of her. Well, I do, anyway. I'd suggest you write her story,' Fay said. 'But I hesitate to let the world know how badly I failed her.'

'You didn't fail her,' Jack replied. 'Speaking of which, has he been in touch again?'

Fay shook her head. Gerry had been on the phone to Fay shortly after she arrived at Hopgood Hall, demanding to know where she was. When she said she was in Lambourn, Seaton had become defensive, accusing her of listening to 'that reporter's lies' and insisting she return home. Alexi heard Fay's end of the conversation and wanted to punch the air when she calmly told him that if he came within ten miles of her, she would release Natalie's diaries to the press.

'No, I've not heard from him since. He must have seen the news and decided to keep a low profile. Natalie's identity and the fact that she was our adopted daughter hasn't yet been released, but I expect it will be any day now and Gerry knows he'll be in demand for interviews.' She curled her lip. 'What's the betting he'll preen in front of the cameras, thanking god that he finally knows where his long-lost daughter was all this time, giving him closure?'

'I certainly wouldn't bet against it,' Jack replied.

Fay nodded, drained her coffee cup, and stood up.

'I shall have to go back to Newbury tomorrow,' Jack said once Fay had left them. 'Will you be all right?'

'Of course.' She smiled at him, surprised at how much she didn't want him to go. 'The press will clear off once Fuller's been before the beak so I'm planning on showing Fay Natalie's cottage tomorrow.'

'What about you?' Jack said. He reached for the coffee again, thought better of it, and went to the fridge for a cold bottle of wine. He poured her a glass without asking if she wanted one and placed it in front of her. Alexi took a healthy swig. 'What do you plan to do now?'

'Actually, the country's growing on me. I might take a rented cottage down here. I like the area and it would be good to be close to Cheryl when she becomes a mother. I fully intend to be a hands-on godmother.'

'I think that's a great idea. Got any places in mind?'

'I've put out a few feelers with local estate agents, but until the furore of Fuller's arrest dies down...'

'I'm glad you're sticking around.' He touched her face with the tips of his fingers. Alexi waited, half hoping he'd say more. Glad when he didn't. 'Let's have dinner once the village returns to normal.'

'I'd like that.'

'Me too.'

He briefly, too briefly, touched her lips with his own. Then Cheryl joined them, which Alexi told herself was just as well.

Jack's mobile rang. He answered it, and listened for a while.

'Just a moment,' he said. 'I'll pass you to Ms Ellis. She can help you.' Alexi flexed a brow in enquiry. 'It's Natalie's solicitor.'

'Oh, right.' Alexi took Jack's phone. 'Alexi Ellis. How can I help you?'

'The name's Denton. I represented Natalie Parker's interests and was very sorry to hear what happened to her. Very sorry indeed.' He sighed. 'I understand Mrs Seaton is there with you. Could I come down and talk with her tomorrow?'

* * *

Alexi drove Fay and Cosmo to Natalie's cottage the following morning. Fay sat in Fabio's passenger seat, lacing her fingers together and twisting them until her knuckles turned white, staring straight ahead and not saying a word.

It had been harrowing for Fay to read her daughter's words. And now she would see for herself how she had chosen to live since leaving the agency. She would be able to touch her clothes, her possessions; walk through the rooms she had decorated and furnished to suit her own taste. Breathe in the essence of the woman she hadn't seen for nearly thirty years but had never stopped loving, worrying over, and wondering about.

'Here we are.'

Fay snapped out of her reverie when Alexi pulled up beside the cottage. She peered through the window, tentatively at first, but revived when she saw the lovely garden in full bloom.

'Cheryl tells me it was a right old wilderness before Natalie got her hands on it.'

Fay walked through the gate, barely sparing a glance for the cottage as she walked round the side of it and into the garden. Rose petals littered the path, their fragrant perfume almost overwhelming. Jasmine and honeysuckle fought with plumbago for pride of place on a trellis against a back wall and flowering shrubs Alexi couldn't put names to filled every bed.

Cosmo stalked ahead of them, tail aloft, almost as though patrolled the grounds to ensure there were no persons with murderous intent lurking behind the shrubbery. Satisfied on that score, he found a patch of sun and settled down to attend to his ablutions.

'Are you all right?' Alexi asked, placing a hand gently on Fay's shoulder.

Fay wiped the tears away with the back of her hand, stopped dead in the centre of a path, and turned to face Alexi, the emotion of reminiscence lending character to her face. 'She remembered the plans we had when we talked of creating a garden from scratch,' she said softly. 'She actually remembered.'

Fay spent half-an-hour in the garden and Natalie's workroom, brightening considerably at little touches that evoked memories. By the time they went into the cottage, Fay seemed more composed.

'Thank you for bringing me here, Alexi,' Fay said softly.

'My pleasure.'

'We can go now. I've taken up enough of your time.'

'Actually, we're waiting for someone.' Alexi consulted her watch. 'Natalie's solicitor needs to speak with you.'

Fay's eyes widened. 'With me? Whatever...'

The doorbell cut off Fay's astounded reaction and barrage of questions. Cosmo growled, so Alexi shooed him out into the back garden. She then went to the front door and wrenched it open. A man of about forty, of medium height and medium build who would be forgettable in a crowd, stood on the threshold. He was dressed in a lightweight, crumpled suit, an opennecked shirt, and wore aviator sunglasses which he whipped off when Alexi opened the door.

'Ms Ellis?'

'Yes. Mr Denton I assume. Do come in.'

'Sorry to be a little late.' He extracted a business card from the top pocket of his jacket, handed it to Alexi, and followed her into the cottage. 'Took a wrong turn and had to double back.'

'No problem.'

Alexi introduced Fay. Ever the hostess, Fay had set her wariness at Denton's arrival aside and put the kettle on the moment the doorbell rang. She was now busying herself by assembling a tray with coffee cups. Alexi carried it through to the lounge, Fay poured and Mr Denton then got right down to business.

'I'm sorry for your loss, Mrs Seaton,' he said. 'I liked your daughter very much. She was a good person.'

'Thank you.' Fay swallowed. 'Did you know her well?'

'I looked after her business affairs for a number of years.'

'I see.'

'Actually, Mrs Seaton, as I told Ms Ellis, Natalie left very detailed instructions regarding her funeral wishes.'

Fay blinked rapidly. 'How could she have known?'

'She wished to be cremated,' Denton said, extracting a sheaf of papers from his briefcase. 'She doesn't want any religious connotations. She was most specific on that point.'

'Given what happened to her,' Fay said, *sotto voce*, 'that doesn't come as a big surprise.'

'No flowers or donations to worthy causes in her name, and close friends only. No announcements in the papers.' Denton cleared his throat. 'On one point, she was most specific. She did not want... under any circumstances, Mr Seaton to be admitted to the funeral or involved in it in any way.'

Denton looked concerned that Fay would object, or have a screaming fit, when he stumbled through that provision. Instead, she straightened her spine and met Denton's gaze head on.

'You have my assurance that he will not be, Mr Denton.'

'Right, okay, well, that's good.' He offered Fay a detached smile. 'So, that just leaves the business of Natalie's will.'

Fay looked shocked. 'She made a will?'

'Indeed. She owned this cottage outright, along with all its contents. She had a healthy bank balance and thriving business.' Denton paused and leaned forward to hold Fay's gaze. 'She left all of it to you.'

Alexi's smile was as spontaneous as it was heartfelt. Fay, on the other hand, looked to be on the verge of passing out. Alexi reached across and took her hand. It was ice cold.

'Me?' Fay shook her head. 'But she must have hated me for...'

'Evidently not,' Denton replied. 'But there is one major stipulation.'

'Of course.' Fay seemed to shrink in on herself, as though she expected someone to jump out from behind a chair and yell 'got ya!'

'If Mr Seaton has any dealings with Natalie's property, then the will is revoked and everything is left to charity. I have been appointed as administrator of this rather unusual bequest. I am to have full access to all accounts, and to the property and business without prior appointment. If I find this clause has been circumvented or abused in any way, I have the power to revoke the bequest and evict you from the premises.' He smiled to take the sting out of his words. 'I hope that won't prove to be necessary and I'm sorry to sound so blunt, but Natalie was adamant.'

'I'm sure she was,' Alexi muttered when Fay didn't immediately respond.

Fay glanced at Alexi, her eyes glassy with shock. 'She didn't hate me,' she said dazedly. 'She didn't forget me. She wanted me to have all this.'

Fay burst into tears. Alexi smiled at Denton, who fidgeted in his chair and looked most uncomfortable, the way men do when women cry in their presence.

'She was offering you a way out,' Alexi explained when Fay's sobs subsided. 'She probably knew you would never leave him otherwise, or that he wouldn't let you and you had no independent means to make it happen.'

'She left this for you.' Denton stood up, handed Fay a sealed envelope, and prepared to take his leave. 'If you have no further questions, ladies, I ought to be going.'

Alexi could see that Fay had a great many but was too stunned to voice them. Instead she fingered the envelope Denton had given her, clearly wanting to open it straight away. Alexi gave her some privacy by showing Denton to the door and then wandering around the back in search of Cosmo. She found him stretched full length in a patch of sun, ever optimistic, beneath the bird feeder.

'They won't come if you make yourself so obvious,' she told him absently, her head full of Natalie's bequest.

* * *

Alexi and Cosmo stayed in the sun for a good ten minutes before they wandered together into the sitting room. Fay had the letter open and was clutching it between trembling fingers.

'Are you all right?' Alexi asked tentatively.

Fay looked up, a combination of relief and sadness clouding her expression. 'She explains it all,' she said. 'She believed him. She was convinced it was her own fault, that she'd encouraged him in some way and that I would think less of her, if I believed her at all. When she was old enough to realise it hadn't been her fault, she was already working as an escort and was ashamed of what she'd become.'

'She wanted you to be proud of her.'

'She says she could have lied to me about what she did for a living but preferred to keep her distance rather than there be more secrets between us.' Fay sighed. 'She was planning to contact me once she'd concluded her business with her natural father. She was blackmailing him and Gerry, not for herself but so she would have enough money for me to be able to move in here with her if I wanted to and help with her business.'

'She knows you would have liked that, I expect, which is why she designed the garden to your specification.'

'Foolish child! She should have told me all this years ago. I would have left Gerry in a heartbeat and lived with her in a hovel if necessary.'

'What shall you do now?' Alexi asked.

'Why, what Natalie wanted me to do, of course: I shall move in here and take over her business. And I shall also sue my husband for divorce and take him for every penny I can.' She tossed her head. 'I'm not quite the doormat he takes me for. I've always known how much we're worth and where all his bank accounts are. Even the ones he thinks are secret. Especially those. I shall make my daughter proud of me, you just see if I don't.'

Alexi believed her.

EPILOGUE

'What do you think?' Alexi asked.

Cheryl grinned. 'I think it's perfect for you. The garden's big enough for Cosmo to stake his claim but not unmanageable.'

'Or I can get a man in.' Alexi grinned. 'I'm not that much of a changed character. A window-box still stretches my horticultural abilities.'

The friends joined Cosmo on the patio and sat in the sun, enjoying a moment's peace and quiet. It was the first they'd had for some time. In the two weeks since Natalie's funeral, life had been hectic. Fay was doing okay. She'd moved into Natalie's cottage and taken over her business. A girl from the village was doing the arrangements while Fay did what she did best and concentrated on ensuring the garden thrived.

The funeral itself had been conducted in accordance with Natalie's wishes, with Jack's solid and reassuring presence helping Alexi to keep her demons at bay. Fuller's name was on everyone's lips, the reverberations echoing far beyond Lambourn, reminding her of her ordeal. She put a brave face on things but clearly didn't fool Jack, who barely left her side the entire day.

Gerald Seaton created quite a fuss, wanting to attend. Fay had told him he would be bodily removed if he attempted it, right in front of the press contingent covering the event. The threat was enough to keep him away. Denton was there to ensure fair play. Athena De Bois attended and Alexi saw her and Fay in deep conversation at the small reception held at Hopgood Hall afterwards. Darren Walker, the man Natalie had dated three times, was also invited. He and Fay had a great deal to say to one another, too, and Alexi understood they'd arranged to have dinner together soon. Alexi was glad. Fay was already making new friends and building an independent life for herself.

Fay had insisted that Alexi write Natalie's story. At first lukewarm about the idea, it had grown on Alexi. She needed to do something while she decided on her future, and this was a story that needed to be told. She already had a publisher interested.

Patrick had been down, they'd had dinner together, and she had told him his offer of employment was a no-go. He seemed sad yet resigned, still convinced she would have enough of the country sooner rather than later and promising to keep the offer open indefinitely. When she was ready he would make it happen. Somehow.

She diverted him by pitching a story that she really did want to write: a three-part series for the *Sentinel* focusing on the effects of incest on its victims and how it impacted the rest of their lives. She had two people willing to contribute. One who had put it behind her and moved on, one who had been in and out of therapy for years and couldn't get past it, and Natalie, the avenging angel. The world now knew of Alexi's involvement in Natalie's case and it wouldn't take a rocket scientist to piece together the part Gerald had played in it, even if she couldn't actually name him or Natalie in the article. It would be the ultimate revenge – the ultimate closure – for Fay.

And for Natalie, too.

She still thought Seaton was getting off too lightly and fumed because she couldn't do more to name and shame him. He'd ruined Natalie's life but was now doing the media rounds, painting himself as a victim. Natalie's murder had broken up his marriage and it was all Fuller's fault. Fay was furious. She knew he was doing it to get back at her. He would have to agree to her terms for the divorce and couldn't claim a half-share of her inheritance, off-setting it against what he must pay her, partly because she'd sued for divorce *before* she knew of the inheritance.

Seaton continued to plague Fay with entreaties, promises, and then demands. In the end, she had threatened him with a restraining order and since then he'd gone deathly quiet.

Cheryl and Alexi tore themselves from the sunny patio and re-joined the letting agent who was patiently waiting for them in the sitting room.

'I'll take it,' Alexi told him. 'How soon can I move in?'

Having told the agent she would call at his office to sign the lease agreement the following day, Alexi drove Cheryl back to Hopgood Hall.

'Oh god!' Cheryl shuddered when she heard shouting coming from the kitchen. 'I'd better go and see what's wrong this time.'

'Leave him to it,' Alexi said, heading for the kitchen. 'You'll only encourage his bad behaviour otherwise. Come on, I'll make some tea.'

'Thanks,' Cheryl said, when Alexi placed a cup in front of her a short time later.

'What's happening about the annexe?' Alexi asked. 'Any news about the future of Fuller's yard?'

'More owners have withdrawn their horses,' Cheryl replied. 'And some of the lads have already been poached.'

'What will you do?'

Cheryl sighed. 'I wish I knew.'

'Are you up for suggestions?'

'Speak!'

'We... ll, I was just wondering if you've considered using your lovely home as a retreat.'

'Conferences, you mean?' Alexi nodded. 'We don't have the facilities. Besides, most conferences are at weekends and that's when we're busiest.'

'Not necessarily. I shall be living down here and I happen to know a lot of people who'd pay through the nose to attend journalist workshops hosted by yours truly, modesty notwithstanding. And I have other colleagues from different aspects of the business who would probably contribute. Then there are creative writing retreats, stuff like that. With the right marketing, it could work.'

'I'll talk to Drew about it, but I already know he's desperate enough to try anything.'

'And what about the annexe? Do you really want to keep that monstrosity?'

'Of course not, but—'

'Why not replace it with a proper extension, in keeping with the main part of the house?'

Cheryl flashed a sarcastic smile. 'And pay for it, how?'

'Hear me out.' Alexi paused to sip at her tea. 'You don't want the tennis courts back. They're a pain in the backside to maintain and no one used them anyway. You said that yourself. But you could have a lovely conference centre on that site, use aged bricks so it blends in better with the main building, get land-scape gardeners to put in courtyards and pretty little bits... and, I don't know, but I'm sure you get my drift.'

Cheryl shrugged. 'There's no harm in dreaming.'

'Hey, pay attention, I'm serious. I was thinking of Marcel and how to keep him. His star's in the ascendency, so lots of wanna-be chefs would pay good money to come here and be yelled at by him.' She spread her hands. 'It takes all sorts. Anyway, you could open your restaurant at lunchtimes and flog their efforts cheaply enough to attract a crowd.' Alexi grinned. 'A crowd who would stump up for wine to accompany the food. Marcel could boss his students about and feel important, and you could reap the benefits.'

'It's a lovely idea, Alexi, but it would cost a fortune to build the conference centre and finish it to the required standard. We just can't—'

'No, but I can.'

'Seriously?' Cheryl blinked. 'Why would you?'

'I need an investment opportunity. My flat in town has already been let for twice the amount I'll be paying in rent down here, I have the money I inherited from my mum sitting in the bank earning diddly squat, my redundancy pay-out has nothing to do, and now the publishers are talking a hefty advance for Natalie's story.'

Cheryl swallowed, looking warily interested. 'You really are serious?' She covered Alexi's hand. 'Thank you, but even if we were tempted, it would be years before we could repay you.'

'Hey, I'm not an easy touch. If you go into business with friends, it needs to be on an official footing. I'd want a binding contract that allowed you to pay back my capital in a timescale that wouldn't keep you awake at night *and* pay me a handsome dividend from the profits.'

'You're overwhelming me, Alexi. I can't—'

'Think about it. Talk to Drew.'

'What if Marcel decides to leave anyway?'

'His ego won't allow it. Anyway, you might want to offer him a share in the profits, which would bind him in.'

Cheryl caught an errant tear on her forefinger as it trickled down her face. 'Why would you do this, Alexi?'

'I know a good opportunity when I see one. Besides, someone has to take care of my godchild's interests.'

Cheryl grinned. 'The idea has merit but it's so ambitious it takes my breath away. Still, if you really mean it, I'll run it past Drew.'

'Don't run it past him, convince him.' Alexi squeezed her friend's hand. 'It's the only way. Don't allow his silly pride to stand in the way of your dreams.'

Cheryl's smile widened. 'You're right,' she said. 'Men don't always know their own minds. It's down to us to make sure that they do.'

'And I shall be here to back you up.'

'And see more of Jack, perhaps?' Cheryl suggested, a sparkle in her eye.

'Jack works in Newbury,' Alexi said. 'Besides, I'm off men. They're more trouble than they're worth.'

Cheryl leaned over awkwardly, her expanding belly restricting her movements, and kissed Alexi's cheek. 'Keep telling yourself that,' she said, chuckling.

ACKNOWLEDGEMENTS

My thanks to all the wonderful Boldwood team and, in particular, to my talented editor, Emily Ruston.

ABOUT THE AUTHOR

E.V. Hunter writes bestselling cosy murder mysteries. She has also written revenge thrillers as Evie Hunter. For the past twenty years she has lived the life of a nomad, roaming the world on interesting forms of transport, but has now settled back in the UK.

Sign up to E.V. Hunter's mailing list here for news, competitions and updates on future books.

Follow E.V. Hunter on social media:

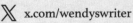 x.com/wendyswriter

facebook.com/wendy.soliman.author

bookbub.com/authors/wendy-soliman

ALSO BY E.V. HUNTER

The Hopgood Hall Murder Mysteries

A Date To Die For

A Contest To Kill For

A Marriage To Murder For

A Story to Strangle For

Revenge Thrillers by Evie Hunter

The Sting

The Trap

The Chase

The Scam

The Kill

The Alibi

Poison
& Pens

POISON & PENS IS THE HOME OF
COZY MYSTERIES SO POUR YOURSELF
A CUP OF TEA & GET SLEUTHING!

DISCOVER PAGE-TURNING NOVELS FROM
YOUR FAVOURITE AUTHORS &
MEET NEW FRIENDS

JOIN OUR
FACEBOOK GROUP

BIT.LYPOISONANDPENSFB

SIGN UP TO OUR
NEWSLETTER

BIT.LY/POISONANDPENSNEWS

Boldw**oo**d

Boldwood Books is an award-winning fiction publishing company seeking out the best stories from around the world.

Find out more at www.boldwoodbooks.com

Join our reader community for brilliant books, competitions and offers!

Follow us
@BoldwoodBooks
@TheBoldBookClub

Sign up to our weekly
deals newsletter

https://bit.ly/BoldwoodBNewsletter